D1617450

The Weight of Love

Jolene Dubois

Visit Jolene Dubois Patreon for lots more stuff,

including the *Plump Fiction Video Series*

https://www.patreon.com/Jolenedubois

Heroes get remembered but legends never die, follow your heart kid, and you'll never go wrong.

- Babe Ruth, *The Sandlot*

For Autumn

The Weight of Love BBW~WG

By Jolene Dubois

Part One

Chapter 1

Mike sat on the cement stoop and looked at the apartments across the street. The building directly in front of him was his, but the old brick one to the left was where Autumn lived.

He took another drag off his Camel Filter. It was an early afternoon in May of 2019 and the sun was shining through his short, dirty blonde hair and bouncing across his handsome face.

He'd only moved to the neighborhood a week ago, but he thought by now he would've seen her, at least once, but he hadn't. Not one time had he witnessed her come out of her apartment, not even for a cigarette.

Did she quit?

She'd been trying to give up smoking back when they worked together.

That was over four years ago.

He had seen her since then. They went on a date, or sort of a date, but still, even that was a few years back.

Fuck.

She was really beautiful, really special.

Why the hell didn't he pursue her further?

Was she too good for him?

Maybe he had become so accustomed to not getting what he wanted, that when he did, he sabotaged himself.

He wanted another chance.

He needed another chance or he would regret it for the rest of his life, and every time he went over to that stoop for a smoke, he kept an eye out.

Countless girls, (mostly Amazon employees) came in and out of her building and whenever he got excited that one of them might be her, he was left disappointed. From a distance, it was hard to tell.

Maybe that's her! No, too tall.

Is that Autumn? No, not pretty enough.

Is that-no, too short.

Maybe…nah.

He laughed at himself.

He'd have a better chance of spotting her if he focused more on the men, and if their heads snapped around when a woman walked by.

Aside from her obvious beauty, and though it seemed superficial and dumb, one of the things he liked about Autumn was her size. She was around 5 feet 5 inches tall and 130 to 140 pounds, a perfect match in his mind for his athletic, 5 foot 11 inch physique. She hit all the checkmarks of the ideal girlfriend he'd always fantasized about, face, body-type, everything.

Maybe that was it.

Maybe she was too perfect and hit too many checkmarks.

He looked at his phone. He thought of texting again but didn't want to come across as needy or overzealous.

He hadn't planned to move in next door, but when he saw the location and the available studio, he jumped on it. He didn't have time to be choosy. Living in the building next to Autumn was just a coincidence, and that was all.

He took a final puff on his cigarette, stomped it out on the sidewalk then grabbed the pack in his jacket pocket but it was empty.

Shit.

It was a skip and a jump to the corner mini mart, down the sidewalk and across the street. The place was guarded by panhandlers and had the selection of a small gas station, but Mike could buy cigarettes there and everything else a single guy could need.

He turned down the aisle and scoured the cold cases for his usual drinks.

Who was he kidding anyway?

Even if he got another chance with Autumn he knew he'd never be able to commit to a long term relationship, which was no doubt what a woman like her would demand.

He was good for a year, two tops.

He grabbed a couple of Red Bulls and headed toward the front checkout counter. He stopped.

There was a girl in his way.

Not just any girl either.

Although her back was turned, Mike could tell that this was a very attractive, and very shapely young woman, and she wasn't hiding much in her black tights and green camisole.

Was it her?

No, it couldn't be.

This girl had some hips on her and Autumn never had quite that much junk in the trunk.

She turned and tossed back her shoulder length reddish-brown hair. "Mike?"

His knees weakened and butterflies fluttered in his stomach. "Autumn."

He blinked and did a double take.

While she was always a stunner she now looked somehow sexier than he remembered, and with the way she filled out those leggings, a bit curvier too. It seemed she was closer to one hundred and fifty pounds than to 130.

He was prepared for that though.

Part of what rekindled his interest was according to Facebook, she had put on a little weight, and there was something about a woman with curves that excited Mike like nothing else. Perhaps because all of his ex-girlfriends were slim and petite.

He gathered Autumn broke her foot or something a while back as there was a photo of her online with friends at an outdoor country music concert, sitting on the grass next to a pair of crutches. She was wearing cutoff jean shorts that displayed softer, chubbier legs. An understandable and slight weight gain no doubt the result of injury.

But injury or not he was surprised by this development.

Autumn was many things, but fat, or anything close to being overweight or out of shape was never one of them. When they worked at Starbucks together she had such a tiny waist she could wrap her apron like three times around and still make a big loopy bow tie in the front.

Standing before him now she flashed a smile of perfect white teeth. "Hey, I thought that was you. Sorry I didn't get back to you, I've been really busy."

God she had such a sexy voice.

He swallowed nervously, his heart thumping as he tried to keep his gaze from lowering too far south of her neckline.

Where did those boobs come from?

"That's okay," he said. "How have you been?"

She gestured at her leg. "I'm alright, still limping around a little."

"Yeah, I saw that, I mean…heard about it."

"Either buy somesing or go!" the tiny asian woman behind the counter said, boldly expressing her traditional Seattle friendliness.

Autumn turned with her bag of Cheetos and iced tea and went to check out. She asked for a pack of yellow American Spirits and paid.

He followed behind and did the same although his eyes couldn't help but focus on Autumn's ass and the delicious way it moved.

They stepped outside and slowly walked together toward home.

"Sooo which building are you in?" Autumn said.

Mike shifted his little brown grocery bag to his left arm and pointed across the street. "The blue one with the white pillars."

"Wow you really are right next door."

He shrugged as the walk sign came on. "It was a good price."

She continued to move gingerly, trying not to put too much weight on her right leg, although she was wearing boots with half inch heels so she couldn't have been in that much pain.

"I think you'll like living on the hill," she said. "It's a fun neighborhood, great restaurants all around this area."

"I'll bet, although I hope you haven't had to walk too much with that foot."

"I manage."

As they approached their buildings Mike knew the moment of truth had arrived.

Would she still be interested in him?

He knew that with girls like Autumn you typically get one chance, and one chance only. She was difficult to read, but the way she looked at him seemed promising.

They stopped walking.

He put his hand in his jacket pocket and crossed his fingers. "We'll have to grab coffee and catch up."

She gazed at him with maybe a hint of a smirk across her usually pouty lips. "I've got a meeting right now but I'd love to have coffee with you. I'll check my schedule and let you know when I'm free."

He exhaled, relaxed his hand, then shrugged, trying to act as nonchalant as possible. "Yeah, sure."

"Bye Mike, good to see you."

She turned to walk away and he packed his Camels against his palm as he watched her go.

Goddamn she had a body.

He could hardly believe how much bigger and rounder her but was. Gone was the cute little barista girl he had known and in her place was a stunning and fully grown sophisticated woman of substance.

"Good to see you too Autumn," he said.

Chapter 2

Victrola coffee shop was adjacent to a small art theater and Autumn walked through the doors the next afternoon. Mike was standing in line with nobody behind him.

He looked good.

He had a mysterious intensity about him, a kind of darkness that made her feel warm and fuzzy inside. At Starbucks, all the girls had crushes on him and she was no exception, although she would never reveal that.

He turned and smiled. "Hi."

"Hey."

He looked her up and down.

She was stunning.

Her long prima-donna legs were showcased in a pair of high waisted blue jeans and on top was a sexy black shirt with sleeves so short, they barely covered her narrow, yet soft shoulders. Her upper arms were so much more plush than they used to be, a clear indicator of her recent weight gain.

"What do you want to drink?" he said.

"I'll get it."

His smile dimpled. "No, it's on me. You walked all the way over here, it's the least I can do."

She looked at him blankly. "Okay." Her dark lashes fluttered for a moment. "I'll have a soy chai, twelve ounce."

"You got it." He was lost in her gaze. Her brown eyes were spellbinding and they complimented her fair skin and auburn hair perfectly.

She had spent some extra time on her makeup that afternoon and he took notice. He wasn't the only one either, as when the line moved forward he saw that the lone male barista was undressing her with his eyes in a less than subtle way.

"Go ahead and find a table," Mike said " I'll bring it over."

Autumn lifted her arm and let the strap of her small Couch handbag fall into her elbow. She nodded. "Okay."

Steam rose and hissed from the espresso machine, drowning out an ambient Norah Jones song. When the hot beverages were ready, Mike put the lids on and walked them over to the small round table next to the window where Autumn was sitting.

"Thanks," she said, putting her phone down.

"My pleasure." He took his jacket off and sat across from her. "So what happened to your foot…or leg I mean?"

She brought her Chai to her nose then set it down. "It was an ankle fracture, kickboxing training at the gym."

"Really, kickboxing?"

"Yeah, messed up my knee too, but that's pretty much healed now."

"That's too bad." He nursed his Americano carefully. He was nervous. This was what he had been hoping for since he moved. A chance to sit down and have coffee with Autumn Murrell. Now it was actually happening and he desperately wanted to make the most of it, but her fuller figure and haughtier beauty was not doing anything to put him at ease. "Cool that you were kickboxing though, I've always wanted to try something like that."

"I wasn't fighting or anything, it was just a way to stay in shape." She adjusted her hips in her seat. "So, when did you move again?"

"About a week ago."

"Why the hill?"

"I needed a place, took one of the first apartments I saw."

She gave him an expressionless stare as if she could see right through him. "Breakup?"

"Yeah."

"Doing okay?"

He sat up straight and looked her in the eye. "Oh yeah, it was my decision and it was the right thing to do, so it's good."

"What happened?"

His americano was beginning to cool and he took a sip. "I don't know." He took another sip. "She was a little bit older, I think we were in different places in life, wanted different things." He looked out the window at the busy city street, then back at her. "How about you? You got a boyfriend?"

She rolled her eyes at his boldness. "Went through a breakup a few months ago."

"Mind if I ask what happened?"

"I don't know." She took a sip of her Chai. "We went to Maui together, got in a big fight and split up when we got back."

Mike figured she was single but he was relieved all the same to hear her say it. He had gone through her Facebook and Instagram accounts and had seen a picture or two of the guy he assumed she was talking about. He was young and handsome, seemingly much more like himself than the huge bodybuilder guy she dated a few years prior. "What was the fight about?"

She sighed. "I wanted to go out to nice restaurants and enjoy myself, he didn't want to spend money."

"Oh."

"I was like, okay, we're here, we're not here very often, I want to go out and have fun…but he wasn't into it. He said he didn't want to waste money on needless stuff and told me I was too bossy."

Mike shook his head, although he knew from his experience of working with Autumn that she most definitely had an authoritative side to her personality. "It's not bossy to want to go out to a nice restaurant."

She rolled her eyes in an exaggerated way that Mike found incredibly sexy, but then again, everything she was doing was sexy. Just watching her lips move mesmerized him.

"I know," she said.

"Relationships are hard. I'm in my 30s now and it seems like the older I get, the heavier everything feels."

She slid her butt to the back of her wooden chair causing it to groan and squeak beneath her weight. "You gotta work at them, and you have to be with someone who is willing to work."

"For sure." He looked into her eyes, then at her drink which she was clutching with both hands. Her hands were small and delicate and her nails were long, and manicured a creamy sea-green color. “You lactose intolerant?”

“Why because of the soy?”

He was testing her. “Just curious.”

“Not really,” she said. “It's just that regular milk upsets my stomach sometimes.”

“So many people around here are gluten free or vegan these days.”

“God yeah.”

“But you’re not?”

“No, I don’t give into trends that easily.”

He smiled. “I like that.”

She passed his test with flying colors. He had dated girls in the past that seemed to be allergic to everything, had multiple dietary restrictions and he found such things to be difficult to navigate, especially as a guy who loved to cook.

They sipped their beverages and made small talk for a while longer but soon came the inevitable awkward silence Mike was trying to avoid.

He took a drink and found himself lost in the hint of cleavage above the hem of shirt. He quickly looked out the window.

There was a guy with an afro wearing an old Sam Perkins Supersonics jersey outside walking his poodle.

He turned back to Autumn. "Got any pets?"

She sipped her Chai. "I have a cat."

"Boy or girl?"

"Boy. His name is Samson." She pursed her lips for a moment and smiled through her eyes. Her facial features were delicate and feminine like her hands.

Mike found it intriguing that despite the noticeable weight gain, her gorgeous face seemed unaffected by the extra pounds, at least in comparison to her hips.

She moved her chair backwards. "You wanna meet him?"

"Yeah." He took a final swig of his coffee then stood. His eyes drew down towards her legs which were packed so snuggly in those designer jeans. Still in her seated position he had a clear view of her hips and thighs. She was even bigger and curvier than he had initially realized.

He had always known Autumn to have a small, tight little hourglass figure, but looking at her now she seemed more bottom heavy and pear-shaped. He watched as she scooted back her chair further and placed her hands on the table.

He reached out his arm. “Need help?”

“I can manage,” she said in a haughty if not breathy voice.

With more effort than he was expecting, she heaved herself up.

He moved a chair to clear a path then grabbed her Chai. It was empty. “I’ll recycle these real quick.”

She nodded then focused her attention back on walking without putting too much pressure on her foot.

He held the door open and they went outside.

He kept in stride with her and they crossed the street and continued to walk slowly until they were in front of her building.

He put his hands in his pockets as a cool breeze chilled the air. “You uh, want a cigarette before you go?”

“I’d need a jacket.”

"You can wear mine."

"No, it's okay." She paused, then smiled as her hair fluttered in the gentle wind. "We can smoke inside."

"You can smoke in your apartment?"

"Not really, but I do sometimes. I just turn the fan on and try to blow it out the window."

"Okay, sure."

Her building was an old and quaint place of 1890's construction much like his. She took keys from her leather handbag, unlocked the door and led him inside to a small maroon carpeted lobby, then around the corner to her ground level studio. They went in and a black cat with a lion's cut greeted her.

"Hey buddy, how are you?" She bent over and stroked his furry mane and ran her slender fingers down his shaved little body.

Mike took a second to regain his composure, then crouched down next to her and brought his hand to the cat's mouth, only to be shunned.

Autumn smirked. "Don't take it personally. He needs a while to warm up to strangers."

"What is he afraid he might like me?" Mike smiled, then stood and looked around. Of the handful of years he had known Autumn, he had never been in her apartment before. Somehow, it was exactly as he pictured.

It smelled good, in a warm, cozy and familiar sort of way.

It wasn't a big place and there was a queen size bed in the center of the main room. To the right there was a canvas propped on an easel, and behind that was a black sofa in front of a wall mounted TV screen above an automatic cat feeder. On the other side of the sofa was a small desk with an open MacBook. She had one of those framed Audrey Hepburn posters on her wall.

Autumn toot a few steps to her right. "Sorry it's a little messy right now,"

"How long have you lived here again?"

"Almost five years, ever since I graduated college."

"You work from home?"

She draped her handbag over the side of a chair and turned towards him, her knee-high boots creaking the old wood flooring in the process. "Mmhmm."

He took his jacket off and hung it on the coat rack against the wall near the front door. “You like that?”

“It’s a little stressful, but it’s been nice with the leg and everything, not having to commute.”

He followed her around the bed and through an open entryway where there was a small kitchen. Her place wasn’t exceedingly clean, but it wasn’t overly messy either. A small red candle sat on the table of a tiny breakfast nook, and couple dirty dishes were stacked in the sink.

“How have you been getting food and stuff? I’d think it would be hard to lug grocery bags all the way from QFC with your injury.”

“I manage,” she said blankly. “I usually get Amazon Fresh deliveries or take an Uber or get Uber eats.”

“Smart.”

She took an empty coffee mug from one of the cupboards, placed it on the table, then turned on the kitchen fan which was built into the partially cracked lath and plaster ceiling. “What about you?”

Mike sat. “What do I do for groceries?”

She shoved the kitchen window upward, then grabbed a silver cigarette case from the sill and opened it. "No, what are you doing for work these days?"

"I just finished a big video editing contract, but got hired at the Google Campus up in Fremont with a facilities company."

She placed a cigarette between her lips and Mike quickly lit it for her with his zippo. She exhaled and looked into his eyes."I love Fremont."

"I actually start on Monday. We'll see how it goes I guess." He lit one himself. "So what are the best places to eat around here?"

Autumn leaned her butt against a wooden ledge that was part of the wall that separated the kitchen from the rest of the apartment. She really did have an amazing figure.

Her thighs and hips were shapely and generous; and while her midsection was small, there was a hint of a soft belly roll poking out just above the high waistband of her jeans causing her top to ride up toward her breasts.

"There's a lot of good places," she said. "There's ramen, Little Woody's, Fogan Cocina across the street, tons of great Thai and dumpling places as well."

"I've been getting Hot Mama's pizza sometimes, it's not bad."

She took a drag on her smoke and sighed. "I tend to gain weight if I eat that kind of stuff."

Mike's heart skipped a beat after she said that. She said it almost as if she was unaware that she had already gained weight.

To be fair, she had seen herself everyday for the past four years while he certainly had not. To him, her curvier, more voluptuous appearance was obvious, but perhaps in her mind she looked the same as she always did.

When they went on that date a couple years ago, she made a big deal over skipping the gym in order to meet with him. She was in really good shape back then, but looking at her now it was evident, and it made sense because of her injury, that she hadn't set foot in a gym in some time.

She was such a mystery and a walking contradiction. Just the fact that she smoked cigarettes seemed to go against her progressive, intelligent and orderly personality; but along with her weight gain it was something he liked about her as it told him that despite her tendency towards a resting bitch face, she wasn't as rigid and stuck up as she appeared.

He flicked ash into the coffee mug and gazed up at her. He was hesitant to tell her how beautiful she was, as she no doubt got that all the time. "You look great," he said.

"Thanks." She took a short puff and looked back at him. His tight shirt showed off his broad shoulders and lean muscular arms. His piercing blue eyes brooded at her so longingly they nearly took her breath away. "You too." There was a moment of silence that to her felt like an eternity. "Still have your motorcycle?"

"Yep, still got it," he said. "You don't have a car right?"

"No. Like I said I take Uber, there's no place to park around here anyway."

"Right." He tried to flick more ash into the mug but there was none to flick. "I uh…I know you probably got a few more hours of work but we'll have to do this again sometime."

She stood up straight and her eyes brightened. "Yeah, I'd like that."

He took a final drag on his smoke then stabbed it out. He rose. "Alight, I should get going."

"Okay," she said.

He took a step forward and they gazed at each other face to face. She was so young and ripe for the taking. Her lips were full and plump and looked so delicious he could hardly stand it and the way she was looking at him was making him crazy. He thought about grabbing her and kissing her right then and there but his nerves held him back.

"Call or text anytime, you know I'll always be close by," he said.

She smiled in her understated way. "Yeah I know where you live."

He walked over to the front door, unhooked his jacket and put it on. "See you later Autumn."

With a finger twisted in her hair, she looked straight into his eyes. She sighed. “Bye Mike.”

Chapter 3

The attraction between Mike and Autumn was powerful and magnetic, but there was a sense of fear that kept them wary. Mike still had his ex fresh in his mind and her memory weighed on his conscience.

He already got what he wanted in some ways. He had proven to himself that Autumn was available and interested, but when it came to moving forward, he felt scared and blocked, as he knew the great responsibility that comes with falling in love.

It was easier to dream about her at night and picture her body naked from the comfort of solitude than to make that dream, and all the attachments that come with it, a reality.

Autumn kept her heart well guarded because she had been lied to by men in the past. She was a hopeless romantic, too pretty for her own good and deep down, she was lonely.

She liked Mike and always had, but wasn't sure if she could trust his intentions. He was so good looking she found herself questioning whether or not he was a player, or if he was capable of being a one woman man.

They did not see each other the next day, nor did they call or text. It wasn't until two days later that Mike received a message from her, asking if she could come over.

He jolted to attention and cleaned up and organized his tiny, sparsely furnished apartment before bolting down the stairs. He opened the door to his building and found her standing on the moonlit steps. She had been crying.

"Hey," he said. "You okay?"

She looked up at him, her eyes big and serious. "Can I come in?"

"Umm, yeah of course." He opened the door wider, then stopped. "Do you want to have a cigarette first?"

"No, I've been chain smoking all afternoon, I really need to quit."

He nodded and let her step inside. She was dressed in black yoga pants and a matching zip up tracksuit jacket that looked like it was purchased 15 pounds ago.

"There's stairs, are you going to be able to…"

"I can manage."

Mike's place was on the second floor and Autumn went up the steps one by one, slowly and carefully. By the time she reached the top she was slightly winded from the exertion.

"Is that hard?" he said.

"It's (pant) not too bad."

He opened his door and they went in. "Sit down, get off your feet and make yourself at home."

She collapsed on his small Ikea sofa and looked at him.

"What's wrong?" he said.

"It's my Dad. He's been having heart problems and I just found out he's in the hospital."

He moved his acoustic guitar to the side and sat in a collapsible wooden chair across from her. "I'm sorry."

She scrunched her nose and sniffled, then wiped some of the smudged makeup from her eyes with a tissue from her purse. "I'm just scared."

"He's down in Oregon?"

"Yeah, I wish I could be there. I'm just having trouble picturing him…that way, you know?"

Mike nodded. "My dad had a heart attack a few years back, had to have open heart surgery."

"Really?" She scooted forward, unzipped her jacket and took it off. Beneath she wore a black spaghetti strap top that also seemed too small. "Is he okay now?"

"Oh yeah, he's good, better than he was before." He stroked his chin and gazed at her. Even in her distressed state she looked amazing. Her breasts had certainly grown over the past few years and the tightness of her shirt squeezed against the softness of her sides, making little creases in the exposed skin above her armpits. "It's hard seeing your parents get older."

"Yeah I'm not used to it. I don't think I'm ready for it."

He was having trouble keeping his eyes from drawing down to her legs. Her thighs were so much bigger shapelier than his ex's, and found them to be wildly and refreshingly attractive. "It'll be okay."

"Thanks," she said softly. "Sorry to come over like this, I'm kind of a mess."

"It's okay, I'm glad you came." He was getting the feeling the health problems of her dad were less serious than she was making them out to be and perhaps her show of distress and vulnerability was more of a test, or an excuse to see him. Not that he thought she wasn't being truthful, but the vibes she was sending were more flirtatious than fearful.

"I guess I just needed to talk about it with someone," she said.

"I'm glad you chose me."

"Me too."

There was a long and deliciously awkward silence, then Mike stood. "Um, can I get you anything?"

"No, just..." She closed her eyes as if she was on the brink of tears.

He stepped forward and sat beside her on the couch. "It's okay, come here."

He put his arm around her shoulder, pulled her close and she nestled her head against his chest.

The comfort of his embrace felt so natural and loving she thought she could dissolve in his arms if she let herself. She lifted her head and stared directly into his eyes with her nose just inches away from his.

His heart rate accelerated.

He didn't hesitate a moment longer.

He did what he had always wanted, yet failed to do since he met her. He leaned in and kissed her plump wet lips, softly, gently.

It was like a weight was lifted from their shoulders as she melted into him and kissed him back.

His hand shifted from her shoulder to her waist and he pulled her tight to his body. She felt heavier than he expected, but she felt wonderful.

.“I just wish everything wasn’t so hard,” she cooed after their lips finally parted. “Work, family, love…it just…” She hesitated for a moment, turned away, then looked at him. “It makes me wish I could just be a house cat.”

“A house cat?”

“Well…yeah.”

“You mean like, never have to worry about anything, not have to work, just lay around and sleep and have someone else feed you?”

She sniffled again, then let out a cute giggle in spite of herself. “Sounds pretty great right?”

“It does actually.”

She looked down, feeling silly for breaking down and expressing her vulnerabilities. “I’m sorry, I’m okay really.”

He put his hand on her knee. “You got nothing to be sorry about.”

"Thanks."

They talked for a while longer until there was another moment of tense sexual silence, as neither of them were quite certain of what the other was expecting of them.

"I know it's a long way down those stairs," Mike said, "but are you ready for a cigarette now?"

She let out a breathy sigh and looked at him lovingly. "Sure."

He sprang to his feet and helped her up.

He lingered behind as she went down the creaky steps.

Her ass was spectacular. It was big, as round as it was wide and it jiggled, bounced and curved severely into her thighs with every sexy feminine move she made.

She left her jacket on his couch, but he didn't say anything as the way she looked from the back in those tights and that revealing top seemed too good to be real. She had a great body, and if she left her jacket purposefully, he couldn't blame her for wanting to show off.

She wasn't fat and he wouldn't call her chubby, but she certainly had a hefty bounty of curves in all the places that made his stomach flutter.

Outside she took a cigarette out of her purse and he lit it for her. He then lit his own and gracefully hoisted himself up onto the concrete ledge that separated the sidewalk from a garden strip in front of the more modern apartment building across the street. She attempted to do the same.

With her hands on the top of the ledge she tried to lift herself into a sitting position. She kicked her boots against the short wall just inches above the ground as she struggled to get up next to him. She failed and lowered back to the ground with a gasp.

"Oh God, (huff) you made that look (pant) so easy."

He reached out his hand. "Here I'll hold that for you."

She gave him her cigarette and tried again. "Come (gasp) on." Her little heeled Frye boots came back down to the sidewalk as her second try resulted the same as the first. She was out of breath, and looked frustrated and confused. "Shit, (huff) what the hell!"

It was clear, and also incredibly hot for Mike to see Autumn coming to the realization she was no longer as light and athletic as she once was.

No doubt once her ankle was healed completely she'd be anxious to get back in the gym so she could shed the extra 15 or 20 pounds she'd gained over the past year and a half.

He hopped down. "Let me help you." He placed the cigarettes carefully behind his ears, bent over then cradled his hands together and she stepped on his open palms and finally climbed up.

"Fewww! God I'm so…"

He jumped back up next to her and gave her back her smoke. "You're so what?"

"Nothing." She looked at him and sighed. "Thanks for your help."

"My pleasure."

She smiled then took a short drag and blew smoke into the clear night sky. "I'm glad you moved here."

"Me too." It was a little chilly. He took off his coat and draped it over her exposed shoulders.

She gazed towards the vast city skyline, the full moon rising above the space needle like an upside down exclamation mark. She looked back at him. "I have trouble getting close to people."

He swallowed and his voice lowered to a slow rumble. "I've been trying to learn guitar. Name me two of your favorite songs and I'll figure out how to play and sing them for you."

"Oh gosh. I'll have to think about that."

"Just whatever two songs pop into your head."

She looked upward. "How about that Miss American Pie song, I've always liked that one."

"I could probably do that, what else?"

She took another drag then let her hand dangle between her knees. "Samson."

"Samson, by who? Sorry I'm totally out of touch with music from the past like 15 years."

"Samson by Regina Spektor, came out like 20 years ago."

"Okay, I'll look it up."

She smiled. "I'll hold you to it."

"Deal."

Chapter 4

Autumn slept at Mike's place that night, but they did not make love. They just laid in bed spooning and she fell asleep in his arms.

He loved the way she felt lying next to him. The way her ass dominated his pelvis and filled up his crotch like a balloon, the way her waist was soft and supple against his hands, and the way she smelled like a delicious combination of cake and flowers.

They woke up early the next morning and Mike walked her to her apartment before hopping on his motorcycle and making the two mile trip through the morning mist and city traffic to Fremont, on the north end of Lake Union.

He felt high and couldn't stop thinking about her. He wanted to buy her flowers and ask her out to dinner, but he was afraid of giving himself away.

Maybe he should've fucked her last night.

Maybe that was what she wanted, and why she really came over.

Maybe it was all a bad idea.

They were neighbors.

What if he fell in love, what if things didn't work out?

He waited until he was off work to text her again.

She said she was at Little Woody's, the burger joint about a block away from their buildings. It was interesting to him that she went ahead and got dinner on her own, but he liked that about her. Autumn was always that way. Independent, self-sufficient and uncompromising. If she wanted to do something, she would do it.

She was sitting alone with a half-eaten cheeseburger and a carton of fries in front of her. He greeted her and ordered something for himself, but she polished off all her food before he was even a few bites into his.

Wearing jeans, her thighs spread out wide and full in her seat. They were thick and meaty and along with her hips they made her waist look much smaller than it was, especially when perched so provocatively on that chair.

She had such style about her. Everything from how she dressed, to the cool and unbending way she spoke, to the way she ate.

Mike's ex would never eat a huge greasy burger on her own like that, and even if she did she would never finish the whole thing.

They strolled back to her place afterwards as rain began to trickle down from the darkening sky. Inside her apartment Autumn turned the kitchen fan on, took out a cigarette from her case and lit up.

Mike lit one too.

"I think it might be time to do these dishes," he said, gesturing toward her sink.

Her eyelashes fluttered as she stared at him expressionless. "Don't worry about it, I'll do them eventually."

"No way, I would love to do them for you and keep you off your feet."

She rolled her eyes. "I'm not helpless you know."

"I know, but I'm still going to do them."

She puffed on her cigarette, then coughed a few times. "God (cough, cough) I really need to quit smoking."

Mike leaned forward in his seat. "Why?"

"Are you serious?" She raised an eyebrow. "It's so bad for you."

"It's just a simple pleasure."

She scrunched her nose. "That's one way of putting it. More like a compulsive addiction that turns your lungs black and gives you cancer."

He smirked. "Cigarettes are old fashioned and romantic, like me."

"Right, if that's what you gotta say to make yourself feel better."

When they were done smoking, Autumn went to lay down in bed and watch TV. Mike, being true to his word, did her dishes and cleaned up her kitchen, even disposing of the cigarette butts and taking out the trash.

When finished, he sprawled out next to her on the mattress.

"We should get something for dessert," he said.

She was lying on her side with her head on one of her many pillows. "Dessert?"

"Yeah, is there anything fun around here?"

She propped her hand against her temple and sat up a little. "I usually try to stay away from sugar, especially at night."

He stared at her. She looked like a beauty queen posing for a photo, with her torso slightly bent and her ass sticking out behind her.

"I'm still a little hungry, I should go grab something," he said. "When you do eat sugar what do you get?"

She gazed at him lazily. "There's Cupcake Royale."

"Where is that?"

She yawned. "I think it's on like…10th and Pike I wanna say."

"What's your favorite cupcake?"

"I'll go with you."

"You sure you're up for walking that far?"

"It's not that far," she said with a heavy roll of her eyes. "Besides, it will be good for me. I'm supposed to be walking as much as I can to rebuild the strength in my leg."

"Are you going to physical therapy or anything?"

"I was, but not anymore." She curled her feet beneath her thighs and sat up. "I'm on my own now."

He rolled over to her side of the bed and gently took her hand. "Okay, let's go, sounds like it stopped raining."

Having Autumn walk with him was not what he had in mind, as he would have happily ran there and back just to let her relax, but she seemed insistent and there was no talking her out of anything. When they reached the trendy little bakery Mike noticed the store's slogan.

Cupcake Royale. Does a booty good.

He smiled and wondered if this place was part of what contributed to the growth of Autumn's rear end, but kept that thought to himself.

She liked chocolate and he bought her a cherry chocolate cheesecake and a salted caramel. He got a donut for himself and took it all to go.

They walked back to her place, and when a belligerent hobo bombarded them from a darkened alley screaming, "Ahhhh! End is near Motherfuckers, end is near! The plague is comin! Ahhhh!" her hand slipped into his.

She made him a cup of tea and they ate and talked and smoked in her kitchen. They couldn't keep their eyes off each other and before too long they were back in bed.

"Mmmm, come here," she cooed, running her fingers up his arm and underneath his shirt. She squeezed his bicep and felt its hardness. "Do you work out?"

"Sometimes, a little bit."

Her eyes and fingertips investigated him. "You have an amazing body."

"Thanks, so do you."

She rolled onto her back, her head elevated by two pillows. She sighed as if she needed to get something off her mind. "Tabitha, one of my best friends, always wants me to go to the gym with her. She's got like a 4-pack and super toned arms and everything, I'm just like, yeah…no, that's just not really my body type anymore."

Mike scooted closer, fascinated that she felt the need to tell him that. "I love your body type."

She ran her hand over his chest. "Well that's good."

He pressed against her and gently caressed her thigh. "I am obsessed with your body."

"I'm glad."

He unbuttoned her jeans, crawled on top and kissed her belly with a lift of her shirt. She had a mostly flat stomach but it was also soft and slightly pudgy, especially in the area around her deep-set belly button. He kissed her lips and began fondling her waist, slowly working towards her breasts.

She stopped him. "Do you umm, want to…"

"I don't have any condoms." He tilted his head and kissed her neck, just below her ear. He looked back up into her eyes. "Should I go get some?"

"It's up to you."

"Umm, okay so..." He gazed at her with a longing that seemed to burn and throb throughout his body. She looked so voluptuous with her jeans undone and her blossoming breasts pushing against her low cut shirt. "I'll just go do that."

Her brown eyes glowed. "I'll be waiting. The keys to the front door are in my purse."

He shot out of her apartment like a rocket, ran over to the corner mini mart and was back in no time.

She was still partially dressed and hadn't moved from her spot on the bed. He kicked off his boots and pounced on top of her, picking up where he left off.

He kissed her lips, her neck, her chest, her breasts, then began peeling off her jeans, which turned out to be tighter around her thighs than he anticipated.

She sat up and took her top off with her legs hanging over the side of the bed and her back facing him. He was completely inthralled by her natural beauty.

Her hips looked so wide and feminine and her weighty ass sank deliciously into the push mattress. She was wearing a black thong and had cute little love handles that sprung slightly over the sides of the taught fabric.

He leaned forward, unsnapped her bra and she gasped with delight as she turned with her boobs hanging free.

She shoved them in his face and savored the feeling of his stubble rubbing gently between.

He kiss her chest.

God she smelled good.

He stripped himself of his clothes she crawled on top on him.

He grabbed her ass with both hands, shook and jiggled it. It felt so big and it moved and wobbled as if somehow separate from the rest of her body.

He had never been with a woman this curvy before and his hands could not keep up with the nagging lust that had taken over his mind.

He slipped off her skimpy panties, tossed them on the floor like a feather, pushed her off and kneeled erect on the bed. He straddled her with his thighs on either side of the narrowest part of her body, her waist.

He took the condom, opened it, then handed it to her with his raging manhood on naked display.

She unrolled it onto him, her pussy throbbing and soaking.

"I want you," she said. "I want you inside of me."

He collapsed onto the warm softness of her body. He smelled her sweet perfume and kissed her neck again.

For a moment his nerves overtook him.

He was falling in love with this woman. He wanted her and he wanted her more than anything, and not just for one night. He wanted to please her and his nerves only came from fear of not meeting her expectations.

He did his best to block those feelings out and let his unrelenting carnal desire take over. All it took was one more look into her pleading eyes.

He squeezed her with his strong masculine hands and slipped inside. She moaned and gasped as he thrust rhythmically back and forth. He grabbed her ass and went in deeper and harder until her moans and gasps turned to squeals and screams.

Fuck her pussy felt good, so warm, so wet, so perfect, and the sounds of her orgasmic bliss came too soon for both of them.

They smoked a few cigarettes in the kitchen with the afterglow shining from their eyes.

She was still naked.

He had never seen a woman so voluptuous in the nude before, and watching Autumn moving around with her soft wide hips, big ass and full breasts, only served to reinforce what he'd been missing out on his whole life.

They crawled back in bed and he noticed that she had a bit of a lingering cough.

He kissed the white skin of her upper arm. "You alright?"

"Yeah I'm fine," she said. "I cough sometimes when I'm sleepy, don't worry about it. My blood sugar feels a little low though."

He didn't hesitate to get up and grab the salted caramel cupcake he bought earlier. "Here you go."

"Oh god, that's not exactly what I meant."

"Do you want me to get you something else?"

"No, this actually looks pretty good right now." She took it out of the small box and licked some frosting off the top. She turned to him like she was looking for approval. "Sorry. I eat in bed sometimes, it helps me sleep."

"I don't mind at all, I do the same thing." He rested his head against her shoulder and lightly caressed her breasts. "Sleep is important and you gotta wake up pretty early right?"

She took a bite of her cupcake, this time more unapologetically. "I do (chew) tomorrow, I need to get up for east coast time."

"We better get some rest then."

She finished chewing and licked her lips. "Can you do me a favor?"

"Sure."

"Can you go to the fridge and grab me one of those orange sleep drinks?"

He sat up. "Neuro sleep drinks?"

"Yeah, how'd you know?"

He got up and headed toward the kitchen. "I drink those too, thought I was the only one."

"Guess we have a few things in common."

"Guess so."

He brought her the drink then held her as she ate the rest of her dessert. He let her fall asleep in his arms before he drifted off himself.

They were together nearly every day as spring slowly brightened into summer. Mike would wake up early and, rain or shine, ride his motorcycle to work, then head back to her place every evening.

Autumn liked having him around. He cleaned Samson's litter box, he did the dishes, did laundry, and happily went on grocery runs for her whenever she needed anything. He cooked for her, although most of the time they would order takeout, which Mike would usually go get himself to avoid delivery expenses.

She was a bit of a foodie.

Perhaps the reason she was always so dedicated to the gym was because it allowed her to eat what she wanted while still maintaining a svelte size 6 figure.

With her injury however, working out the way she used to was out of the question, which was why she had graduated to a size 10 by the time Mike came back into her life.

Now, after being in a relationship for two months, even her 10's were feeling snug.

"Have you been washing my clothes on hot?" she said.

Mike put his phone in his pocket and turned her way. It was a muggy evening in late July and she was standing next to the bed struggling to fasten the top button of her jeans, the same ones she wore on their first coffee date back in May. "Umm, I don't think so, I usually just do the normal cycle. Why?"

"Because these pants (gasp) used to fit."

He stepped forward. The short sleeves of one of her favorite black shirts looked even shorter from extra pudge in her arms. Her jeans appeared painted on, and the seams of the denim pulled tight over her legs, especially in the hip and thigh areas. "Did they shrink?"

She faced him and showed how she could no longer close the gap of the fly over her softening midsection. “I don’t know, you tell me.”

He shrugged, acting clueless. “I’m sorry, I don’t think I did anything. I usually just throw stuff in the washer and press start.”

She glared at him like he was stupid, then sighed. “It’s okay, I probably just need to get back in the gym.”

“You think your leg is ready for that?”

“My leg is basically healed, I just need to ease myself back into a routine at some point.” She tried to get the button closed one more time but failed miserably. “Okay these (gasp) pants are not happening today.”

“What’s wrong with that dress you had on earlier?”

She wore dresses most of the time during the work week because they were stretchy and comfortable while still being presentable enough for video calls.

“Did you like it?”

His eyes widened. “Did I like it? You looked incredible in it.”

"Really? I thought it was a little revealing, you know, just from the waist down." She gave him a little smirk and started to peel her jeans towards her thighs. "But then, I guess that's why you like it."

He glanced at his phone again. "Well put something on, ride will be here soon."

"You know we could just walk."

He looked at her little feet and the way her calves so elegantly tapered into her ankles. "In heels?"

"Okay, good point." She sat on the edge of the bed and continued to undress. "Just give me a sec."

He went outside for a smoke to let her get ready in private and when he came back his jaw nearly hit the floor.

"Jesus Christ, you look amazing," he said.

"It's not too tight right?"

"Does it feel too tight?"

"I mean it's stretchy but…" She tugged on the straps of her dress and gave him a spin. "It's not like it's leaving much to the imagination."

That was an understatement. It wasn't the same dress she had on earlier. It was something he had never seen her wear before, a knee length body-con little black number that clung to every curve of her figure like a glove.

He was surprised. Although he had been with her nearly everyday, or maybe because of that, he hadn't fully realized the changes in her body.

She was getting bigger, and it wasn't his imagination.

She had been avoiding her bathroom scale and had not been weighed since her last doctor's appointment, but gazing at her in that dress, Mike thought she looked a good 10 pounds heavier than she did when they started dating.

He didn't know why but he really wanted to know how much she weighed.

She was five foot five, maybe five six. He remembered thinking she was a hundred and fifty pounds or so when he first bumped into her at the mini mart.

Mike's weight estimations came mostly from the knowledge that his skinny ex-girlfriend was 5 foot 3 and 117 pounds, and he himself was a hair under 6 feet and 165.

Damn. Did Autumn really weigh almost as much as him now?

10 pounds in two months?

It was possible and it certainly made sense.

Autumn's lifestyle consisted mainly of sitting in front of her laptop, whether it be in bed or at her desk. As far as Mike could tell she got almost zero physical activity throughout her work weeks, especially since he entered the picture and started doing her chores and errands.

Her thighs were thicker, her cute little knees were less defined and dimpled. Her breasts seemed larger as well but it was her rear end that Mike could not pry his eyes away from.

She had great genetics, and was well proportioned; but it was clear that most of her weight was continuing to settle in her hips and butt. He had never before seen her ass look so big, so round, or so spellbinding.

He was speechless for a moment and blinked his eyes a few times to come back from his lust fueled stupor. "Just, um, throw a jacket on or something."

"You sure?"

"Yeah I'm sure." He drew closer and took in the dazzling sight one more time. She was such a knock-out, and even if she did weigh as much as him, he wouldn't change a thing.

His shoulders dwarfed her shoulders, but her hips dwarfed his hips, and when they embraced, they fit together like perfectly matched puzzle pieces.

Suddenly the idea of her wanting to get back in the gym saddened him. He gave her a quick peck on the cheek so he wouldn't smear her lipstick and his hand drew to her hips as if beyond his control. "I mean I can't wait to strip it off you later tonight, but I'm sure."

"Uh, whatever." She pushed him away as her phone buzzed. She looked at it quickly. "You're in for the softball game tomorrow right?"

"Yep, I'll be there. You gonna play?"

"I don't know. I don't think it would be smart for me to test my leg like that just yet, but I want to see you play." She took her stylish bomber jacket off the coat rack. He noticed there was a little more jiggling happening when she moved than there used to be.

"Alright, let's go," she said. "I'm starving."

He smiled, gazing at her deepening cleavage and then into her eyes. “Me too.”

Chapter 5

Mike was in his own apartment fingering his guitar when he glanced at his phone and realized he was almost late for the softball game.

He was nervous about going.

Once he met her friends, he knew be in a real relationship again.

No more bachelor life, no more freedom it would be official.

Was it too soon?

Fuck, now he had to go.

He threw on some hiking boots and a sweatshirt, grabbed his glove and headed out the door.

The game was at a city park only about 4 blocks away, but running short on time, and perhaps wanting to make more of a dramatic introduction to Autumn's friends, he took the motorcycle.

He parked between some cars on the side of the street and hopped off. A few heads turned beyond the chain link fence and Mike scanned the faces until he saw Autumn, sitting in the dugout.

The day could not have been more beautiful. The whole city seemed to be out and about. Couples were having picnics, moms were pushing strollers, and a few homeless men were sitting in the park bleachers, passing a bottle around, perhaps hoping to catch some eye candy, as well as a softball game.

Walking toward the field Mike saw a few people playing catch beyond the first base line. He entered through a gap in the fence. He had arrived just in time.

Autumn turned and leaned forward in her seat. She was dressed in capri style blue jeans, white Chuck Taylor high-tops, a t-shirt with three quarter length sleeves and a Seattle Mariners baseball cap.

Mike was surprised about the jeans because he didn't think she had any left that still fit.

"Hey look who it is," she said. "Thought you were going to flake out on us."

He smiled. "Sorry, I lost track of time."

Autumn shifted her hips around on the bench and gestured to the guy sitting next to her. "Okay, just a few quick introductions. This is Ryan, one of my best friends. I told you about him, remember."

Mike stepped forward and looked down. The guy was in his mid to late twenties, right around his age if not younger. He had a slim build, and a splotchy blonde beard shaved clean at the neck. They shook hands. "Hi Ryan, I'm Mike."

Ryan smirked. "Nice to meet you."

"And this is Sydney," Autumn said. "Mike Sydney, Sydney Mike."

Sydney smiled, her eyes beaming with kindness. She was pretty, and about the same height as Autumn but she was round and chubby and looked to outweigh her by a good 50 pounds.

"Nice to meet you," Sydney said.

Autumn, still seated, continued as another friend entered the dugout. "And, there's Tabitha."

Tabitha stepped forward and adjusted her glittery trucker hat. "Hi you must be Mike, I've heard about you. Good we can finally meet."

Mike remembered Autumn mentioning Tabitha before. She was the gym girl with the abs and she certainly looked the part, wearing leggings and a loose crop top that flattered her well-defined arms and tiny waist. She was very attractive, but compared to Autumn, she was plain.

"Yeah likewise," Mike said.

An umpire in chest pads and a baby blue shirt, called out from home plate. "Visiting team ready?"

Autumn stood and shouted back. "Yep, we're ready."

Mike watched his her with pride.

Goddamn she looked good in jeans, and nobody could pull off that cute and sporty baseball-cap-look the way she could.

"Okay, let's play ball!" the umpire said.

The game went on as expected. No one was very good but some were more competitive than others. When it was Mike's turn to bat, he felt the need to show off his skills and do something impressive.

"So are you serious about this guy?" Tabitha said. She was sitting next to Autumn on the bench, watching Mike step into the batter's box.

Autumn shrugged. "Meh, we'll see."

"He's super cute." Tabitha gazed over her shoulder at the street behind them. "Cool motorcycle too."

Autumn rolled her eyes. "Let's see if he can hit."

The pitcher delivered the ball with a slow underhand lob. Mike geared up, swung with all his might, and struck nothing but air.

Tabitha snorted. "Oohh, strike one. Literally."

Mike gritted his teeth, embarrassed. Even Ryan had been able to put the ball in play, and Mike refused to be shown up by the likes of him. Whether he was one of Autumn's best friends or not, he didn't like the way he had been eying her, and it caused a sense of jealousy to rise up within.

He kicked his shoes into the dirt and tightened his grip on the wooden handle. Unlike most of the people there, Mike played ball in high school, and he was good, at least he used to be, although hitting a 40 mile per hour softball was a lot different than hitting a 90 mile an hour baseball.

The pitch came in and Mike drew his elbows back, shifted his weight to his right foot, and swung again.

This time he made solid contact right on the sweet spot and the ball jumped off his bat like a missile. It sailed high in the air and it landed on a Honey Bucket just beyond the boundary of the field, a home run.

Tabitha rose to her feet. "Whoa, nice!" She turned to Autumn. "Okay, maybe I approve of this guy."

Autumn stood as well, but maintained that haughty look of indifference on her face, a look that she seemed to keep as the game went on.

In the 4th inning, a guy on the team had to take off early, leaving them a player short, and Autumn volunteered to take his place.

"You sure you gonna be okay?" Mike said.

Autumn rolled her eyes. "Yeah, I can at least stand in the outfield."

He smiled. "Okay, just take it easy, watch out for sprinklers and divots and stuff."

In the top of the 6th, Tabitha hit a ground ball up the middle and ran gracefully to first base. She was quick, agile and moved like a gazelle.

Next it was Autumn's turn.

Although she was right handed, she batted from the left side and Mike had a clear view of her backside as she stepped to the plate.

With a slight bend to her knees she reached back her arms and awaited the pitch. Mike clasped the chain link fence with both hands and watched closely. She was a sight. Her hips and thighs filled out those jeans marvelously and Mike had never seen a hotter ass in his life.

Was it really that big or was it something about those jeans?

He was utterly enthralled. The whole concept that a hot girl could actually gain weight like that was new to him, and he found it fascinating. Autumn was just so much of a good thing, it didn't seem fair to other girls.

After letting the first ball go by, Autumn swung at the second and hit a dribbling grounder down the third base line. She dropped the bat and ran towards first as the pitcher cut off the ball.

Watching Autumn run was something of a spectacle all to itself. To put it mildly, she ran like a girl. Her wide hips and bottom heavy figure jiggled and gyrated in a hypnotizing fashion, and it appeared she was moving in slow motion, as if her body could not keep up with her mind's expectations.

The throw to first was high and floated clear over the fielder's head, allowing Autumn to trot on safely. Ryan was up next and was somehow hit by a pitch which loaded the bases for Mike.

Mike belted a line drive that was hit so hard it bounced off the wall in right center. Tabitha scored, Autumn rounded third and she scored and so did Ryan. Mike flew around the bases with speed far superior than anyone else at the game, and with a wild throw to the plate, he scored as well. It was a base clearing, inside the park grand slam and the team cheered like it was the world series.

After a few high fives, Mike entered the dugout and found Autumn sitting back down on the pale aluminum bench, trying to catch her breath. Tabitha sat to her right and Sydney sat to her left.

Tabitha raised a fist in the air. "Way to crush it slugger!"

"Thanks," Mike said bashfully. He turned to Autumn. "How's your leg holding up?"

She fanned herself with her hand. "It's fine, I'm just (pant) not used to running like that."

"Don't push it too hard, be careful."

Autumn rolled her eyes. "Noted."

Tabitha grabbed her phone and started taking selfies.

Mike observed the girls as he paced around in the dugout. He knew that all three of them were more or less the same height, but the shapes of their bodies were vastly different. Autumn's hips spread out significantly wider than Tabitha's, and they were actually almost as wide as

Sydney's, despite the weight difference. He also noticed that Autumn sat higher than Tabitha, solely due to the fact that she carried so much more weight in her thighs and butt. Autumn was the prettiest one too, on either of the teams by far, and he found it refreshing that the prettiest one was also the curviest, and he felt incredibly lucky that she was with him.

They all socialized after the game albeit briefly, while some other teammates loaded up equipment before going their separate ways.

"That was fun," Mike said, turning toward Autumn as they made their way to the street.

"You're pretty good there with your home runs and everything."

"Chicks dig the long ball right?"

Autumn glared at him. "Chicks?"

He swallowed. "Sorry…umm, women appreciate the long ball."

She punched his arm. "Okay stop it."

He smiled. "You're not bad yourself."

"Ooooh, I don't know." She sighed. "I was in much better shape the last time I played."

He put his arm around her shoulder and pulled her close as they continued to walk. "You did great. You probably just haven't built back all your leg strength quite yet."

"Yeah, I guess so."

They stopped in front of his motorcycle and Autumn fiddled with her purse.

"Are you hungry?" He said.

She lit a cigarette. "I could eat."

He opened the back bubble-like Givi storage container on his bike and put his glove inside. "Let's get out of this place, go somewhere fun."

She took a short puff from her smoke. "Wanna get a car2go?"

"No way, we'll take the bike." He smiled, placed her glove next to his, then from the case pulled out a black, faceless half-helmet. "Still got an extra one."

She bit her lower lip and gave him a look that just about made his heart melt. "Okay."

He let her finish her cigarette, then mounted his bike and she climbed on behind. His motorcycle was a Ducati Enduro, and though it was a sportbike, it had room for two and a decent backrest attached to the Givi.

He had given her a ride on the same bike before, but that was a few years ago when she was maybe 20 pounds lighter. Now, the suspension sagged beneath her weight, and the bike felt heavy in a way Mike wasn't used to, but he relished in the sensation of her body clasping snuggly behind him. Her breasts pressed against his back, her thighs straddled his narrow hips and the feeling of her closeness sent a wonderful shiver up his spine.

He fired up the engine. "Okay, just don't fall off."

"Okay!"

She leaned forward and wrapped her arms around his waist as they rode away. With it being such a nice summer day, he took her on the most scenic route he could think of. They went through the high-rises and skyscrapers of downtown, then across the West Seattle bridge all the way to Alki Beach. He parked in front of Duke's seafood and chowder house and they got off.

"This okay?" he said.

She unbuckled her helmet and brushed back her hair. "Yeah, looks good to me."

Mike put his name in at the restaurant but it was busy and there was a 20 minute wait time. In the meantime, they went and sat on a bench that overlooked Puget Sound and smoked cigarettes.

Passenger Ferries drifted along the water and people on the beach began staking out campfire spots as seagulls squawked in the distance.

It was a warm evening, but that didn't stop Mike from holding Autumn tight and close to his body. The sun hovered just above the Olympic Mountain range in the west and highlighted the city's skyline to the northeast while wandering wisps of a breeze stirred romance in the air.

Autumn tilted her head up from Mike's shoulder. "Still nothing?"

He glanced at his phone. "Not yet."

She stood and put out her cigarette. "I'm just gonna go check."

He watched as she went so confidently toward the restaurant just on the other side of the paved bicycle path.

He loved the way she walked. Shoulders back, head high, with a little wiggle in her hips as she so elegantly and dramatically did something as simple and mundane as place one foot in front of the other. Even in her jeans and with her baseball hat back on, she had a way of standing out in a crowd, and the heads of strangers turned as if the spell of passing beauty was too strong to ignore.

Just moments after entering the restaurant, she came back out and waved at him to come in.

He sprang up and scurried toward her.

"Is it ready already?" he said.

"Yeah, come on."

"How'd you get a table so fast?"

The corners of her lips turned upward seductively. "I have my ways."

"Right." He knew exactly what she meant. He had forgotten that doors open up a little quicker and tables become miraculously available when in the presence of a gorgeous woman.

She ordered fish tacos and clam chowder with a glass of New Zealand sauvignon blanc, and Mike got fish and chips and a cup of coffee. He watched as she so expertly crushed oyster crackers into her bowl and listened to the way she analyzed and judged her tacos like a professional critic. Despite her denunciations, she was hungry and finished her entire meal well before he did.

"I hate it when I eat everything and the other person still has lots of food on their plate," she said. "I need to get better at slowing down and savoring each bite."

"You can have some of my fries if you want."

She smiled. "No, that's my problem. Everything tastes so good I want it all at once and I end up eating too much."

He set his coffee down. "I like that you're not afraid to eat." As he finished speaking, a very overweight woman squeezed her massive body directly behind his chair, then carefully navigated herself toward her table in front of him.

Autumn noticed the way Mike's gaze drew toward the woman's massive hips and billowing breasts.

Autumn locked eyes with Mike, then gestured toward the woman. She leaned forward and lowered her voice to a whisper. "Can you imagine being that big?"

He was taken aback, as he knew she had caught his wandering eye in mid wander and he was anticipating a scolding. He was unsure how to respond. "Um, no, but I'm not a woman."

Autumn took a few fries from his plate. "I mean like (munch, chew) what do you see when you see someone like that?"

After a quick peek, he turned and looked back at Autumn curiously. "I see a woman, who clearly enjoys food."

Autumn smiled. "Yeah, me too." She leaned in closer, still whispering. "I know it sounds terrible, but when I see someone who's really hugely fat like that, I don't think…like, oh, that's too bad..." She bit her lower lip as if deep in thought. "I think more like, how…delicious, it must have been to get there."

Mike erupted in a grin, as the words she was saying conjured up a million thoughts in his brain. "I like the way you think."

She shrugged before stealing a few more fries. "I don't know, (chew, munch) food is definitely my biggest weakness. I eat when I'm depressed, I eat when I'm happy, I eat when I'm bored."

He chuckled. "That's better than being the type of person that's always on a diet, treating their body like it's some sort of enemy."

"I guess so." She took a sip of her wine. "You don't mind that I drink, do you?"

He shook his head. "Not at all. Just because I don't drink anymore doesn't mean I can't enjoy it through you."

He stared into her eyes. Her hat was off and her beautiful hair was tied back in a messy ponytail that was both chic and wildly sexy. If his relationship with Autumn was budding before, now it was blooming and becoming solidified. He met her friends, she had ridden on the back of his motorcycle, and he had yet to find anything about her that he didn't like.

He never met a woman who could be so casual and unassuming, yet so severely feminine at the same time.

He looked at her face. He had a feeling that it was a face the'd be seeing again and again, for a long time.

She finished the rest of his fries and after he got the check, they rode back to her place in the magic hour of the setting sun.

They were always together as the summer unfolded, and spent a lot of time outside, taking advantage of the long days and perfect weather.

With her injury healed, Autumn tried to make a conscious effort to get more physically active, and at least get her body back to a place where she could fit into jeans comfortably.

Mike rented a canoe a few times and they had fun paddling around Lake Washington, and even went on a couple short hikes in the Cascade mountains. They would walk and talk their way to the Seattle Art Museum or the Museum of Pop Culture and tried to catch the classic movies that would sometimes play at the local independent theater down the street.

Autumn participated more in the softball games and by the time August ended, she was able to button her pants with ease and had seemingly gotten her weight back under control without having to sacrifice dinners out, or her favorite foods.

But things must change and so too did the weather as August became September and September became October. The morning air turned crisp, and the melancholy of the fall season harmonized life with nature like a second spring where every dying leaf becomes a flower.

The sunny Saturday motorcycle rides and the evening walks were replaced with pumpkin spice lattes and movie nights on the sofa with soul warming comfort foods, and Mike got the feeling Autumn's days of being able to squeeze her hips into her size 10 jeans without difficulty, might be short lived.

Chapter 6

Autumn awoke to the sound of rising chimes from her phone on the nightstand. She rolled over and turned it off. She wanted more than anything to stay in bed and go back to sleep as waking up early seemed to be getting more difficult as of late.

The door to her apartment opened, and she could see Mike's silhouette in the darkened entryway. He turned on the bathroom light then walked her way.

"Here you go babe," he whispered, placing a latte and hot breakfast sandwich on the table next to bed. He leaned in and kissed her cheek. "Just one more day to go."

She sat up a little, stretched her arms and yawned as the wonderful smell of espresso and crispy bacon hit her nose. "Thank you baby, yeah I can't wait."

"Okay, gotta run. Have a good day." He kissed her again, this time on her neck while running his hand over her hip and giving it a squeeze. "I love you."

Again she yawned, gazing at the outline of his face. "I love you too."

He gave her hip another squeeze, then went out the door and off to work.

She cuddled with Samson for a few moments then flung her legs over the side of the mattress and turned on the light. After using the bathroom, she grabbed her warm beverage and toddled over to the breakfast nook in the kitchen and lit up her first cigarette of the day.

Sitting on her kitchen chair, she sipped her drink. It was a creamy and delicious 16 ounce triple shot vanilla soy latte.

Mike was so sweet.

He'd been going to the bakery nearly every morning during the past month and buying her a coffee and a bacon egg and cheddar sandwich. Autumn appreciated it, as she was a big believer that breakfast was the most important meal of the day.

It was November, and Mike had basically moved in with her. She wasn't the type of girl that needed a man to be happy, but she had to admit living with one was quite nice.

When she was single she had to fend for herself and make her own breakfast, usually something like a bowl of oatmeal with yogurt and berries on top and a cup of green tea.

She flicked ash into the mug on the table and took another sip of her beverage. It was sweet. She hated to think about how many calories it contained, and she'd been meaning to tell Mike to get plain soy lattes instead of vanilla, but it tasted so good she kept putting that off.

She sat up straight and tugged downward on her white camisole. The skimpy top was a bit skimpier than it used to be. She placed her hand on her stomach and felt the roll of pudge protruding over her panties.

She sighed. All that wining and dining with Mike, the stress of working a demanding job, and the lack of exercise during the last few months were taking their toll.

After finishing her cigarette she went to the bathroom, jumped in the shower and got ready for the day.

At her dresser next to the bed, she slipped on a clean pair of panties that felt way too tight as the elastic fabric dug uncomfortably into her belly and hips. She wiggled back to the bathroom and gazed into the mirror.

Oh god.

She was gaining weight again.

She twisted around and investigated her backside.

Oh god!

Where did those hips come from, and why did her tush look so big?

She took out her little bathroom scale, placed it flat on the tile floor next to the litter box and stepped on.

172.8.

Shit.

She knew she had put on a few pounds, but she wasn't expecting to be more than 165, let alone 170.

It was frustrating because she had done so well over the summer. The last time she weighed herself was in August when she'd gotten back down to 157.

It was now late November.

Did she really gain almost 16 pounds in 3 months?

Why hadn't Mike said anything?

She stepped off the scale and investigated her reflection again. She had never seen her body look so voluptuous and she wasn't used to it.

For most of her adult life she had stayed within the one hundred thirty to one hundred forty pound range, and when she was a cheerleader in high school she was in the 120's.

She was amazed by the sight of her boobs and butt. She had never been this curvy, nor had she ever been this heavy.

It was too much.

With a naturally petit figure and bone structure, a number like 172 was very alarming.

No wonder none of her clothes fit.

She needed to lose at least 5 pounds by Christmas.

She went back to her dresser and squeezed her topless body into another camisole. She didn't feel like wearing a bra, they were all too tight anyway.

She went back to the bathroom and with her belly pressed softly into the tile countertop, fixed up her hair, did her makeup, then crawled back in bed with her laptop.

She unwrapped the sandwich that Mike brought and the smell made her mouth water and also seemed to somehow erase the depressing memory of stepping on the scale just moments prior.

She took a big bite.

It wasn't that warm anymore but it was still like heaven on an English muffin, so cheesy and buttery and toasty. She knew it must be packed with fat that she certainly didn't need, but she was tired and hungry and felt justified in eating it. After all, breakfast was the most important meal of the day.

Around noon she set her laptop aside and forced herself out of bed. She was hungry again. She went to the kitchen and looked around for something to snack on.

God.

Why did she let Mike do all the grocery shopping?

The man ate like a 14 year old boy.

There was a pack of blueberry muffins, a whole thing of jumbo sized croissants, a family sized bag of potato chips, a tray of black and white cookies, three slices of cake in the fridge and half of a cherry pie on the counter next to fucking pop tarts.

How the hell did he stay in such great shape with all of this food around?

Did he have the metabolism of a hummingbird or something?

She turned the fan on and lit up another cigarette. She really needed to stop smoking so much inside, but with the window cracked she could hear the rain patter on the street. It had been raining all week, all month come to think of it.

No wonder she was gaining weight. With the dreary fall weather, she rarely walked around outside anymore, especially when she had a boyfriend brought her every she needed.

She looked at the plastic container of croissants as her tummy gurgled. She wanted one badly, but couldn't rationalize indulging in that amount of empty carbs, knowing she was now over one hundred and seventy pounds.

After all, things were going so well and having turned 27 in October, she was happier than she had been in a long time.

In the past she thought her relationships with men were too one sided, always feeling like the guy was way more into her than she was into him; but with Mike it felt equal.

She had no doubt he adored her, just as she had no doubt she was in love with him. The last thing she wanted was for him to lose interest over something as stupid and trivial as her not being able to keep her weight in check.

Mike finished responding to his last email, then ran down to the campus gym to blow off some steam. It was all part of his after work routine.

50 pushups, 50 pullups, and 2000 meters on the row machine. He could do it all in less than 30 minutes

and he liked feeling all pumped up and ripped when he returned to Autumn in the evening. Although she would rarely say anything, he knew she appreciated his lean, strong, masculine physique, and the idea of being able to impress a woman like her, motivated him to be his best like nothing else in the world.

After a quick shower in the locker room, he got on his motorcycle and rode home. When he opened the door to the apartment, he was greeted by the sight of his beautiful girlfriend, standing next to the bed, wearing nothing but panties and a tiny spaghetti strap top.

"Why hello there," he said, smiling. He had been aware that her body had been going through some changes, but he was amazed looking at her now.

He wondered if other guys would be concerned if they saw their formally classically hot girlfriend gain as much weight as Autumn had so early on in a relationship.

For him it seemed the opposite. Perhaps it was because he had never dated a curvy woman before, or perhaps he was simply discovering things about himself that he was previously unaware of, but whatever the case, and whatever was going on with Autumn's weight, he was loving everything about it.

"I like your outfit," he said.

She scrunched her nose in disgust, but in a way that he found incredibly cute. "Thanks but, it's not like I have much of a choice."

He tossed his gloves off, hung his rain dampened jacket on the hook then stepped towards her. "How do you mean?" He put his arms around her and drew her close, noticing how far her butt jutted out behind her still narrow waist.

"Because hardly anything fits me anymore." She pushed him away and wiggled toward the kitchen. She held her hand up as if to signal she wasn't in the mood for any of his consoling comments. "Don't even say anything."

He followed her to the kitchen with his eyes on her ass. Her hips were significantly wider than her shoulders and he had never seen her butt look so full and prominent before. He couldn't get enough of the way each oversized cheek wobbled and jiggled with every step she took. "I'll go shopping with you if you want."

She lit a cigarette and sat down. "Yeah I should probably bite the bullet and go up a size. I could use a wardrobe upgrade anyway."

He lit his own and sat across from her. "No sales tax in Oregon."

She paused for a moment and blew thick gray smoke in the direction of the window. "Good point."

He was hardly listening, as he was so distracted by her naked legs and the way they settled in that chair. He was astounded by how much wider her thighs and hips looked when she was seated. She caught him staring and he turned away. There was a crumpled paper bag on the counter.

"Potbelly for lunch again?" he said.

"What?"

He pointed. "Potbelly sandwiches."

Her long eyelashes fluttered expressionless. "Yeah, I just did Doordash because it's so rainy out there."

"You don't need to do that you know. There's plenty of food here, we should try and use it up, save money."

She giggled abruptly with a cute and quiet feminine snort. "Whatever, I make more than you do." She puffed on her cigarette. "But also, I can't just keep eating all the crap you get, that's why my clothes are so tight."

He gave her a crooked smile and his eyes drew towards her thighs again. "What's wrong with tight clothes?"

"Stop it. You have no idea how easy men have it. You can probably just buy the same size jeans over and over on Amazon and never have any problems."

He leaned in and touched the bare skin of her knee. She was right. He had been buying the same Levi 501's with the same size 30 waist for years. "That's because a man's body is just for working and getting around and stuff. Your body, on the other hand, is a work of art."

She quivered from his gentle touch. "A work of art huh?"

He drew his hand back and nodded while maintaining eye contact. "A beautiful work of art."

She shifted her hips in her seat, causing the chair to squeak. She smiled cooly. "Mmm, I think I like that."

There was a moment of silence, as they both stared at each other.

Mike cleared his throat. "I'm starving. We should eat before I take the bike up to mom and dad's." He stood and put his cigarette out. "Little Woody's alright with you?"

She sighed. "Yeah, that's fine. But you don't need to get me fries, I really think I need to slow down with all the eating."

"What? Thanksgiving is tomorrow."

"I know! All the more reason I need to watch it." She took another puff on her cigarette. "I haven't even met your parents yet and I've already gained the relationship 15."

"Well you'll meet them this weekend."

Mike stopped in the kitchen's doorway as the last thing she said suddenly registered in his brain.

The relationship 15?

He turned and spoke without thinking. "Did you weigh yourself or something?"

She gave him a death stare and pointed her cigarette at him. "Don't even think about asking." She put her smoke out, but quickly lit another.

He stood, slack jawed.

Fuck.

How much did she weigh?

He didn't know why he cared but he did.

They'd been dating six months already and she still wouldn't tell him, not that he had the courage to ask.

She tapped her foot on the wood floor and glared at him. "Aren't you supposed to be getting food?"

After dinner Mike made the 30 minute ride north in the dark of night to his parents house in the suburbs. He parked his motorcycle in their four car garage and exchanged it for his Dad's Honda CRV. The next morning he drove with Autumn down interstate 5 to Beaverton, a town just outside of Portland, where Autumn's parents lived.

Mike met Autumn's dad Gary, who seemed to be doing better after his health scare earlier in the year. He was a large man in his late 50's, just over 6 feet tall and at least 200 pounds. He was soft, clean shaven and pudgy, with a slight beer gut protruding over his belt.

Mike thought Autumn's mom Patty was quite attractive for an older woman. She was regal and classy, perhaps slightly overweight but with surprisingly big hips and full weighty thighs, considering the bony lightness of her top half.

Autumn was one of two children, as was Mike, and her older brother Steven also made the trip to Oregon for Thanksgiving. Married, he brought with him his wife Julia, and their two children, Lily, age 4, and Noah, age 2, all the way up from their home in the Los Angeles area.

Steven was handsome, slightly built, and somewhat nerdy, but he bonded effortlessly with Mike as did his wife and parents.

Autumn got through the family holiday without receiving any comments about her weight, other than her mom telling her several times that she looked very happy. Her parents seemed thrilled with Mike, and she was thankful that she didn't have to answer a million questions about her love life for once.

On Saturday, they drove back north, and she finally got a chance to meet Mike's parents, John and Debbie, as well as his younger sister Megan, her husband Kevin and their two little kids, Liam and Willow.

For Mike, the meeting of the parents was a big deal and it was good to get it out of the way. His mom and dad loved Autumn, just as he knew they would, and, coming from a similar upbringing, she fit in with his family seamlessly.

Mike's dad gave him a double-thumbs-up look of extreme approval when Autumn's back was turned, as if surprised his son was capable of landing such a knock-out.

The month of December had never seen Mike and Autumn so happy. Their love for each other had not wavered in the slightest and if anything, it was getting stronger by the day.

They began to talk more about the possibility of getting a bigger apartment and moving in together officially. The eight month lease on Mike's place expired in January, and Autumn had the option to renew her's in February. Getting rid of Mike's studio was a no-brainer, as he hardly used it, but for Autumn, giving up her apartment took more convincing.

She had lived there for almost the entirety of her adulthood, and she was grand-mothered in with a cheap fixed rent that was hard to let go.

On the other hand, she had to admit her place was too small for two people, and was a ground level unit in the heart of the party district that was becoming increasingly noisy and potentially dangerous as the homeless population swelled.

It wasn't until Mike's dad offered to sell him the Honda for a family rate that Autumn became more serious about moving.

As much as she loved riding on the back of Mike's motorcycle, she could only do that for a few months out of the year, and the idea of having full time access to a car sounded nice. Of course, that meant that they would need parking and that was not an option if they stayed put.

"Did I hear that right, you guys are moving to Belltown?" Tabitha said as she sat down next to Autumn on the sofa.

Autumn took a sip of champagne. "Yeah, Mike found a really nice place, seems too good to pass up."

It was December 31st, and Mike and Autumn had gone to Tabitha and her boyfriend's Derek's apartment for a new year's eve party. There were about 20 people there, including Sydney and Ryan, as well as a few others from the co-ed softball league.

"Where is it exactly?" Tabitha said.

Autumn slid her butt toward the back of the couch. She looked exceedingly beautiful. Her skin-tight long-sleeve beige bodysuit was tucked beneath high waisted white jeans and the outfit highlighted and worked in perfect harmony with the alluring curves of her body. "Over on 2nd and Wall, right near The Whisky Bar and Rocco's, it has a view of the Space Needle too."

"Ooohh, Rocco's pizza!" Tabitha leaned forward and put her hand on Autumn's forearm. "Better watch out, that could be dangerous."

Autumn looked at her curiously. "Why would that be dangerous?"

Tabitha jolted backwards, smiling wide in her bubbly sort of way. "Are you kidding? That's the best pizza in the city, I'd probably be going there everyday if I lived that close."

Autumn rolled her eyes and the glitter of her earrings clashed on the surface of her perfectly made up face. The notion that living next to a pizza joint would be dangerous for her size 2 friend was laughable to her. "Well, Mike and I are getting a gym membership."

"Omigod yay! I'm so excited your leg is finally better and we can workout together again. What gym is it?"

"Just Anytime Fitness. It's actually right on the bottom floor of the building so I'm going to have no excuses."

"Good for you."

Autumn looked down at her thighs, feeling a little self conscious sitting next to her friend who was obviously much smaller than her. She remembered a time, not too long ago when Tabitha and her were the same size.

Good intentions not withstanding, the holidays had not done Autumn's waistline any favors. It was too busy and hectic, with too many temptations in the form of Christmas treats, decadent desserts and lavish feasts.

Instead of losing the weight like she hoped, she gained an additional 6 pounds since Thanksgiving; having discovered she was embarrassingly, one hundred and seventy-eight pounds when she stepped on the scale that morning.

She could feel it too.

Her size 12 jeans had been slightly loose around the waist and snug at the hips when she bought them a few weeks ago, and now they already felt uncomfortably tight all over.

“I know,” Autumn said, running her hands over her thighs. “I definitely need it. I’ve put on a few pounds.”

Tabitha shrugged, unsure of what to say at first. It hadn’t gone unnoticed that Autumn was looking a little fuller and curvier than usual. “Don’t worry about it. It’s just love weight and you look great. I mean really, you look so happy you’re like glowing.” She froze for a moment and her eyes suddenly widened. “Wait, you guys aren't pregnant are you?”

"Oh my gosh no! I'm drinking aren't I?" She was abhorred that Tabitha would even think such a thing.

Had she really put on so much weight that people thought she looked pregnant?

It wasn't like she had a belly or anything, well, not really.

She gulped the remainder of her champagne as if to drive the point home. "We haven't even been together a year, and you know I don't have interest in having kids anytime soon."

Tabitha raised her brows. "What about Mike?"

Autumn glanced at her boyfriend. He was at the edge of the kitchen chatting with his friend Cameron. She smirked and lowered her voice. "He seems to agree with pretty much anything I tell him."

"You got him wrapped around your little finger don't you." Tabitha turned her head toward Mike then looked back at Autumn and giggled. "You did good, he's definitely a keeper."

"I know." Autumn was beginning to slur her words. Wanting to feel skinny, she'd been abstaining from consuming anything other than champagne all evening, and it was finally catching up with her. “Don’t ever tell him I said this but, he’s like perfect.”

Tabitha sat up straight and animatedly fanned herself from the sexual undertones of her friend’s remark. “Is it getting hot in here or something?”

She pushed Tabitha’s arm. “Stop it.”

“Okay okay, don’t worry. Your secret’s safe with me.” She shot Mike another quick glance. “But seriously you two are so cute together, you’re the best looking couple I know.”

“Thanks.”

“Omigod what time is it?” Tabitha looked at her phone then sprang to her feet. “Quick, we need more champagne!”

Autumn rose as well, but at a much slower pace than her limber friend. She calmly sauntered toward Mike in the kitchen with her empty glass in hand.

Ryan was in the other corner of the room next to his friend Landon, watching Autumn’s every move from a short distance. "Damn," he whispered. "Is it just me, or is Autumn starting to get thick."

"It's not just you," Landon said. His eyes darted back and forth, paranoid of someone overhearing. "She's so hot though. If they break up, she's mine."

Ryan snorted. "In your dreams." He continued to stare at her in that devastatingly gorgeous outfit as her healed knee-high Italian boots clicked across the laminate wood flooring.

Despite being nearly one hundred and eighty pounds, she didn't look fat, but rather, soft and ultra curvy. Her legs were poured into those pristine jeans, and together with her tucked-in body suit, they had a shape-wear effect, shrinking her waist and pushing her breasts up and out.

"Jesus," Ryan said. "If she farts them boots gonna fly off."

Landon laughed, as the idea of a woman as beautiful as Autumn actually farting was somehow mind boggling to him.

His laughter was drowned out by Tabitha yelling out to the entire room. "Okay everybody! It's 11:58, make sure you got enough champagne!"

Autumn looked at Mike seductively and held out her glass. "Refill please."

He smiled and grabbed the open bottle of Taittinger Brut from the counter. "Yes ma'am."

Autumn watched as he filled her clear chalice nearly to the brim with the golden liquid. "You got your apple juice?"

He put the champagne down then held up his cup. "Yep."

"Okay, come on, I want to see the show." They locked elbows and she pulled him in the direction of the living room windows.

Tabitha's apartment was in the lower Queen Anne neighborhood, not far from the Seattle Center and the traditional fireworks display that was about to shoot out of the Space Needle. Mike and Autumn leaned against the glass and looked up.

"This is going to be a great year babe," Autumn said after a sip of her drink.

Mike put his arm around her waist and pulled her close. "I think so too."

She loved the way her body dissolved so easily into his. His hard angular straightness against her soft meandering curves, and even though she was now slightly heavier than him, they did look perfect, like they were destined to be together. Tabitha wasn't kidding when she said they were the cutest couple she knew.

Autumn gazed up at Mike with love beaming from her eyes. "I'm excited about getting a new apartment." She placed her free hand on her hip and stuck her butt out a little. "I'm excited we'll be able to go to the gym together too and I can lose some of these holiday pounds."

Mike gave her a half-hearted smile. Her words were delicious yet unswallowable. His eyes went from her beautiful hair, which she wore down, to her breasts, which looked as large as he had ever seen them, to her womanly waist and the way the top front button of her jeans seemed to be hanging on for dear life against the softer flesh of her belly. "You know you don't have to workout or lose anything to impress me. I think you're perfect just the way you are."

She smiled, pressing softly into him. “You’re really sweet, you know that?”

“I know.”

Tabitha started yelling out a countdown for all to hear as the final seconds of the year ticked away. “5, 4, 3, 2, 1. Happy New Year!”

Everyone kissed their significant others, let out their celebratory cries and clanged glasses in a toast to the end of 2019, and the promise of 2020, but something was off.

Mike stared at the Space Needle. It was still and quiet.

“Where the hell are the fireworks?” Ryan said from across the room.

Tabitha touched her nose to the window. “Did something go wrong?”

Autumn turned to Mike. “Check your phone, see if there's news.”

“Shit,” Mike said. “We’re only seconds into 2020 and already we got problems.”

“Bad omen?” Autumn said.

He smiled in his calm and comforting way. “Don’t know. Could be bad, could be good, we’ll just have to wait and see.”

Chapter 7

They moved into the new apartment at the end of January. It was a modern building, huge, and compared to Autumn's old place it was a palace.

It was on the seventh floor of an eight story building, but the apartment itself had two different levels, with carpeted stairs going up to a master bedroom and an office on the top; and a living room, spare bathroom and bedroom on the bottom.

The two floor loft style design gave the main living room incredibly high ceilings, making it seem posh and excessively spacious. It also came with a parking spot in an underground garage, which Mike used for the Honda he bought from his dad, and it had free motorcycle parking in a designated area.

At just under 3 grand per month it was significantly more expensive than what they were used to individually, but with Mike no longer paying for a place of his own it was easily affordable between the two of them and they were able to set a good percentage of their paychecks aside after Autumn changed companies in the beginning of February, moving from T-Mobile to Oracle, receiving a substantial bump in pay, while continuing to have the option to work remotely.

Mike punched in the electronic code on their front door then went up the stairs after returning from work. Autumn was laying in bed gently stroking Samson's furry neck.

"All done?" he said.

She sat up and moved her laptop to the side. "Been done for about a half an hour, although this learning curve is killing me."

"Did you stay in bed all day?"

She yawned and stretched out her arms. "Yeah, my neck starts to hurt if I sit at the desk for too long."

"Up for going to the gym?"

She made a face of disgust. "Uhhh…I need to eat something first." She tossed the comforter aside and swung her legs over the edge of the mattress. She was wearing only panties and a white camisole with her black bra visible beneath, which seemed to be her typical outfit as of late when she didn't have meetings. "Do you have anything planned for dinner?"

He blinked.

In the month leading up to the move Autumn talked incessantly about how she couldn't wait to get into a workout routine, lose weight and get back in shape; but now she seemed apathetic and disinterested.

They had been living there for a week, and in that time they had only been to the gym together once, as Autumn was so sore the day after the first time, she hadn't been able to muster the will to go back.

"Umm, not yet," he said. He sat beside her, noticing the deep creases she'd recently developed where her thighs folded into her hips. "But there's that weird German Turkish place downstairs I've been wanting to check out."

She leaned forward and arched her back, causing her cute little belly to poke out beneath her top, while also making her hip-cleavage all the more pronounced and distinct. "What do they have?"

"I don't know. It's like gyros, sandwiches and fries and stuff. That sound good to you?" He didn't think that she would want fries, as she had explained many times that she needed to eat less carbs, but he figured he'd at least put out the offer.

"I don't care," she said, "but I need something before I pass out."

"Didn't you get lunch?"

She gave him a blank stare. "I just got one pizza slice delivered, but that was like 4 hours ago."

"Rocco's?"

"Yeah, their slices aren't as big as I remember them being." She shifted her hips toward him and playfully nudged him in the side. "Can you just go please?"

"Alright alright." He decided not to say anything about getting a delivery charge from a pizzeria that was literally across the street from their building. Instead, he kissed her, went down the stairs and out the door. He knew a hungry girlfriend after a long work day was not someone to be questioned.

Despite his lack of enthusiasm about her wanting to lose weight, he respected her desire to do so and was going to support her, but he was confused.

She wasn't going to lose anything if he kept buying her takeout every evening, especially if she was ordering pizza by the slice for lunch.

He brought back two lamb and beef sandwiches and an order of fries. The food was delicious, and the sandwiches were dripping with creamy sauce, Middle Eastern spices and vegetables, and the fries were sprinkled with feta cheese. Mike hated feta so she ate most of those in addition to the rest of her exuberant meal.

Was it just him, or was her appetite getting bigger?

After dinner she squeezed herself into a pair of yoga pants, put on her purple Balenciaga athletic sneakers and a big fluffy faux fur coat and they went outside to their private balcony.

"So much for not smoking on the porch," she said.

Mike got up from his chair and peered over the railing, cigarette in hand. He looked down at the honking city street below, then looked left, right, and up. "I'm sure it's fine. Nobody else would be outside when it's this cold anyway."

"I don't mean that, I just mean like it's going to be harder to quit when it's this easy."

He sat back down and zipped up his jacket. "Well in the old place it was even easier."

"I know but we really weren't supposed to be doing that. It was more of just a bad habit that I started because I was too lazy to go all the way to the street."

He puffed on his cigarette. "How long have you been smoking?"

"Ohhh, almost, wait… seven years I guess."

"What made you start?"

"When I was in college I did a quarter in Delhi." She took a long slow drag on her cigarette and blew ribbons of carbon monoxide into the frigid air. "Seemed like everyone (cough) smoked there and I was curious. You know I was like 20 and I told myself I wanted to fit into the culture."

As wrong as it seemed, Mike loved watching her smoke. Something about that repetitive motion of caressing her mouth with the cigarette and manicured fingers, the subtle suck of her cheeks and exhaling from plump pursed lips. She was putting pleasure before health, and it was oddly erotic and sexy to him. "That's right I forgot you went to India, that's so cool that you did that."

She shrugged. " I suppose. Been smoking ever since though."

"Did you ever quit?"

She rolled her eyes. "Dozens of times. How about you?"

He pointed at himself. "Did I ever quit?"

"When did you start?"

"College, same as you." He gave her a crooked smile. "But I blame it on too many Humphrey Bogart movies. Watch like two or three of those in a row and you'll find yourself buying a pack of cigarettes without even knowing why. I don't know, since I got sober I tell myself I can keep smoking."

"It's still so unhealthy though, we're going to need to stop eventually. Hopefully the gym will help."

"Yeah." He took another puff, then extinguished it in the bowl they were using as an ashtray. "You ready?"

"No." She sighed and wiggled in her seat although the arm rests of her chair didn't give her much room. "I'd much rather have a glass of wine and take a bath, but I really need to get my butt in gear before it gets any bigger."

Her rosy face was illuminated from the lights coming from their spare bedroom on one side, and the high-rise apartment building on the other, and with her fur coat and the contrast of the evening sky he thought she looked like some sort of elegant ice princess.

He stood. "Why does it turn me on so much when you talk like that?"

She rose as well and put out her cigarette. "Oh I don't know. Probably because you like me." She gazed up at him, expressionless and in a whisper said, "And you're deeply in love with my ass."

He blushed.

Fuck she could be such a tease sometimes.

They rode the elevators down to Anytime Fitness. It was so easy and convenient, being able to access the gym without needing to go outside.

Autumn did the same routine she did last time. She was not a runner, and unwilling to push her cardiovascular system to anything close to strenuous, she hung out on the stair-stepper and maintained a slow and steady speed.

Mike found it funny she chose that machine yet would never take the stairs in the building, always using the elevator.

The gym was quiet and Mike did mostly body-weight exercises like dips and pullups, trying not to get distracted by the sight of his girlfriend slowly wiggling her hips and looking like the queen of the universe on the towering pedestal that was the stair machine.

It was just so hard to look away, no wonder it's called a stare master.

She came down from her podium only minutes later, sweating and breathing heavily. "Are you (pant) done yet?"

"I can be." Mike let go of the overhead bar and planted his feet on the springy foam mat. "You don't want to do anything else?"

"No, I'm (gasp) exhausted." She fanned herself. "I'm so out (pant) of shape. I'm more winded now than I was when we went on that hike last summer."

"You're doing great. It takes a while sometimes to get back into it."

"I'm definitely ready for that bath and glass of wine now."

He smiled. Her face was flush and her breathing was labored, but goddamn if she wasn't the most beautiful sight in the world. "You deserve it."

The days passed, and although her eating habits didn't change much, she kept forcing herself into the gym, twice a week, then three times a week, and by the end of February she seemed to be getting into a healthy routine.

"Babe, guess what?" Autumn said..

Sitting on the sofa, Mike muted the TV and looked up at her. "What?"

Wearing a black crop top and matching boyshorts, she raised her arms and wiggled her hips. "I lost 4 pounds."

He jolted to his feet and came towards her. "Hey take it easy, don't lose too much." He held her and began massaging her upper arms.

Smiling, she pulled away. "Don't worry. I'm actually starting to like my, umm, fuller figure." She twirled around, gave her booty a shake then looked back at him. "I still need to lose like another 10 though and I want to tone up more, but I already feel like I have more energy."

He sighed, and sat on the sofa's armrest, facing her. "That's great baby."

It was happening.

That wonderful period of carefree love handles and early relationship romantic bliss was ending. Mike knew it couldn't last, as much as he loved the way she gained weight, he knew she couldn't go on that way forever. Maybe it was a good thing.

"I think my cough has gone away too," she said.

"The nighttime cough?"

"Yeah, I've only had 4 cigarettes today." She crossed her arms and raised her eyebrows. "How many have you had?"

He turned towards the TV. "I don't know but I'm about to have another one."

She followed his gaze and stepped forward. "Why what's this?"

He shrugged. "Governor declared a state of emergency."

"Cause of that corona thing?"

"Yeah, they seem to be taking it pretty seriously."

She wiggled towards him and lowered her butt into his lap. "Interesting." She put her arm around his shoulder and rubbed against him. "I hope they don't close the gym."

He looked down at her ass and lower back, then held her hips with both hands. He grabbed her waist and pulled her tighter to his body. "That would be a shame."

Anytime Fitness shut down completely in the first week of March as covid-19 spread across Washington State and the rest of the world.

The campus where Mike worked closed soon after. Nobody knew for how long, so he was kept on retainer, which meant he would continue to be paid his full salary just to stay home as his job was not one that could be done remotely.

He felt bad that he had unlimited free time, while Autumn still had to wake up early and slave away in front of her laptop, so he did his best to make her days as easy and comfortable as possible.

"Oh wow, this looks amazing," she said, sitting up in bed.

He handed her a huge plate of food and a fork, then set a steaming mug of coffee on the nightstand. "Most important meal of the day right?"

"Right." She smiled and wiggled her hips beneath the down comforter. It was her all time favorite breakfast. A big fluffy German pancake smothered in melted butter and real maple syrup along with two strips of crispy bacon on the side. Her boyfriend knew her well. "Maybe it's not such a bad idea, having you home all day. I could get used to this."

He grinned. "Enjoy it while you can. I'm sure I'll have to be back at work within a week or two."

She took a bite. "You (chew, chew) think so?"

"I'm guessing."

She licked her lips. "Okay, then I'll be sure and take full advantage of it."

He sat on the edge of the bed and caressed the bare skin of her upper arm. "I live to serve you."

She took another bite. "Hopefully (chew, chew) the gym opens back up soon."

"I'm sure it will." He continued to fondle her arms and shoulders as the morning sun brightened the room. "Good thing we got this place when we did. Would've been pretty cozy if we had to shelter-in-place in your old apartment."

"Yeah, you wouldn't be able to practice much guitar." She was only half way paying attention to him, as she seemed to have one eye on her breakfast, and the other on her laptop screen.

"You gotta get to work?"

She sighed. "Uhh, always."

"Okay, I'll let you be." He stood. "I'll head over to Whole Foods later, text me if you think of anything we need."

"Sounds good." She shoved another forkful of pancake in her mouth. "Oh (chew) before I forget, (chew) can you grab some of that ice cream I like?"

"Which one is that again?"

"You know, the Turkish Coffee one."

"Sure." He leaned in and kissed her syrupy lips. "Love you."

"Love you too."

The beauty of Whole Foods was that no matter what Mike bought there, Autumn somehow seemed to approve of it, whereas if he went to Safeway or QFC, she'd accuse him of buying too much unhealthy junk food that was going to make her fat.

As long as it was organic, or "orgasmic" as she would say, Mike could buy pretty much whatever decadent little treats he wanted, knowing they all would find their way between her lips, and eventually on her hips. Tiramisu cake, chocolate croissants, pistachio macarons, peanut butter cookies, to name a few of her favorites.

When he returned from running errands, he went upstairs to check on her. She was still in bed, and her breakfast, which he knew was way more food than she would ever eat in one sitting, was actually, completely gone. He tried to act natural.

"Did you like your breakfast?"

"Yes, it was good, you know how to make that well."

He didn't think that anyone could possibly still be hungry after eating such a carb heavy, high calorie meal, but he decided to press his luck anyway. "What can I get you for lunch?"

Her eyes flashed towards him. "Are you kidding? I'm still full from breakfast."

He stepped forward and took her plate and fork away from the nightstand. "Okay, well, let me know if you get hungry."

"Don't worry about me, I can fend for myself."

He looked at her lovingly. "I know, I just like to take care of you."

"I appreciate it."

Early the next morning, Autumn pried herself away from Mike's spooning clutches and silenced her phone's alarm of overlapping chimes. She rolled over and pressed into him as he gently kissed her neck and caressed her thigh and hip.

He loved cuddling her. She smelled so delicious and her body was so warm and soft to the touch that he would've happily laid in bed with her all day if he could.

She yawned and gazed at him dreamily, slowly trickling her finger along the muscles of his chest. "I'm hungry."

"Okay baby." He put his hand on the side of his head and propped himself up. After the previous morning's lavish meal, he knew that she would probably want something healthy and light, or maybe a soy latte and sandwich if he was lucky. "I can head out and grab something from the coffee shop."

"No." She spoke with a sensual coo, almost a pout. "I want what you made me yesterday."

He sat up. "German pancake?"

She nodded. "Mmhm."

He was shocked. The frisbee sized pancake, along with bacon was a breakfast fit for an old time Bavarian lumberjack that spent his day chopping beech trees; not a work from home girl who spent most of her time in bed.

Did she really want that two days in a row?

He smiled. "As you wish."

She rolled her eyes. "What are you, the Dread Pirate Roberts or something?

The coronavirus continued its worldwide spread as March turned into April and the state government was closing down restaurants, bars and even schools.

It was turning into pandemic and beginning to seem unlikely that Mike would be going back to work anytime soon.

There was only so much guitar he could practice and only so many pushups and situps he could do before it all got repetitive and mundane. Wanting to find other ways to fill his time, he started getting more into cooking and baking.

He had perfected the Dutch Baby or German pancake to an exact science, and had been making it for Autumn almost every morning. Amazingly, she didn't seem to get tired of them.

Day after day it was the same routine. He would wake up, preheat the oven, mix up a batter of eggs, whole milk and white flour, then melt a half a stick of butter in a 12 inch cast iron skillet. He would then pour the mixture over the melted butter, put the pan in the oven, then fry strips of bacon on the gas stovetop as the pancake baked and rose like a soufflés.

When it was done he'd cut it into segments of 4, put it on a big dinner plate and drizzle it liberally with maple syrup; and along with two pieces of bacon and mug of coffee with steamed half and half, he'd carry it up the stairs, so Autumn could eat in bed.

The amount of fat, sugar and carbs she was consuming every morning seemed unfathomable to him and he kept waiting for the day when she'd tell him she wanted something lighter, or that she was sick and tired of the same old breakfast, but that day didn't seem to come and it was starting to show.

The 4 pounds she lost before covid hit came back in the blink of an eye and they brought some friends with them.

Mike didn't know if it had something to do with the shelter-in-place or the quarantine and 6 feet apart mandates, or if it was the end of the world type of atmosphere that hovered over the city, but Autumn's pink cloud of enthusiasm towards wanting to get in shape had seemingly evaporated.

Did she not care?

Didn't she say that she wanted to lose weight?

It was as if the closing of the gyms gave her the excuse she needed.

Maybe she liked having an excuse.

Maybe that wonderful period of early relationship romantic bliss wasn't ending just yet and this whole corona thing was inadvertently extending it.

Whatever the case, Mike went on serving her breakfast in bed, six, sometimes seven days a week and Autumn went on eating.

Like the frog in the boiling water, it was difficult to notice any changes in Autumn's body on a day to day basis; but after a few weeks, after a few months, they were undeniable, at least to Mike.

After loading the dishwasher, he ran up the stairs like a twelve year old boy.

It was a Sunday evening in late May, and Autumn was in the bedroom, struggling to fit into a pair of skinny jeans.

By now he was used to seeing her try to squeeze into undersized pants, and he could tell right away it would be a losing effort. He spoke hesitantly. "Do you like em?"

She gave him a look. "Yeah, (gasp) but, I don't think they're the right size." She was pulling hard on the waistband and gasping from the effort, the jeans still below her hips. "This is why I (pant, gasp) can't buy anything without trying it on first."

"They won't let you do that now, I don't even think you can take stuff back once you wear it anymore."

She glared at him. "I know."

"Can you return stuff online?"

"Maybe." She managed to slowly slide them over her butt, then, with her back turned and a bend in her knees, she tried to fasten the front button. "It's just so hard (gasp) to find clothes that fit my body shape."

Mike stared at her like a kid in a candy store. It had been a while since he had seen her in jeans and he was having trouble believing his eyes.

Her ass.

It was getting wide.

Was he even ready for that thing?

He had been hearing a lot of people complain about packing on pounds during quarantine, and his girlfriend was clearly no exception.

Never had he seen her look so big before, 10 or 15 pounds heavier than she was at Tabitha's new year's party, at least.

The weight crept onto her body much like it had before.

Her upper arms had become a little softer, her breasts a little fuller, but the majority continued to find its way to her hips, thighs and butt.

And what a butt it was, especially in those jeans.

As Mike's eyes zoomed in on the overstuffed taut denim of her back pockets, his mind flooded with obsessive torturous yearning. He put his hand to his mouth to make sure there wasn't any drool.

"Looks pretty amazing from the back," he said.

"Yeah, but look at the front." She turned toward him, still tugging with both hands, trying to close the gap of the unzipped fly to no avail. She let go and flung her arms up in frustration. "Maybe I shouldn't have tried to do this right after dinner."

They had just finished eating a home cooked feast of chicken alfredo pasta, but Mike knew that one meal wasn't to blame for what he was seeing. Her stunning hourglass figure was filling out in awe-inspiring fashion.

Her proportions were more amplified. She had real honest to god thunder thighs now, and the denim around her hips looked to be on the brink of splitting at the seams.

Her waist was more than just soft now too, and she was starting to get a belly, evident with the way it was filling the void of her unzipped fly like risen dough.

"Do you need help?" He stepped forward, wrapped his arms around her from behind and grabbed the tops of her jeans with both hands, pressing himself into her butt as if pulled by magnetics.

"No!" She wiggled away and plopped down on the edge of the bed. The force of her body caused the springs of her old queen size mattress to squeak like a rusty door hinge. "Uhh, who am I kidding? There's no reason for me to be wearing jeans anyway. It's not like we can see people or go anywhere so I might as well just be comfy."

He smiled and sat beside her. "Good idea, no pants are the best pants."

His eyes drew downward. He couldn't get over how enormous her thighs looked when she was sitting.

Why was that so incredibly hot?

She pursed her lips, then moistened them with her tongue. "You'd like that wouldn't you."

"Of course."

She sighed. "I can always just keep wearing leggings and dresses."

His heart felt like it could beat right out of his chest in such a way that he hadn't experienced since he was a teenager. Her belly was protruding onto her lap and oozing over unfastened pants and yet he wasn't the least bit repulsed.

On the contrary he could think of nothing he'd rather do than kiss it, squeeze it, knead it, and bury his face in it until he couldn't breathe.

What the hell was happening?

What were these sensational feelings that were making his heart throb and electrifying his body?

Why did Autumn's weight gain turn him on so much and make him crazy with lust?

Why did he find himself wondering what she would look like if she gained even more weight?

What was it about a woman with curves that was so fucking sexy?

"Come on, let's get these things off you," he said. He stood and began peeling the brand new pants down the swollen flesh of her legs. "They're really nice jeans, maybe get the same ones and just go up a size." Once off completely, he brought them over to the Amazon box in the corner of the room.

He folded them and glanced at the tag on the inside of the waist.

Size 14.

Chapter 8

Mike may not have been much for breakfast, but he made up for it by being a dessert fanatic. With covid still spreading like wildfire, and a return to work nowhere in sight, he had gotten in the habit of not eating during the day, and consuming all of his calories in the evenings.

He liked this routine because it made Autumn less self-conscious about matching him in portion sizes at dinner time, and it seemed to give her a sort of self-appointed permission to indulge in dessert without feeling guilty or greedy.

It didn't matter that they didn't always eat the same things.

Mike was a big fan of pie and donuts, while Autumn, in her more sophisticated way, was fond of gelato and ice cream, chocolate in all forms, cream puffs, cheesecake, cupcakes, or any cake; and although she was still consuming a massive breakfast each morning, she was also having dessert every night before bed.

She scraped another forkful of creamy cake from the store-bought plastic container and took a bite. "All of these (chew, chew) Planet Earth shows are really just about sex."

Mike set his half eaten slice of cherry pie down, scooted to his right and put his arm around her shoulder. "Animal instinct I guess."

It was July, and they were enjoying another quiet night together in front of their fairly new Philips 65 inch flat screen after a dinner of takeout Thai food. They already burned through their favorite British TV dramas and were left with mostly nature documentaries, travel and cooking shows.

Autumn pointed with her free hand. "The females don't even have to do anything. Look, see they just sit there and wait while all the males fight over her."

Mike turned the volume down a few notches then gave her arm a loving squeeze. "Just like humans."

She continued to clean the bottom of her container with her fork as if she was trying desperately to get every last morsel of whipped cream into her already bloated looking belly. "Not really."

"What do you mean?"

She licked her lips, leaned forward and put her now empty container on the coffee table. "Are you kidding? Girls are always in the gym, trying to change their bodies, all because they're competing with each other to attract guys."

Mike stared at her like a man in a trance. It hadn't gone unnoticed that she was eating much faster than she used to. Her body had become accustomed to a diet of high glycemic foods which no doubt caused fluctuations in her blood sugar, creating a vicious cycle of a subconscious, yet constant craving for more carbs.

The extra ten pounds or so that she added to her figure in the past month, was to Mike, very much evident. Dressed in skimpy loungewear shorts and a matching spaghetti strap top, she was leaving little to his imagination.

"Yeah but girls don't need to," he said. " They only think they do because society makes them think that.

You know, because society can make money off people's insecurities and stuff."

She tossed a wisp of hair away from her face and batted her eyelashes. "Do you really believe that?"

"Yeah, I do."

"What about me?"

"What about you?"

She curled her legs beneath her butt and adjusted her posture to face him directly. "Do I need to workout? Do I need to lose weight to attract you?"

Her thighs were squished together and her shorts were riding up her hips. He remembered when those very same shorts fit her the way they were designed, loose and lax. Now they were so small that the hems were digging into her flesh.

He lowered his head and kissed her above her knee like a man in deep worship. "I think you know the answer to that. You don't need to do anything."

"Really?" She slid backwards, placed her hand on her belly and looked at him blankly. "Because I think I've officially gained the covid 15, maybe even the covid 19."

He gazed into her eyes, recalling a time not so long ago when she complained of the relationship 15. "You look beautiful."

"I need to get some exercise." She unfolded her legs and let her butt plop back on the leather surface of the sofa, causing the cushion to make an airy noise of deflation. Her belly puckered into overlapping rolls. "Can we go for a hike this weekend? It would be nice to get out of the house and see some nature."

His shoulders slumped knowing she still had a desire to lose weight, but he supposed it was inevitable, whether he wanted it or not. "Um, yeah sure. If that's what you want to do." He gawked at the way her newly developed love handles were poking out and over the sides of her shorts. "You wanna take the car or the motorcycle?"

"Uhhh, car." She scrunched her nose cutely. "I need jeans for the motorcycle and I still don't have anything that fits. Another reason why I need exercise."

"Come here." He put one arm around her waist, the other beneath her knees and attempted to pull her body onto his lap. She felt heavier than he expected, but he managed.

"I want a cigarette," she cooed.

Her big ass dominated his much narrower pelvis and he grabbed the outer sides of her butt cheeks with both hands. He savored the sight and feeling of it. He couldn't imagine her getting any bigger, and he knew full well that before long the pandemic would end, gyms would reopen and she'd be back into some sort of workout routine but goddamn, he was going to enjoy this sense of heaven while it lasted. "Okay baby."

He took her to Denny Creek trailhead the following Saturday.

An hour's drive east on Interstate 90, it was a popular hike due to its gentle, family friendly grade and the spectacular waterfall at the end.

It was a warm day, but the canopy of old growth forest kept them in the shade for the most part. Mike found Autumn's walking pace to be almost unbearably slow, but he stayed by her side and helped her along.

After a quarter mile, she paused and took a deep breath of the clean mountain air. "Mmmm, it smells so good out here."

Bright green ferns, salmon berry bushes, and pink, yellow, and purple wildflowers surrounded them in every direction while sharp rays of light shot through out-stretched branches of Douglas-Firs and Western Hemlocks above.

Mike slapped a mosquito away from his arm, and adjusted his backpack. He looked straight at her. Her brand new Lululemon camo pattern leggings highlighted her alluring shape, and to him, she looked like a dream. "Yes, breathtakingly gorgeous too."

She rolled her eyes. "I'm excited to see this water-fall, how much further?"

"It's not far."

They continued their trudge upward over exposed roots and rain-rounded rocks. Autumn had been a fairly decent hiker, at least, she did okay the previous summer, but Mike was amazed by how different she was now. With no gap between her thighs, her walk had turned into more of a wiggle, and she was moving so slowly that little kids, dogs and families were passing them at seemingly every turn, and it wasn't long before she needed to stop completely.

"Can I (gasp) have some water?" she said breathlessly. She was panting and sweating and her face was flush.

Mike unzipped his backpack and handed her a 24 ounce bottle of Smartwater. "You okay?"

"Yeah, I (pant, gasp) just need to catch my breath." She took a drink. "Are we close?"

He shrugged then turned his head toward the traversing trail that zigzagged uphill and disappeared into the trees. "Maybe another mile."

She fanned herself with her free hand. "Are you kidding? I feel like we've (gasp) been walking forever."

An older couple wearing disposable masks appeared from around the bend and Mike led Autumn towards a mossy boulder off to the side to let them pass. The couple, a man and a woman, looked to be in their 70s, but they were fit and trim and moved with ease.

"Hello," the older woman said in a mask-muffled, yet cheery voice.

Mike gave her a nod. "Hi."

Autumn stared at the old woman with what Mike thought was a look of contempt before sitting down on a clean, shelf-like piece of granite. She took another sip of water and watched the couple dissolve into the forest. "God, (pant) it's like the coronavirus everybody has turned into professional hikers all of a sudden."

Mike gave her a few more minutes before helping her up.

He loved walking behind her. She had naturally wide hips, a small waist, and narrow shoulders and now with the extra pounds these features were just that much more amplified.

She was extremely curvy without being very strong, and because she stored so much of her weight in her butt and breasts, she was able to maintain an hourglass figure even with her climbing body-fat percentage.

Damn her ass was getting big.

After another quarter mile, they reached a wooden bridge that crossed the babbling brook the trail had been following from the beginning. Autumn was visibly exhausted.

"You know, (gasp) maybe I don't (pant) really need to see the waterfall," she said matter-of-factly. "This is pretty enough right here."

Mike put his hands on the knotty log that was the railing of the bridge. "You sure? It's not that much further."

She sighed. "I know but my feet hurt, (gasp) and my neck is sort of acting up again."

He looked at her, his eyes kind and sympathetic. Her outfit didn't hide much, and she was constantly tugging on the waistband of her leggings, as if pulling them upward would disguise her belly. "Okay, we can just head back I guess."

By the time they got to the car Autumn felt weak and drained. Mike gave her the bottle of water then took her cigarettes out of his backpack. He placed one between her lips and lit it for her.

She took a puff with a worried look on her face. "Oh my god (cough, gasp) I'm so out of shape." She leaned against the Honda as if her legs were too tired and sore to support her own weight. She sucked on her cigarette like a lollipop and exhaled repetitive clouds of smoke into the air. "We really (cough) need to quit smoking."

He lit one of his own. "Easier said than done."

"Maybe it's just (pant) that my blood sugar is low, I feel a little dizzy." Her breasts heaved beneath her low cut black tank top with each breath she took, and the late afternoon sun beamed across her radiant white skin and auburn hair like nature itself was trying to highlight the rare beauty that she was.

Mike could not articulate the reasons why; but he found himself extremely turned on by the way Autumn struggled so mightily with the short hike, so much so that she was unable to even finish.

Perhaps it was the panting and heavy breathing, or maybe it was refreshing to see her be vulnerable for once.

He wondered if this hike was it.

The event that would push her over the edge and cause her to get serious about making some lifestyle changes.

Maybe this was the first of many hikes.

"Drink water," he said. "We can stop at a drive-through on the way home." He put his arm around her, she was sweaty but cool to the touch. "Sound good?"

She gazed at him blankly, plucked a wedgie out her butt and nodded. "Yeah."

Sydney waited for Autumn to finish her cigarette in a parking lot near Shilshole Bay and Golden Gardens park in the northwest corner of Seattle.

It was a lovely September day, and the sky was so clear that the Olympic mountain range was completely visible beyond the silvery blue water of Puget Sound.

"You don't smoke in the car?"

Autumn took one last drag, tossed the filter on the asphalt, and stomped out the cherry with her heeled boot.

"God no. It would get all gross and stinky and Mike would probably kill me." She opened the door to the CRV and climbed in.

Sydney entered on the passenger's side.

"Anyway..I think sleep has been the hardest part for me during this whole thing," Sydney said. "I'm tired during the day and then I just toss and turn all night."

Autumn shifted her hips in her seat and shut the door. She started the engine and turned toward her friend. "Mike's been buying these CBD gummies."

Sydney stretched the seatbelt over her hips and belly. "Do they help you sleep?"

Autumn flipped down the overhead sun visor, checked herself in the mirror, then flipped it back up. "They work really well actually, you should try it. Helps with my anxiety too."

Sydney pointed at the bright red warning light shining from the dashboard. "Um, I think you need to put your seatbelt on if you want that beeping to stop."

Autumn grabbed the metal latch plate to her left and looked around for the buckle to her right. “Yeah I know I just can’t find it.”

Sydney's eyes drooped towards Autumn’s hips. She had seen her friend a few times since covid hit, but she was no less surprised looking at her now. She had gained so much weight, one look at her butt and that was obvious.

Her jeans hid nothing and she was sporting a belly that started just below her breasts and pushed its way onto her lap, and yet it somehow still looked tiny in comparison to her hips and thighs.

“I think you’re um, sitting on it,” Sydney said.

“Oh am I?” Autumn tilted her buttcheek up and felt around the seat with her hand. “Let me just…”

Sydney reached in. “Here, got it.”

Autumn contorted her neck, took the buckle and finally managed to click herself in. “Thanks.”

Sydney's eyes darted over her friend’s body and the way it jiggled from the effort. She cleared her throat. “Right… yeah, CBD might be good for me. I tend to just pig out on comfort food to deal with my anxiety.”

Autumn backed out of the parking lot. "I do that too. I've gotten so out of shape since this whole thing started. Over the summer Mike took me on what he said would be an easy hike, and I seriously felt like I was going to die…and I've probably gained another 5 pounds since then."

Sydney shrugged. "Whatever, everybody is gaining weight these days. How could you not?"

Autumn's took a right on Seaview Avenue. "Gaining weight is one thing, but I've literally outgrown my entire wardrobe, apparently I'm plus size now, but even these jeans are a size 16 and I can barely get them buttoned now, I used to be a size 6!" She immediately felt a little silly for saying that out loud, knowing that Sydney had been overweight most of her life.

Out of their little group of friends; Sydney was usually described as the fat one, while Autumn was the hot one, just as Tabitha was the athletic one; and the last thing she wanted to do was to make Sydney feel even fatter by complaining of her own body issues.

The two girls had such different body types. Sydney was apple-shaped and top heavy. She carried a lot of fat in her face, neck, shoulders, breasts and stomach, while Autumn was the exact opposite, with the exception of her breasts.

"Oh please you wear it super well and you're so pretty you can hardly notice," Sydney said. "Besides, who cares about that stuff anymore anyway? There was no softball this year, everything is canceled, Donald fucking Trump is still president, and with the riots and people dying all over the world, worrying about weight seems like such a meaningless first world problem."

"You're probably right." Autumn stopped at a red light and rolled her window down a crack. "I just think back to when I lived on the hill, before I hurt my leg I was walking everywhere, and now I barely even move. Especially with the way Mike's been waiting on me and treating me like an invalid."

Sydney raised an eyebrow. "Sounds pretty nice if you ask me. You should enjoy it while you can."

"I just feel bad for him," Autumn said. "He's been so sweet, and he probably expected me to stay the same size that I was when we started dating. I can only imagine what he must be thinking now."

"Has he said anything?"

Autumn tilted her head. "No, that's just it. All he does is compliment me. He hasn't criticized my weight at all, not even once."

"Of course he hasn't." Sydney adjusted her posture, turning herself slightly toward Autumn. "How could he with that booty?" She raised her eyebrows. "He probably loves you with some extra padding."

Autumn's mouth slipped into a hint of a smirk as she wiggled her hips in her seat. "Yeah and he's like, you know, ready to go 24 seven. It seems all I do is work, eat and have sex."

"Really…" Sydney smiled. "I've been meaning to ask you…how is he?"

Autumn gave her a quick glance and pursed her lips, a coy expression on her face.

"Come on," Sydney said. "Here I am, single and bored out of my mind, the least you can do is give me a few details."

Autumn sighed, then smiled dreamily. "He's really good. He's really…passionate. The way he makes love to me makes me get just like, so in the moment, so present. He makes me feel so like worshiped and all of a sudden I have like no fears, no self-conscious, like I could just surrender to him until I melt…"

"Nice penis?"

There was brief silence, then Autumn broke into a mischievous smile.

Sydney rolled her eyes. "Omigod. I'm so jealous of you sometimes. I think you should put your window down more cause its fogging up in here."

Autumn turned the wheel and went left onto Holman Road. "Speaking of penises, do you have time for a Dick's burger?"

"Omigod, I always have time for Dick's. I wasn't going to say anything but all that talk about gaining weight made me super hungry for some reason."

"Oh my goodness," Autumn said with a giggle. "We are so bad."

After dropping Sydney off at her place in the Green Lake area, Autumn came home to an empty apartment. Mike was still out on a motorcycle ride with his friend Cameron and wouldn't be back for another hour.

Autumn, still a bit full and bloated from the deluxe double cheeseburger and fries from Dick's drive-in, poured herself a big glass of red wine and plodded up the stairs.

She felt heavy and lethargic.

Were the stairs getting steeper?

She drew a bath, and waiting for the tub to fill she noticed her scale beneath the towel rack in the corner. She'd been avoiding it like a parking ticket she had no intention of paying.

The last time she weighed herself was in February, back in the pre-covid days when the world was normal and she and Mike were working-out on a semi-regular basis. She was 178 pounds then, happy to be on the right side of 180, and excited about the prospect of getting back down to the 160's.

God.

That felt like a lifetime ago.

She shuddered to think of what the numbers might say now.

Chapter 9

Mike came home later that evening. The apartment was dark and quiet. He flipped on the lights, set his helmet down next to the shoe rack that displayed Autumn's vast array of boots and high heels; hung his jacket up, then went upstairs.

She was lying in bed, deep beneath the covers. He carefully moved her knees, sat down beside her and ran his hand gently through her hair. "Hey."

Still with her head on the pillow, she shifted into a fetal position. Her eyes remained closed.

He gave her shoulder a nudge. "You okay?"

She grabbed the corner of the comforter and drew it up so it covered her body from the neck down like a cocoon.

He kissed her on the cheek. "What's wrong?"

She opened her eyes, let out a disgruntled sigh, then squeezed her eyelids shut again.

"Are you hungry?" he said. "There's cake in the fridge, I can bring it up for you if you want dessert in bed." He slowly pulled the blanket off. She was naked except for a pair of beige panties. Her body was tense and her hands were balled into fists. He stared at her, confused. "Does that sound good, cake?"

She opened her eyes."No Mike!" She sat up abruptly, swinging her legs over the mattress and shoving her pillow aside. "No more cake. No more desserts all the time!"

He stood. "Hey, what's the matter with you, what's wrong?"

She sniffled and glared at him. "Everything."

His eyes, as if beyond his control, dissected her body from head to toe. She was clearly upset about something, but despite that, or perhaps because of it, she looked unbelievably gorgeous to him. Her naked breasts were an exhibit of youth and beauty and beneath was a soft tummy that spilled over her panties like a ball of pudding.

Although her belly wasn't small, it was dwarfed by her ass and thighs and her hip cleavage had become a fully formed and distinct thighbrow of symmetrically folding flesh spreading wide across milky white skin.

He stepped forward. "What does that mean?"

With her arms at her sides, she clasped the bottom sheet with both hands and sniffled again. "Nothing. Nothing is wrong and everything is wrong."

He sat next to her again. "Baby, have you been crying?" He stretched his hand around and placed it on her far right hip. It was getting to be a bit of a reach.

His eyes drew downward to her pudgy sides and subtly budding back-fat. He had never realized it before, as he always thought of her as having such a narrow midsection, but her waist in her sitting position was actually quite a bit thicker than his own.

"Why? Come on, talk to me," he said.

"Nothing, I just…" She became silent for several seconds, then turned her head so she could look him straight in the eye. "I weighed myself."

Mike inspected her face nervously. He swallowed. "Okay…well, so what."

"So what?" She stood, then spun back around to face him. "I'm two hundred and sixteen pounds. That's what!"

Her words hit him like a ton of bricks.

Two hundred and sixteen pounds?

Was she serious?

Damn that was a lot of weight.

He didn't know how to respond, so he just sat there dumbfounded for a few seconds before muttering, "Umm, well…"

She stomped her bare foot on the carpet like a child that didn't get her candy and her entire body jiggled in rippling waves. "Two hundred and sixteen pounds! I couldn't believe I was over 200, let alone 216."

He stared at the brown leather of his boots for a moment, then slowly looked up. He examined her closely.

Two hundred and sixteen pounds.

He was having trouble believing it himself.

Could she actually be that heavy?

It was baffling because she really wasn't a big person.

She had small graceful hands, small dainty feet and ankles, a small ribcage and narrow, almost fragile looking shoulders. Her facial features too were smallish, slight and delicately feminine.

He cleared his throat and spoke without a thread of conviction. "Maybe the scale is…broken?"

"It's not broken Mike, I checked like 4 times!" She crossed her arms beneath her boobs. "I've gained like over 30 pounds since January and this fucking year isn't even over yet! Do you realize what this means?"

"What?"

"It means that I'm clinically overweight."

Mike thought about that for a second.

Clinically overweight?

5 foot 5, 216 pounds, with her petite bone structure?

It seemed more likely to him that she was now clinically obese, not clinically overweight.

Holy shit.

He shook his head. "You're not clinically overweight honey."

"Yes I am Mike! I'm getting fat. I can't find any clothes that fit me anymore, I can't even walk up the stairs to the bedroom without getting out of breath and it's your fault!"

"What did I do?"

Her eyes bored into him, penetrating and severe. "You're constantly buying desserts, constantly bringing me food and constantly encouraging me to eat."

"Well I just… want to take care of you. My love language is acts of service."

"Don't throw my love language stuff back at me."

"Sorry." He drew closer, wondering if maybe she was going through nicotine withdrawals or something. "You want to go outside? Do you need to put some clothes on?"

He reached his hand toward her waist but she turned away and collapsed back into bed.

He gazed at her and pulled his hair with both hands. He sighed. "I'll…be outside."

He already smoked two cigarettes when the door to the balcony opened. Autumn, wrapped from head to toe in a fluffy blanket, stepped outside and squeezed herself between the railing and the small round table. She sat in the chair across from him.

She was empty handed so he pulled out one of his own cigarettes, placed it between her lips and lit it.

She took a long, soothing drag, then stared at him silently for a moment.

"You look like you were electrocuted," she said, finally.

"I do?

She leaned forward and ran her fingers gently against his scalp and fixed his hair, then settled back into her seat and took another drag on her smoke. "I'm sorry I got upset."

"It's okay."

"It was just that the number was so shocking. I can't believe how much I've let myself go."

Her hair was wavy, slightly tangled and looked wickedly sexy as did the pouty part in her plump pink lips.

Why did she have to be so goddamn good looking?

Even with all of the extra weight, her face had changed little, and from the neck up there was scant evidence of the bountiful and ample curves that lay below.

“I’m sorry too,” he said. “I think you’re every bit as beautiful as you were the day I met you, but I suppose it doesn't matter how beautiful I think you are.”

Her eyes, still puffy from the tears, flashed into his. “Why not?”

“I mean, well…I want you to feel beautiful too.”

“I do feel beautiful, and I appreciate how much you love my body…” She trailed off as a police siren wailed in the distance.

There was a ponderous moment of silence. Mike lit a third cigarette and sat up straight. He cleared his throat. “You remember that time back in the Starbucks days, when it was Black Friday and they were doing the

Christmas tree lighting? I had to go get more supplies or something…"

She raised her brows. "A DSL?"

"Yeah I had to do a DSL and there were so many people outside I could barely get through the crowd with my little cart or whatever, and I can't remember why but you were outside too and the lights were on and Christmas music was playing and everything…"

She looked straight into his brooding blue eyes. "I remember."

"You came to tell me something. We were like right next to each other and there were so many people we could hardly move and I thought…what if I just kissed her right here?" He smiled in a subdued and melancholy kind of way. "Thought it would be super romantic, like in the movies or one of those famous black and white photos."

"Why didn't you?"

"I don't know, got scared I guess. You were always so hard to read and I didn't know how you would react. Thought you were too…uptown for me." He flicked ash into the bowl on the center of the table. "What would you have done? Would you have kissed me back?"

She was smiling through her eyes. "Yes."

"Damn, wish I would have."

"I wish you would've too." She adjusted her blanket so it covered her naked shoulders. "Look, I am very grateful to have you and I'm grateful for the way you've stood by me and the way you've taken care of me during this whole crazy year…" She paused. "But I feel like my weight has gotten out of control, and it's really not healthy for me to be this big." She placed her cigarette between her lips, sucked in her cheeks then exhaled a mist of smoke. "I don't know, (cough) maybe It's just that you're in such great shape and I'm starting to feel kind of… self-conscious."

"Okay first of all, I am not in great shape." He held up his burning cigarette. "And second of all, isn't that part of what makes attraction so beautiful? The contrast… the differences in our bodies is what attracts me to you."

"I know but I've never struggled with my weight like this before, and I really need to put a stop to it before I get any bigger."

As much as he hated to admit it, he knew she was right. He felt as though he was playing with house money anyway, as he never expected her to get this big.

Two hundred and sixteen pounds was a lot, especially considering she had gained so much of it relatively quickly.

He looked into her eyes and nodded. "I love and adore your body, and I think you are gorgeous and perfect just as you are right now…but I understand what you're saying, and I will support you in any way that I can."

She leaned back in her chair. "Thank you."

He paused for a long moment. "Do you ever miss having a job where you actually go into the office?"

She scrunched her nose. "Not one bit."

"Guess you were already used to it, and now the whole world's doing it."

"What about you, any more news with work?"

He shook his head. "Nope, looks like we won't be going back anytime soon."

"God, it's so crazy they're still paying you."

"I certainly can't complain." He shrugged. "You getting sick of me being home all the time?"

She puffed on her cigarette. "No, I like it, and I'm kind of dreading the day when you have to go back."

"Me too. We've done okay with this whole corona thing so far, could be a lot worse, so many people are struggling out there."

"I know. This year has felt like 5 years," she said. "I was thinking about when we lived on the hill and it seems like that was so long ago."

"I know what you mean. Feels like we've been together forever too. In a good way."

Her head became still and she stared at him long and hard. "What kind of a relationship do we have?"

"What do you mean?"

"I don't know, our circles of friends have like shrunk, we can't even really see family anymore and… sometimes I feel like we're the only two people on earth." Her eyes drifted toward the vast illuminated skyline of the city, then darted back to him. "But we never talk about what like, we're actually doing."

He leaned forward and gazed at her as the feeling of romance waxed heavy in the evening air. "I know that I love you."

Her eyelashes fluttered and her lips parted slightly before she spoke. "I guess what I'm saying is that I want to feel secure in this relationship. I don't really see a point in getting married, but I need to know that we're committed."

He extinguished his cigarette and his eyes beamed into hers. "I am committed. I don't want anyone else but you."

She smiled, her gaze warm and melting. "Same."

Chapter 10

Things were different the next day.

Autumn was different.

She was less affectionate, refused her bacon and German pancake breakfast in the morning, and didn't seem to eat much of anything during the day aside from fruit and yogurt.

Mike caught her exercising in the bedroom on her lunch break, doing pilates through an app on her phone.

She was a sight to see, to say the least, but she didn't want him watching..

He decided that if she was serious about getting back in shape, then he would get serious too and step up his game.

"Oh wow, there's no way I could do that," Autumn said.

Mike had installed his pullup bar in the door of the guest room downstairs, and having finished her workout, Autumn watched from behind as he gripped the bar, slowly lowering himself down, then shooting back up with explosive bursts of strength.

His shirt was off, and she admired the way his hardened back muscles, biceps, and shoulders bulged and contracted with each movement. His hair was getting longer too, and she liked it that way.

What could she say? She had a hot boyfriend.

He let go of the bar and faced her. "I could help you try, if you want."

She shook her head, but stepped beneath the bar. She rolled her eyes. "I have no upper body strength."

"Can you grab it?"

Lifting to her tippy toes, she curled her fingers over the foam covered grips.

He bent down and wrapped his arms around her thighs, smooshing his head into her butt in the process."Okay, ready?" He heaved her upward, lifting with his legs as she pulled with all her strength. She felt very heavy, but he managed to get her chin just above the bar. He lowered her down slowly, then let her hang for a second.

"This is actually (pant, huff) a good stretch for my back," she said, gasping from the strain of her own weight. She tried to pull herself up but couldn't move an inch. "God, I can't believe (gasp, pant) you can do this." She let go and lowered her sock covered feet back to the carpet. "I think (pant, huff) I'll let you do your exercises (pant), and I'll stick with mine."

Mike gazed at her. She was driving him crazy with her workout outfit and loose ponytail and the sexy way she was panting and trying to catch her breath.

Why did her labored breathing turn him on so much?

He gently caressed her waist with his fingertips. Her body was warm. He gestured toward the upstairs loft. "Are you doing okay up there?"

She stayed at arm's length, and did not draw closer to him like she normally would. "Yeah why?"

He shrugged. “I don’t know, just seeing if you're hungry or if you need anything.”

She crossed her arms. “No. I’m not hungry and you don’t need to keep asking.”

“Alright alright.”

Her eyes darted over his naked, pumped up torso, then she glared at him like a teacher reprimanding a student. “Don’t worry about me.”

He nodded and gave her a dismal smile of defeat. “Okay.”

Since the start of the pandemic, Mike and Autumn had been making love at least every night, sometimes twice a night and in the mornings.

It had now been three days since Autumn stepped on that scale and it had been three days since Mike had gotten even a sniff of her delicious pussy.

Fuck.

Had she really become ashamed of her curves, ashamed of her weight?

God, he missed her.

He missed their evenings together on the couch, watching conversation stimulating shows while he held her in his arms and she ate creamy rich desserts without a care.

He wondered if she missed it too.

He laid in bed, twiddling his thumbs thinking about it.

The toilet flushed and Autumn emerged from the bathroom. She was wearing a black thong, but had thrown on a loose fitting t-shirt as if to hide herself.

She sat on the edge of the bed for a moment with her back turned.

He marveled at her shape from behind, and the way her hips sunk into the mattress, and the way the entire mattress seemed to slope towards her butt.

He was so hard he was practically throbbing. The lack of physical contact was killing him. He reached for her.

"No, please. I'm tired and not in the mood." She flung her legs on top of the bed and laid on her back with her knees bent and the covers off.

He reached for her again, trickling his fingers against her thighs.

She could feel his desire burning through her and turned toward him coldly. "Come on. It's hard for me to get aroused when I don't feel sexy." She sighed and looked at her knees. "I don't even recognize myself anymore."

Don't feel sexy?

How could she not feel sexy?

Weight gain or not, she couldn't be unsexy if she tried.

He laid on his back and bent his knees as well, mimicking her position exactly. Dressed only in boxers, he compared his thighs to hers. His were thin, toned, hairy and there was a huge gap between them.

She had no gap between her thighs. Her thighs were squished together and they were thick, soft, silky smooth, and seemingly twice as big as his in every direction.

"You have very nice legs," he said.

She let out a disparaging gasp and without a trace of enthusiasm said, "Thanks."

He stretched out his arm, slowly dug his fingers between her legs and caressed the softest spot of her inner thigh, gently and lovingly. He did this for a while and then drew his hand away. "I'm sorry, I'll let you sleep."

"No." She turned, her mood suddenly different. "That actually feels really good."

Oh hello.

Was he actually getting somewhere?

Did she feel as sexually deprived as he did?

He put his hand back and continued. Her skin was like butter. After a while he moved from her crotch to her belly. He rubbed it, slow and prudent. "Does that feel good?"

Her hips shifted. Her eyes were closed and her lips were parted. "Mmhmm."

"I love your belly," he whispered.

She opened her eyes. "You do?"

"Yeah." He sunk his fingers deeper into the flesh around her navel and massaged her like he was worshiping a deity. "Do you feel safe with me?"

She gasped, feeling wonderfully woozy and dreamy from his masculine touch. "Yes." She became still for a moment, then looked at him skeptically, yet also with a lusty trace of hedonism. "Why do you like my legs so much?"

"Because they're sexy and shapely and soft…and because they're yours."

She looked back to the ceiling. "Do you think I have… thick thighs?"

Okay. Where was she going with this?

"I think you have amazing thighs, perfect thighs."

She turned and stared at him. "But do you think they're thick?"

His eyes darted from her legs to her face, still unsure of what she was getting at. "Umm…yes."

"Mmmm," she cooed with a sound of deep pleasure.

He looked at her, confused.

He couldn't comprehend how her moods could change so quickly, but he understood what went through a woman's mind like he understood a foreign language.

He sat up, then got on all fours and crawled on top. He lifted her baggy shirt, lowered himself between her spreading legs and kissed her belly. "Do you like that?"

"Mmhmm." She had an odd expression on her face and softly squished and jiggled her legs against his sides. "Do you think my thighs are…chunky?"

Her words sent shockwaves of excitement from his stomach to his throat. Now he was really confused.

How could she go from crying her eyes out over her weight, to vowing to diet and exercise, to becoming turned on by receiving verbal confirmation that her thighs were in fact thick within the time span of a few days?

Was it simply because he had made her feel safe somehow?

Was it all some sort of test?

"Umm…do you want me to think that?" he said.

"I want your honest answer."

He grabbed the thickest part of her left thigh. It was so big that even his two large hands couldn't come close to going all the way around it. "Yeah, I love your chunky thighs."

A tremor went through her, and she wiggled and sank deeper into the mattress. "Oooh, baby."

He continued fondling her doughy flesh and the way she was reacting encouraged a boldness in him. "I love how thick and lush and chunky they are."

She melted. "Mmmm, ooohh god, Mike!"

He was hard as a diamond.

He pulled her panties off, then stripped himself of his boxers.

He lunged back on top and put his lips to her belly again; then fell into her breasts. After several wonderfully torturous minutes of poking and teasing her clit, he slipped inside. He rocked back and forth and she gasped and moaned with delight, groping his ass with both hands.

He rolled off and removed her shirt. He laid on his side, shoved his arm beneath her waist then pressed himself into her and kissed her mouth.

Fucking hell.

The bare skin of her belly felt so delicious as it oozed against his abs.

With a good amount of effort, he rolled her on top, and let all 216 pounds of her pin him to the bed.

He grabbed her love handles, shoved her chubby torso closer to the headboard, then slid back inside of her warm wet pussy and continued thrusting into her as the steady rhythm of sex took over.

He had never seen her so turned on before, but with the heat of the room, and the added weight, she was beginning to sweat, and he was having trouble getting her to climax.

All of the usual dirty talk wasn't working and after a while she was gasping for breath and getting nowhere. He decided to try something audacious, something different.

He gazed up into her steamy, sex-starved eyes and in a low whisper said, "You want me to make you breakfast tomorrow morning, help keep those thighs nice and… chunky?"

She squealed. "Ohhh…yes (pant) baby." She gave him an exceedingly sexy and pouty look, then brought her rocking cadence to a stop. She gazed at him with beseeching, pleading eyes. "I'm (gasp) hungry right now, (pant, gasp) can you get me some cake?"

He grabbed her by the shoulders. "You want cake right now?"

She smiled and nodded. "Mmhmm." She let him slip out, then she rolled off and onto her back.

His eyes were like saucers.

What the hell was happening?

He stared at her for a moment, then jolted out of bed and ran downstairs naked as the day he was born. He returned seconds later with a big slice of cheesecake and a fork.

They didn't need to explain it, they just knew.

Her lips parted expectantly and he didn't hesitate to feed her.

"Oh God, (chew, chew) mmm, more," she gasped between bites.

He kept feeding her and she kept chewing and opening her mouth after each bite and did this until all of the cake was gone. She wheezed wearily and licked her lips. "You really (pant) like how…chunky I'm getting?"

He put the empty plate and fork on the end table. "Yeah, I fucking love it." He mounted her again and slid back inside. He was losing control and reached down, grabbed a handful of her belly and shook it.

She reacted like it was the best feeling in the world. "Oooooh, (gasp) God baby."

He continued thrusting into her violently, passionately and with reckless abandon. "I love how big and soft and curvy…"

She moaned louder. "Ohhhh, (pant) mmmm."

Her response to his words astounded him, but in the heat and fervor of the moment, they were so reassuring, and he was so intoxicated with desire he decided to go all the way, drawing his mouth to her ear and whispering, "And how… fat you're getting."

That put her over the top. Her eyes rolled back, her mouth fell open and her entire body quivered and contracted in euphoric spasms.

"Ohhh (gasp, huff, pant) fuck, (huff) ohhh God baby (gasp, pant), oooohh, (pant) Mike!"

She rolled over, still catching her breath. "Oh my (pant) God. That was amazing, I think I orgasmed like (pant) three times." She slowly sat up. "I feel almost like ashamed."

"You have nothing to be ashamed about." He gazed up at her glossy eyes. "Did you like it?"

She turned her head. "Yes. I did."

"Then why feel shame?" He sat up as well and rested his back against the headboard. "We're all taught from a young age…in this country especially, that sex is sort of bad and taboo and stuff, but that's all wrong. It's a natural expression of love, and there's nothing wrong with giving into your sexual desires. It's a beautiful thing."

She brushed a lock of hair away from her eyes. "I liked it when (pant) you fed me."

"I could tell."

"Why was that so hot?"

"I don't know? Food is sexy. It engages all the senses…smell, taste, sight, the sound of your lips…"

"Stop it, you're going to turn me on again." She gave him a little smirk then got up and went to the bathroom.

Mike watched her naked derriere wiggle away, then collapsed back into a lying position, trying desperately to wrap his head around what just happened.

Was this for real?

Was he dreaming?

He was still wondering about it when she came back.

She looked down at him. "Oh my god babe, you're still so hard."

He tilted his head. "Yeah I know."

She got into bed and curled up next to him. "Why are you still so hard?"

"Why do you think?"

She let her naked leg fall between his knees and ran her fingers over the hairs of his chest. "Is it because you love my body?"

He let out a blissful sigh, then smiled. "Something like that."

She brought her voice down to a slow and sensual whisper. "You love how chunky I'm getting don't you."

God that word again.

Chunky.

He looked into her eyes. "I love everything about you."

With mild struggle, she lifted herself on top of him and kissed his lips. She let all her weight collapse onto his body. "Do I need (pant) to let you go again?"

Chapter 11

It was like Autumn had been holding back a secret, and after almost a year and a half of dating, unleashed it on Mike in a flood of orgasmic bliss. It was magic, and she finally used her magic and it entered his soul and consumed him like a spell.

The question as to whether or not it had been real dissipated over the following weeks. She never said as much, but her actions spoke louder than her words.

It was what she didn't say that gave Mike the permission he needed.

He went back to making her breakfasts every morning that were calorically dense as a weekend brunch and she didn't refuse them. When he would come by to check on her during the day, she would often show him how her plate was empty then give him a little wiggle of her hips and a knowing look that could just about make him swoon.

He wasn't sure if it was something she had worked through, something he did, or the oddly romantic sense of isolation that came from the ongoing pandemic that caused such a change in his girlfriend, but she stopped criticizing herself, and became much more relaxed, at ease, and confident with her curves.

It was utter bliss.

Everything was sexy.

Everyday was Christmas morning.

They understood each other on a deeper level.

In October, she weighed herself again and let him watch.

She was two hundred and twenty two pounds, but she didn't seem upset about it in the slightest. She just looked at him with that expressionless bat of her eyelashes and moments later they were ripping their clothes off and tumbling into bed.

When she stepped on the scale in November she was 227, and by Christmastime, Mike was sure that she had added another 5 pounds to her amazing figure.

"I got something for you," he said.

Autumn pulled the spoon from her lips and placed it in her carton of McConnell's ice cream. She took the soft little plastic wrapped cube from Mike's hand. "What are these?"

"They're like the CBD gummies, but they have a little THC in them. Thought it might help with your foot and neck pain."

She studied it, then looked up at Mike from her spot on the couch. Samson was sitting next to her and he looked up at him too. She put her ice cream carton on the end table, then turned the volume down on the TV. "What about like, you know your sobriety?"

Mike stood next to the coffee table and shrugged. "You took away my sobriety a long time ago."

"What is that supposed to mean?"

He gazed down at her and gave her a dimpled grin. "I get a buzz just from looking at you."

She rolled her eyes.

"It's okay," he said. "As long as I stay away from alcohol I'm fine."

"I haven't smoked weed since college."

"Me neither, I haven't since it's been legal."

"Okay I'll try." She attempted to unwrap it, but gave up quickly and reached out toward Mike. "Can you open it for me?"

He smiled again and took it from her. "Sure."

He tore the plastic off, and popped it in her mouth. She chewed and went right back to her snack and TV show. He ate one too, then walked over to the kitchen to finish putting away the groceries.

He wasn't sure what compelled him, but he stopped by Shawn Kemp's Cannabis shop earlier that day while running errands. He planned on just picking up some more CBD gummies, but with his curiosity and a little push from the sales girl, he walked out of there with 100 milligrams of THC edibles. He wanted to try it himself, and he did think it would help the aching neck Autumn had been complaining about, but it was more than that.

She had started snoring at night, and he was having trouble sleeping.

Also, covid cases were surging again and the lack of work and social activities were making their world feel much smaller and more enclosed.

Both their parents canceled the usual Thanksgiving and Christmas gatherings, and it felt more than ever that Mike and Autumn had no one to lean on except each other.

She finally rose from the sofa and brought her empty ice cream carton to the kitchen and placed it on the counter. Dressed for comfort as well as style in green velour joggers and a matching zip up sweatshirt, she looked gorgeous beyond Mike's comprehension.

"What time do you want to leave tomorrow?" she said.

His eyes danced over every inch of her body.

She looked like a fucking model.

"Earlier the better," he said before closing the fridge.

"God, I am so looking forward to sleeping in though." She sighed and watched him tend to the boiling pot of water on the stove. She leaned her elbows against the counter and subconsciously wiggled her hips. "Will dinner be ready soon?"

"About 15 minutes," he said.

"Okay, I'm going to go outside, want to join me?"

"No you go ahead, I need to keep an eye on this."

"Okay." She gazed out at the far window next to the balcony. "Is it cold out there?"

"Not cold enough to snow yet, but it's getting close."

She stood up straight and unzipped her top, revealing the skimpy white camisole beneath.

Damn.

She really was getting chunky.

Her arms had gone through noticeable changes in the past few months. She had no muscles to speak of, her deltoids looked nonexistent, and yet the upper part of her arms had become kind of big and wobbly.

She bent over to put on her Pikolino boots, then grabbed her fluffy white coat from the wall hook. She put it on but struggled with the sleeves.

It was too small for her now, and she could no longer button it together in the front because of her boobs.

Just the simple ordeal of changing a few articles of clothing, had left her slightly winded in a way Mike hadn't noticed before.

He watched her wiggle away and felt vibrations from the clicking steps of her heels radiate throughout the floor of the apartment. Her strut had become a slow languid slog of swaying hips and bouncing breasts, somehow still perceptible even beneath her winter coat.

Damn, she was getting big.

Was she getting too big?

He wondered what his mom would say if she saw Autumn now; what his dad would say, what his sister and his friends would say.

Life had become like one big sexy game that he never wanted to finish.

It wasn't a game though, it was real, and there would be real consequences.

He sometimes worried that Autumn had perhaps passed the point where she could just start exercising and drop down to a weight more reasonable for her body type, or to the way she used to be.

It couldn't be good for her to carry around so many extra pounds, but if that's what he really believed then why did he love it so much?

Why had their sex life been so turbo-charged?

Why could he not stop fantasizing and wondering, what her ass would look like if it got even bigger, and why was he currently pitching a tent in his jeans just thinking about it?

He dished up a helmet sized bowl of penne pasta with chicken and mushrooms, swimming in a sea of buttery parmesan sauce.

He turned and gazed across the living room toward the balcony. She was still outside. Looking over his shoulder he grabbed a bottle of olive oil and drizzled it over her pasta dish for several seconds, likely pushing the meal to well over 1000 calories.

When she came back in she squirmed out of her coat, kicked off her boots, and plopped on the sofa.

He brought her the sumptuous dinner and gave her a quick peck on the lips. "Here you go babe."

"Mmmm, thank you." She held the bowl with both hands and looked at it wide-eyed. "This thing is huge!"

"Just eat what you can, I made a ton."

"Where's yours?"

"Grabbing it now." He went back to the kitchen and made himself a bowl that was less than half the size of the one he made for her. He turned off the lights, then sat next to her on the couch. "Yellowstone?"

"Sure, (chew) season two I think. This is (chew, chew) really good though."

"Glad you like it." He reached over her lap and took the remote.

They watched, and ate.

When the episode was over, she leaned forward and put her bowl on the coffee table. It was empty.

"Ooooh, (pant) I'm so full," she cooed in a breathy voice. She placed both hands on her bloated belly.

"Ooomff, (gasp) I wish I could take all this, and just like move it to my boobs and butt."

"But your belly is so sexy."

"Maybe (hiccup) to you."

"Who else do you need to impress?" He leaned in, lifted her camisole and kissed her navel.

"You really do like it don't you."

He smiled. "I really really do."

She curled her feet beneath her thighs, stuck her butt out and batted her eyelashes. "I think you like my ass better."

He kissed the velvety fabric that covered her enormous round hip. "I love everything."

"Would you…oooof…(gasp) still love me if I got fat?"

If she got fat?

His eyes scanned the buxom contours of her body. She seemed to be all hips with the sexy way she was sitting.

His smile widened. "Of course, there'd just be more of you to love."

She adjusted her posture and made a face of discomfort as she pulled down on the waistband of her pants, letting her belly spring out freely onto her lap. "Ooohh, (gasp, hiccup) too tight."

"Maybe it's time for some new pants."

She sat up and tried to cross her legs a couple times, but her thigh kept sliding off and back down into the depressed seat cushion. She gasped and scowled. "Again?"

"Yeah, again."

She leaned back and threw up her hands. "Maybe I'll just let myself go. (pant) You'd probably love that."

He smiled and wrapped his arms around her. He fondled her thighs, then squished and kneaded her belly with both hands. "Yeah, I probably would."

She squirmed away. "Slow down lover boy, (pant) I need a cigarette before you get me all hot and bothered." She rocked forward in an attempt to stand, but felt too stuffed and heavy to move.

He wasn't entirely sure if her struggle was genuine, or if she was playing the overfed damsel in distress character for his pleasure, but either way he found the act incredibly hot.

She reached out her arm and gave him a puckering, pouty face. "Help please."

When they returned from the balcony the THC was beginning to take hold.

Autumn flopped back on the sofa and with tired and glossy eyes said, "I'm hungry."

Mike made his way toward the kitchen and hung both of their jackets on the wall. "There's gingerbread cookies, and fudge."

She made a face. "Uhhh…diabetes in a tin. Is there no cheesecake?"

He walked her way, shaking his head. "No, you finished it this morning."

She raised her eyebrows. "All of it?"

"Yeah."

She glared at him and crossed her arms. "Isn't it your job to make sure I always have cake when I need it?"

"I'm sorry." He smiled. She always looked so pretty when she pretended to be mad. "We still have that box of peanut brittle. What sounds good?"

"I don't know, I'm just like starving all of a sudden."

"Okay so…"

"Just bring the tin of fudge and cookies and, why not… get the peanut brittle too."

"Okay baby." He did as he was told and sat beside her as she grazed on the Christmas treats during another episode of Yellowstone.

The edibles were more potent than he expected, as he could feel the intense hunger rising in his stomach along with a sensation of mind numbing relaxation. He watched Autumn pop fudge into her mouth like M&M's. He reached for one from the metal box on her lap.

"Hey!" She slapped his hand away and looked daggers into him. "Don't even think about it. Get your own."

He smiled, drew close and put his arms around her.

As ravenous as he felt, he was more than happy to starve if it allowed her to eat to her heart's content.

Just the sound of her lips moving aroused sexual thoughts.

He put his hand on her belly and savored the way it moved in and out with each breath. He kissed her breast, wiggled his fingers between her sprawling thighs then whispered. "We'll have to stop at every fast food place we see tomorrow, so you can just stuff your face for the whole drive."

Her eyes closed and her neck cocked after biting the head off of a red and green frosted gingerbread man. "Mmmm…yeah, (chew, munch) I'd like that."

"You would?"

She grabbed his hand and placed it on her belly. "Yeah." She shoved the rest of the cookie in her mouth.

No longer paying any attention to the TV, he brought his lips to her ear. "Keep that belly full, make those thighs even…chunkier?"

She squirmed in her seat like a purring kitten. "Ooooooh, (chew, munch) yes baby, so chunky." She flopped her arms limply to her sides. “Feed me,” she cooed.

He took a square of butterscotch fudge and plopped it in her mouth.

She chewed quickly like she couldn’t get enough. “Mmmm (chew, chew) more, more,(gasp) more,” she said.

He fed her a chocolate one, then another butterscotch, then he broke into the peanut brittle and fed her several big chunks. Her eyes were getting glossier, her breathing was accelerating and her belly seemed to be protruding out in front of her further.

“You’re (gasp, huff) going to have to (pant) help me up the stairs after this,” she said. “Either that or we’ll have to move the bedroom down here.”

He rubbed her belly as if she was carrying his baby. “Stairs too hard for you?”

She nodded. “Mmhmm.”

He rested his chin on her shoulder. “Okay baby.”

“Mmmm, more.” Her lips parted.

He fed her another piece of peanut brittle, then gave her belly a gentle slap, creating enough of a ripple effect to make her boobs jiggle. "You like that?"

She was so blissed out that she answered with her eyes closed. "Mmhmm…yeah, (munch, chew) that feels so good." She quivered pleasurably from all the things his hand was doing. "Ooohh, mmmm, (gasp) more please." Her lips parted again.

Chapter 12

Autumn unbuttoned her size 20 jeans with a gasp of relief. Placing her hands on her belly, she turned toward Mike who was driving. "Ooohhh…god (gasp) I'm outgrowing these already. Is it (pant) normal to feel sexier from gaining weight?"

Mike kept his hands on the wheel but snuck a peak at his girlfriend in the passenger seat. With arms exposed in a black camisole, she was distracting to say the least. "If everyone looked like you it would be."

She shifted her hips and grabbed her crumpled Starbucks bag. "I think a little fluffiness and a few extra curves is a major turn on." She took another bite of her bacon gouda breakfast sandwich. "It makes (chew, chew) me wonder what a few more pounds would look like. Is that weird?"

He let out a short lusty sigh and shook his head in elated disbelief.

God how he loved this woman.

"I don't think so," he said. "I think it's the opposite."

"Yes (chew) exactly. Why would (chew, chew) losing weight be sexy? I don't understand that anymore."

"You and me both."

"Gaining weight makes me feel more like, girly and feminine somehow, more powerful almost. I think I'm obsessed." She shoved the last of the sandwich between her lips with her thumb and forefinger. "It's (chew, chew) kind of like, addictively liberating."

"Is that right?"

"(chew)Yeah." She nodded and finished chewing. "I don't know. Who cares? The world as we know it will never be the same, makes me want to be more present in the moment, enjoy what we have right now."

"I couldn't agree more." He put his blinker on and began merging toward the offramp. On Interstate 5, a few miles north of Vancouver, Washington; they were headed to the Oregon coast for a Christmas getaway, just the two of them; but they planned to stop in Beaverton for a quick drive-by visit with Autumn's parents.

"Where are you going?" she said.

"Burgerville."

She sighed and held up the paper bag which still contained some cake pops and a cheese danish. "Baby, I haven't even finished all of this yet."

He slowed as he approached the stoplight and smirked. "What about all that talk about going to every fast food place we see?"

She exhaled in a relaxed and dreamy sort of way. "Were you expecting me to take that literally?"

"Um…were you?"

She let out a cute little snort giggle. "No."

"Do you not want to stop?"

She placed her hand on his knee and noticed his erection. "I didn't say that." She gently rubbed his cock for a moment, then looked up at his face. "As long as you're willing to explain to my dad why I'm too full to get out of the car on my own."

He grinned. The line between sexy teasing and reality seemed to be getting more blurry. "It turns me on when you talk like that."

"I know. It turns me on too."

He took a left into the parking lot of a vast strip mall as a few snow flurries began dotting the windshield. "Are you nervous about seeing your parents?"

"Why would I be nervous?"

He gazed at her blankly for a moment. "I don't know, just because you haven't seen them in so long."

She giggled. "I've gone longer than this without seeing them before."

"Right."

"You mean my anxiety?"

He pulled the Honda into the drive-through line. "Do you even have anxiety? You always come across as tough and confident to me."

She sighed. "Maybe on the outside, but I might try another one of those gummies. You brought them right?"

He turned toward the backseat. "There in my backpack. You want one now?"

She flashed her eyes at him sheepishly. "Umm, maybe."

"You like them?"

"I don't know, they definitely helped me relax."

"Go ahead, if you can reach them." He watched as she twisted and contorted her body around, noticing the substantial rolls forming around her sides beneath the fabric of her top. She was developing a bit of a spare tire around her waist and back. "Take two if you want, I don't mind driving."

"Enhh! (gasp) okay."

Autumn's mom Patty greeted them from the front door of the big suburban house. "Hello!"

"Hi mom," Autumn said with a strained smile. It had been no easy task getting her jeans refastened, and they were painfully digging into the swollen flesh of her waist.

"We'll have to do pretend hugs for now," Patty said, mimicking a fake embrace and turning her head away from the gentle yet frigid breeze.

"Better safe (pant) than sorry," Autumn said, walking up the wooden steps of the porch with Mike at her side. After everything she consumed on the drive down, she was so stuffed that the act of moving under own power felt difficult, and she was breathing heavily from the simple excursion of climbing the short flight of stairs. "Where's (gasp) dad?"

"He's inside," Patty said curiously. "You can come in but be sure to wear your masks."

"Right," Mike said.

Autumn rolled her eyes but put her face covering on and Mike did the same before entering the comforting warmth of the foyer. They went into a spacious living room and found Autumn's dad sitting on the recliner near the gas fireplace.

He put his newspaper down and rose to his feet. "There's my pumpkin," he said with joyous crinkled eyes and outstretched arms. Autumn drew close and they embraced.

Patty looked at them disapprovingly from the kitchen. "Gary, no hugging!"

He squeezed Autumn tighter. "The day I can't hug my daughter is the day I can't do anything."

"How are you (pant) doing daddy?" Autumn said.

"Good, had a check up appointment on Monday, clean bill of health."

"His cholesterol is still too high," Patty said.

Gary sat back down in his chair. "I've cut out red meat, and am down below 200 pounds for the first time in…"

"Since I met him," Patty said, still in the kitchen.

Autumn and Mike sat on the sofa. "Good job daddy."

Mike's brain churned in amusement for a second.

Under 200 pounds?

He'd always thought of Gary as kind of a big guy, but if he was under 200 pounds that meant that he was significantly lighter than his young daughter and that thought blew his mind.

Patty handed her husband a steaming mug then turned to Mike and Autumn. "Why don't you take your jackets off and stay a while."

Mike cleared his throat, feeling a little awkward and uneasy wearing his mask inside. "Well, we don't want to stay too long, still have another couple hours of driving to do and we don't want to get there too late."

"At least have some coffee," Patty said. "Mike, how do you take yours?"

"Black is fine."

"And Autumn, a little oat or soy milk?

Autumn unzipped her coat and took it off, revealing herself in her jeans and tank top. "Actually I'd prefer half and half if you got it."

Patty's eyes became visibly bigger at the sight of her daughter's body. It was her thighs and hips, never before had she seen them look so wide before, and was that a belly?

"Oh, okay," Patty said. She stared for a second before walking back to the kitchen. Next to the island countertop, she turned her attention toward Mike. "Brenda next door made a pie, would you care for a slice?"

Mike looked up. "Um…what kind?"

"Pumpkin."

"Yes please, that sounds great," Mike said. Having just had a cheeseburger less than an hour prior, he wasn't at all hungry, but he wanted to be as polite as possible.

Patty turned to her daughter with her eyebrows raised. "Autumn?"

"I'll have some if you have whipped cream."

"Ohhh, me too!" Gary said, sitting up.

"No dear, you shouldn't be having pie at all, let alone whipped cream."

"Come on mom it's Christmastime," Autumn said.

Patty sighed and looked at her husband. "Okay, you can have a small slice, but no cream." She took the pie out of the fridge and began cutting it up. "Autumn, you want big, small or medium?"

"Um, just like a normal sized piece is fine."

Patty made a gesture of passive aggressive disapproval. "Well, okay, if that's what you want."

Autumn shot Mike a look, then whispered in his ear. "She makes me want a cigarette."

Mike smiled beneath his mask and nodded.

Moments later Patty came into the living room and served the refreshments. She then sat down, six feet away. “So how have you two been holding up?”

After removing his mask, Mike took a sip of his coffee then set it down. “I’m good, but she’s the one who’s been working, I’ve got it easy.”

Holding her plate and fork, Autumn finished chewing. “Mike’s been taking good care of me.”

“Yes I can see that,” Patty said. With her mask still on, her eyes fixated on the girth of her daughter’s arms. “Gary and I have been going on long walks every morning and we just love it, daily exercise is just so important.”

Autumn licked a dollop of whipped cream away from her lips and placed her hand on her boyfriend’s knee. “Mike’s been making me breakfast every morning. It’s so nice having him home, makes my work days much easier. Can I have some more whipped cream by the way?"

"Oh Autumn don't you think you have enough already?" Patty said.

"Umm, no...you gave me such a little squirt, why would I ask for more if I thought I had enough?"

"Don't worry babe I'll get it for you," Mike said, rising to his feet. "Alright if I grab it from the fridge Mrs. Murrell?"

"Yes, if you must."

Mike returned with the can of extra creamy Reddi-wip and ejected it on Autumn's pie until it was completely covered. He looked across the coffee table at Patty. “No pie for you?”

“Oh no I couldn’t possibly, have to choose calories wisely at my age.”

“She’ll eat it when nobody’s watching,” Gary said.

“Don’t listen to him, that is not true,” Patty said, embarrassed.

They continued to make small talk and Patty watched as Autumn took bite after bite of her dessert until her plate was clean, void of crust, whipped cream and all. Her eyebrows arched in amazement. “My goodness you must have really been hungry.”

Autumn set her plate and fork down and gasped in mild discomfort. The half-pound bacon cheeseburger, chocolate milkshake and basket of fries she consumed earlier, not to mention the cake pops and the cheese danish, (which she also finished) had made her bloated, but the THC gummies somehow still stimulated her appetite outside the limits of her willpower.

She let out a weary breath through her mouth and tugged downward on her top, exposing inches of cleavage between her ample breasts. “Brenda’s (gasp) baking is always (hiccup) so good.”

Patty leaned forward, noticing the mellow redness in her daughter’s brown eyes. “You look a little tired, is everything okay?”

“Yeah, (pant) I’m fine.”

Mike cleared his throat. “We should probably get back on the road though.” He put his mask on and stood, then helped Autumn up with both hands.

Patty rose as well. “Okay, well it was so nice to see you both, sorry no big Christmas dinner this year.”

“That’s okay, gives us an excuse to do something different,” Mike said. “Change can be good sometimes.”

“As long as there’s not too much change,” Patty said, staring at the way Autumn was struggling to get her wobbly arms into her jacket. "I'm sure we'll all be back to normal next December."

Mike nodded. "I'm sure. Happy Holidays Mrs. Murrell, Mr. Murrell."

"Please Mike, Gary and Patty, you're family at this point," Gary said.

"Okay."

Patty walked them out the door and down the steps to the street. "Drive carefully, they say it might snow on the coast tonight."

"I'll be very careful, thanks for the pie and coffee," Mike said, opening the passenger door for Autumn.

"Of course, just let us know when you get there safely."

Mike waved. "Will do."

Patty went back into the living room after watching them drive away.

"Nice of them to stop by," Gary said.

Patty shook her head. "Autumn doesn't look like she's been missing too many meals, I'm actually a little shocked, she's really put on some weight."

Gary shrugged. "She looks great, seems happy."

"I don't know. I don't think it's healthy for her to be that big, and did you see the way she polished off her pie like it was nothing? It's not like her to eat like that."

"Come on hon it's the holidays during a pandemic, nothing wrong with a little extra winter padding."

"She's put on more than a little padding. It's just a shame because she's always been such a beauty, I'd hate to see her ruin her figure."

Gary leaned back in his recliner. "That boy is definitely in love with her."

"I know. He worships the ground she walks on, which makes me worry because I know he'll never criticize her if she lets her weight get out of hand."

"Come on she's happy and in love, just stop fretting and be glad for them. They're young, they'll figure it out."

Patty sighed. "I'm sure you're right."

As Mike merged onto highway 26 towards Cannon Beach, Autumn shimmied out of her jacket while the heater blasted warm air against her feet and chest.

"It's too cold and wet to smoke outside," she said, "Are you sure we can't just crack the window and have one in here?"

He turned his head and smiled.

Everything she did made him weak in the knees. He was astounded by how sexy her behavior was becoming, and how much her perfect body was blossoming and filling out in every direction.

From her ass which spread to the edges of her seat, to the way her thighs were poured into those jeans, to her belly oozing over her sides and jutting onto her lap.

She was flawless, and he was ready to jump in front of a speeding bullet if it meant that she could indulge in one of her many vices.

"Yeah, go ahead baby," he said.

"Really?"

"I don't mind if you don't."

She lit up, then started searching through her crumbled fast food bags for something to munch on. "Are there no more snacks in here?"

"Are you seriously still hungry?"

She blew smoke out the window. "I don't know, maybe."

"Let me know if you see anywhere that you want to stop."

"I'm really craving french fries again for some reason."

"Well, that's an easy thing to fix."

She smiled and rubbed his thigh. "You're sweet."

"Not as sweet as you."

Chapter 13

"Shit," Autumn said, standing in the lobby of their building. "Are they serious? How the hell (pant) is it possible for both elevators to be out of order at the same time, is that even legal?"

Mike shrugged, holding brown paper Whole Foods grocery bags, one in each hand. "We'll have to take the stairs."

She shifted her weight to one hip and swung the leather strap of her purse over her right shoulder. She sighed deeply. "That's okay, (gasp) I guess the universe is telling me that I need some exercise."

She spoke in a tongue in cheek kind of way, but deep down Mike knew she must on some level agree with that sentiment.

They were already four months into 2021 and he hadn't seen her even attempt to exercise all year, not once.

The Anytime Fitness reopened in February, but she didn't show interest, especially with the mask mandates still in effect.

But she was getting really out of shape, it was kind of unbelievable.

The last time she weighed herself was in March, and she was 234 pounds, up 10 from late January, and looking at her now, it was obvious, she wasn't getting any smaller.

They walked together to the stairwell and he opened the door for her, then followed behind as she trudged upward with echoing claps of heels. It wasn't long before she was gasping from the effort.

"You okay?" he said.

She slowly placed her knee-high boots on each step, carefully and one at a time as if the task demanded extreme concentration.

He asked again. "Are you okay?"

She turned and glared at him. “Yeah, (huff, pant) why?”

He gazed at her, still a few steps behind and below..

Her black and white checkered patterned skirt-set was squeezing her curves and her dumptruck of an ass now was so big it seemed to take up much of the width of the staircase, or was that just wishful thinking?

The recently formed back rolls visible beneath her tank top most definitely wasn’t his imagination.

“No reason,” he said.

She went back to hauling herself up, huffing and puffing as she went. Her butt looked so heavy and it swayed back and forth, wiggling with each laborious movement like she was deliberately throwing in a little extra action for his benefit.

After a while she stopped and leaned against the wall.

“Hang on, (gasp, pant) I just need to rest (cough, wheeze) for a sec. I think these spring allergies or something make it hard (pant) to breathe.” Her face was flush and a bead of sweat trickled down her forehead. She fanned herself, her fleshy arms jiggling wildly. "God (pant, gasp, cough) this only the fourth floor?"

Four months of doing nothing but sitting her ass, lounging around, eating, smoking and drinking to her heart's content came with its repercussions. She was really struggling with these stairs and her breath was so choked and wheezy that it was making a slight whistling sound from the back of her throat.

"Come on, I'll push you." Mike put both grocery bags in his right hand then pressed against her squishy butt cheek with his left, and they continued making their way towards their seventh floor apartment.

By the time they got there she was so winded she could barely talk.

"Holy shit, (gasp, wheeze, cough) I'm so out (cough, cough) of shape," she said as she reached in her purse and pulled out her pack of Camels. She had recently made the switch from her usual American Spirits to the more chemically enhanced cigarettes.

He scowled. "You don't need to smoke now do you?"

"Fuck, (gasp, pant) do not micro mangage me (huff), I'm fucking pissed that we pay all this money for this place and still (huff, wheeze) they can't figure out how to make (cough) an elevator work." She had a look of both worry and frustration on her face as she fought to get oxygen into compromised lungs.

She flung her purse on the kitchen counter and with her phone and cigarettes in hand, stormed off toward the balcony without a jacket.

Mike put the groceries away then went outside to join her. After lighting up himself he said, "Maybe it's time."

Autumn took a drag from her cigarette and gave him a look. "Time for what?"

He nodded at her pack, half empty on the outdoor table. "Time to quit."

Her eyes narrowed. "Why (pant) just because I got (gasp) winded from the stairs?"

"I got a little winded too," he said. "I don't know, the only way we're going to be able to quit is if we do it together."

She sighed. "Yeah, I know."

"What do you say?"

"It's not going to be easy, (cough) we'll have to get some patches."

"Yeah, or a Juul or vape or something."

She adjusted her posture, but even that was a struggle. Her hips had become so big and blubbery that they squished against the plastic armrests of her chair, and it looked like she was a cupcake away from being permanently stuck.

"I (gasp) don't know I need to do some serious (huff) mental preparation if we're going to actually do it," she said.

"What's the date today?"

She looked at her phone. "Sunday the 11th."

"What month is it again?"

"Are you serious?"

"What? It's a pandemic, it's like Groundhog Day."

She smirked. "Even if you are still getting paid, I think you've been out of work too long." She took a drag off her smoke. "It's April."

"Okay so, you want to say like starting May 1st, no more cigarettes?"

She pursed her lips. "Yeah, (cough) I could be on board for that."

"In it together."

She took a short final puff then stabbed out her cigarette. "Deal."

"Okay then."

She took another smoke from her pack and lit up.

He raised his brows. "What are you just going to chain smoke for the rest of the month?"

Her eyes narrowed. "You know (cough, cough) I really don't need your judgments right now. I feel light-headed and I (gasp, pant) think my blood sugar is low. I haven't had anything to eat since lunch."

He rose. "Okay, umm…we've got lots of cake in the fridge…or should I just run over to Roccos and grab a slice or two?"

She fluttered her eyelashes and stared up at him blankly. "If you were smart (cough) you would have done that (huff) already, and if you were really smart you'd get a whole pizza instead of slices. It's cheaper (gasp) in the long run that way. Maybe I'll have some tiramisu while I'm waiting."

He nodded. "Okay, I'll be back." He opened the door to go inside.

"Mike."

He turned. "Yeah?"

With her cigarette held between French tipped nails, and the gray afternoon sky behind her, she looked like some sort of red headed barbie doll that had let herself go completely. She was smoking quickly, almost frantically. "Bring me a (gasp) couple of those gummies before you leave, need to (cough, cough) calm my nerves."

"Okay."

He went inside and came back out moments later and placed two gummies between her lips. She ate, put out her smoke, rocked forward and put both hands on the table so that she could get into a standing position.

Simple tasks were not as easy for her as they used to be. With a look of discomfort she rose, but the chair was coming up with her.

"Oh god babe, little help?" With her knees and back slightly bent she gave Mike a worried look. "I think (gasp, pant) my butt is too big for these chairs." She bit her lower lip.

He swallowed, and he could feel a strong arousal rising below his belt. "Oh my goodness, poor baby."

While incredibly hot to witness, this had to be one of those harsh reality moments. If it wasn't the wake up call or the metaphorical straw that broke the camel's back that would get her to change her ways and go on a diet then what the hell would?

As much as it saddened him to think that all the sexy fun was over, he knew that it was probably for the best.

Maybe it was time.

He jolted forward and helped wiggle her hips free, letting the chair fall to the epoxy painted floor with a light thud.

She stood up straight with a sharp gasp and a toss of her hair. "Babe?"

He looked at her attentively and waited for the inevitable speech about how she had let herself get too big and she needed to lose weight. "Yes?"

She stared at him haughtily, almost proudly. "Honey-do list time. Can I (pant) count on you to order some bigger chairs that are a little more comfortable and roomy?"

His jaw fell open. "Ummm, yes, I can do that."

"Good. (cough) Now go and get the pizza, (pant) I need to go sit down."

During the rest of the month of April, Autumn indulged in food, cigarettes and wine, well into excess; like she was trying to squeeze in all of her vices and guilty pleasures before giving up smoking in May.

Mike was flabbergasted and actually taken aback by how incredibly self-indulgent she was, but he cherished it, nurtured it and encouraged it while it lasted.

It was really fucking hot, and when the first of the month arrived, she had noticeably put on more weight.

Quitting cigarettes was no easy task, especially during the first few days.

Even with nicotine patches and e-cigs it was a joyless battle. Autumn was cranky and irritable and seemed to curb her withdrawals by snacking and gorging on as much food as she could get her hands on.

Whenever a craving hit, she'd reach for a bag of chips, a box of cookies, a cupcake, or handful after handful of chocolate-covered almonds.

Together they got past day one and day two, and after much grappling with willpower made it an entire week without so much as one cigarette contacting their lips.

Mike threw himself into physical exercise, replacing tobacco with more pushups, pullups and brisk runs along downtown Seattle's waterfront streets and parks.

Autumn dove into her work and found she could focus at her desk for more extended periods of time as she no longer had to get up and go outside every hour, although she constantly felt starving and made zero attempt to hide or suppress her increasingly obsessive desire for food.

Mike thought she had been eating a lot and gaining weight at an alarming rate before quitting smoking, but after giving up her cancer sticks, that pace only seemed to pick up steam.

He was making it easy for her.

Still with lots of free time, he made sure she never had to lift a finger. He brought her food, he took away her dishes and he threw away her wrappers. He did everything for her.

After all, she was the one that had to work.

It got to the point where she could go through an entire workweek without leaving the apartment, often getting no physical activity during the day except for the 40 or so steps it took to get from the bed to her desk and back. She slept a lot, took frequent naps, yet complained of having little energy.

She worked hard and her job was quite draining, but away from her laptop screen she had an extremely indulgent and pampered existence, and she was getting used to it.

Chapter 14

"She's not my ex, it was never like that. We're just friends. I'm like her brother from another mother," Ryan said to his girlfriend Siya.

Siya rolled her eyes as she and Ryan approached the apartment building. "Whatever, I've seen pictures of you with her."

Ryan glanced at his phone. "Well of course, so what?"

Siya stared at him for a moment as they waited next to the glass front doors. "So…she's really beautiful. I find it hard to believe that there wasn't some kind of attraction going on there between you two."

"Stop it, we just clicked in different ways," Ryan said. "You don't have to worry about that stuff, we're both in relationships now anyway, right?"

Siya sighed in a lighthearted manner. "Right. I know, just curious that's all."

The doors opened and Mike stepped outside. "Hey, happy fourth!" he said. "How is it going?"

Ryan smiled. "Good. This is my girlfriend Siya."

"Nice to meet you, I'm Mike. Come on up." He led them into the lobby and toward the elevators. He pressed the button to go up and the three of them waited.

"Sorry, only one is working right now, sometimes it takes a while," Mike said.

"Do we need to wear masks?" Siya said.

Mike shook his head. "Nah don't worry about it."

Ryan put his hands in his pockets and shifted his weight from one foot to the other. "How long does the elevator take usually?"

Mike shrugged. "Hard to predict."

"We can take the stairs," Siya said.

"Are you sure? We're on the seventh floor."

Siya pointed at the fitness tracker around her left wrist. "Fine by me, gotta get my steps in anyway."

Mike sighed. "Okay."

He led them to the right of the elevators and through the door to the building's stairwell and they began climbing upward.

"This is a good way to melt off that quarantine weight. Do this everyday and you'll be in pretty good shape," Siya said, somewhere around floor three.

"Does Autumn usually take the stairs?" Ryan said.

Mike turned and looked at him blankly. "Not usually."

When the three of them entered the apartment they were greeted by the smiling face of Tabitha. "Yay, Ryan and Siya are here! You're just in time, we're about to head up to the roof."

Mike closed the door. "Everybody make sure not to let the cat out."

Siya nodded. "We'll be careful."

"Where's Autumn?" Ryan said.

Tabitha grabbed an Oreo from a paper plate on the kitchen counter and took a small bite. "Umm, (munch) I think she's in the bathroom, she'll be out in a sec. Omigod, I need to get away from these cookies!"

Siya set her purse down and smiled. "I know right? The struggle is real these days."

"I really need the gyms to open up again while I can still fit into my pants," Tabitha said.

Siya gave her jeans a tug. "You and me both."

Both girls laughed until they turned toward the heavy sound of Autumn's boots clicking towards them.

"Ryan, (pant) you made it!" Autumn said with arms raised.

Ryan's jaw nearly hit the floor.

It was as if he wasn't at first entirely certain whom he was looking at. It was confusing because from the neck up it was definitely Autumn, but the body that laid below was unrecognizable. His eyes darted frantically and he found himself at a loss for words. "Umm…"

Autumn smiled and turned to the young woman standing next to him. "Hi, (pant) you must be Siya, I've heard a lot about you."

"Nice to meet you, great place you have here," Siya said with a big smile on her face.

"Thanks." Autumn stepped forward and plopped an entire cookie in her mouth like she was on autopilot. "Grab a beer, (munch, chew) make yourself at home, Mike will start barbecuing (munch) soon."

Ryan's eyes were glued on Autumn as he was still struggling to comprehend what he was seeing. Her burgundy summer dress did nothing to hide the amplified curves of her figure.

She was enormous.

She still had her hourglass shape but her thighs were like trunks, her breasts were like melons and she had a soft puffy belly jutting out as if she was daring someone to ask how far along she was. If it wasn't for the obvious rolls and pudgy love handles around her waist he might wonder about that himself.

"I heard you quit smoking," he said.

Autumn smiled and took another Oreo. "Yep, (munch, munch) it's been over 2 months now."

"Congratulations, proud of you," Ryan said as he stared flabbergasted by her boobs and the amount of cleavage exposed above the low cut hem of her dress. "How'd you do it?"

By eating yourself into obesity?

Autumn looked at him curiously, as if she could read his thoughts. "We've been vaping, but I don't (pant) know, I usually (huff) end up reaching for too many cookies whenever I get a craving…as you can probably tell."

Ryan cleared his throat. "Don't sweat it…"

As the party moved up to the shared community rooftop deck, Ryan found Tabitha alone, looking out at the golden city skyline and nursing a Michelob Ultra. "Holy shit, what the hell is going on with Autumn? She got fucking huge!"

Tabitha scowled and brought a finger to her mouth. "Shhhhhh…"

"What?"

Tabitha looked at him seriously then nodded. "She's gained a lot of weight, that's for sure."

"Are you worried?"

"I don't know, it's probably just like relationship weight, mixed with covid, and then quitting smoking on top of that…I guess it makes sense."

Ryan threw up his hands. "Makes sense if she gained 15 pounds or something, not fucking 50 or whatever. She even sounds like she's out of breath from just talking."

Tabitha took a short sip of her low calorie pilsner. "What can I say? She seems happy, and honestly she's such a fucking knock-out that the all that extra weight still somehow looks good on her."

Ryan turned around and peered out at Mike and Autumn who were mingling with Sydney on the far side of the deck. "I wonder what's going through his head."

Tabitha followed his gaze and smirked. "Probably can't get enough of that booty."

"Yeah, that thing is fucking massive! I thought she was getting big when I saw her at that New Years party a couple years back, but that was because she broke her leg. What the hell is her excuse now?"

"There is no excuse…that's why it's so important to workout, we're not all 22 anymore you know? Please don't say anything though, I'm just happy she quit smoking. I'm sure she's aware she needs to lose weight."

"Just look at those arms."

"I know."

"I never thought I'd say this, but I think Autumn is actually as big as Sydney now."

Tabitha lowered her sunglasses. "Damn…you're right, at least in some places. That is so weird to think about."

"Mmm, (chew) Oh my God (pant) that was so good!" Autumn said after she finished her second bratwurst.

Sydney licked her lips and smiled. "Hell yeah it was. I love a good sausage in my mouth."

Autumn placed both hands on the armrests of her seat in an effort to stand. She then grabbed her plate and wiggled back over to the grill without saying a word. She returned a moment later with two more bratwursts and Sydney watched in amazement as she plopped back down and continued eating as if the heavy food was nothing more than a light snack.

After finishing her third, all dressed up with ketchup and relish and packed into a bready hoagie bun, she paused and fanned herself.

"Pheww!"

Sydney studied her. "You okay?"

Autumn drained the contents of her beer then set it back on the table in front of her. "Yeah (pant) it's just so hot, too (gasp) hot for me right now."

"It's a little warm," Sydney said, standing up. "I wasn't going to have more but since you are, I guess I will too."

Autumn shoved the fourth oversized hot dog between her sumptuous lips then turned to her friend. "Can (chew, chew) you get me another IPA?"

Later that night, after all their friends had left, Mike was cleaning up in the kitchen and Autumn was on the sofa scrolling through her phone.

"Oh god, (pant) I look fat in these pictures! Am I seriously that much bigger than Tabitha?"

Mike closed the door to the dishwasher then walked her way. He leaned against the couch next to her and looked at some of the photos that were taken during the course of the evening.

"You look so gorgeous, this dress is... unbelievable."

"Uhh, I don't know. I look like I'm 8 months pregnant."

He gently massaged her plush shoulder with the tips of his fingers. "You look so good baby."

Autumn continued swiping through her phone. "Oooh, (pant) I look like such a chubby-wubby."

"You look fantastic."

She gave him an odd glance then took his hand and placed it on her belly which was folding into rolls and spilling onto her bloated thighs. She held it there for a moment and sighed with pleasure. "Mmm…does that (pant) feel nice?"

He began fondling her fat, softly and lovingly. "Yes, it really does."

She patted her belly with her other hand and adjusted her posture. "Oooff, (gasp) I know it does, especially because I'm so stuffed. I ate so much tonight baby. I feel like I can hardly move under my own (gasp, huff) like strength right now."

"Really?"

"Yeah." Her mouth waxed sultry. "I never thought (pant) that I would actually enjoy (gasp) gaining weight like this." She became lost in the sensualness of her body for a moment, Mike did too. She gazed up at him and saw the look of extreme happiness on his face. "What?"

"Nothing, just…" He trailed off, came around in front of her, bent his knees and buried his face into her pudding-like midsection with only the thin silky fabric of her dress between his mouth and the lush skin of her belly.

"What?"

He came up for air and stared into her eyes. "I love you so much."

Sensing his lust, she played with the ends of her hair and basked in his touch, teasing him, taunting him and testing her growing powers of seduction. "Would (gasp, pant) you love me if I weighed 300 pounds?"

"I would love you if you weighed 500 pounds."

She mushed her butt deeper into the sofa. "Real-ly?"

He squeezed the sides of her waist and stood. "Yes. I would have a permanent erection, but yeah, I would love you, always."

"Mmmm…I'm glad you said that (gasp) because I don't seem to be able to stop (pant) gaining weight."

"How do you know that?"

"I know because (gasp) I keep outgrowing my clothes." She arched her back and sat up. "God, (pant) I have no idea how much I weigh right now."

A small smirk formed on Mike's face. "Should we go find out?"

She tilted her head up and gave him an exceedingly cute, yet slightly worried look. "What if I gained…like a lot?"

He leaned forward and kissed the skin just above her heaving tits. "That would only make me love you more."

She raised an eyebrow. "Are you sure about that?"

"Yes I'm sure."

"Promise?"

"Promise."

Her eyes pierced him and she reached out her arms. "Okay, (huff) just help me up."

In the bathroom, Mike opened the cupboards beneath the sink and pulled out the scale. He placed it flat on the tile floor then turned to his beautiful girlfriend.

She looked at him with suspicion, still trying to catch her breath after the climb up the stairs. "This is (pant) fun for you isn't it."

"Why do you say that?"

"Because (gasp) it's obvious."

"Is it fun for you?"

She gave him a sly, sexy smirk and then stepped on the scale. It creaked and groaned beneath her bare feet and immense weight and she tilted her chin down, trying to peer over her boobs. She saw the numbers shoot up and dance into the 280's almost immediately.

Her hands flew to the sides of her face in total shock and surprise. "(gasp) Oh god!"

Mike crouched down and took a look at the numbers. "285ish."

"280 what?"

He looked up. Her blossoming double chin was slightly blocked by her tits which seemed to be blooming larger before his eyes and exploding out of her undersized dress. "285.6"

She looked at him, aghast. "Oh fuck. (gasp) Oh my fucking god, baby!"

He was smiling from ear to ear. He knew she had been eating like a mad woman since she quit smoking, but 285?

That was fucking huge!

285 meant that she had probably put on 20 pounds in the last 2 months alone if not more.

"That's really really really hot," he said.

She stepped off the scale, stretched out her jiggling arms and twirled around in front of the bathroom mirror. "Yeah, it really is, (huff, pant) I mean I definitely don't think I look 285 but…I feel soooo sexy, ooohhh god (pant) I fucking love it."

Mike's eyes were wide and his mouth was agape. "You do?"

She looked at him as she caressed the sides of her hips with her fingertips. "Yeah, I don't know…they say late 20's is when a lot of women's bodies change and (pant) metabolism slows down…but god…why does this (gasp) make me feel sooooo….horny?"

"Because it's sexy."

She flashed him a devious smile as she wrapped her pinky in the ends of her hair. "Did you notice (pant) the way everyone was looking at me tonight?" Shifting her weight to one hip, she stuck her ass out, a subtle yet provocative movement that seemed to add a good inch of height to the tent in Mike's jeans. "Do you think (pant) they were shocked, seeing me this big?"

He came closer and put his arm around her waist. "I think people are in awe of your beauty."

"I think (gasp) they were stunned by how much weight I've gained." She paused and squished her lips together, "and that fucking (pant) turns me on."

"It does?"

She pointed her finger, then placed it firmly in the center of his chest. "Yes…they probably think (gasp) I'm a fat lazy piggy…and I know it turns you on too."

She pressed her boobs into him as lightly as a butterfly touches a flower. He could smell the sweet pheromones, perfume and the alcohol on her breath and her alluring scent brought ripples of tantalizing shockwaves down his spine and to his knees. "You do?"

"Mmhm, (pant) of course I do."

"Do you want to-"

"I don't want to lose weight."

He drew his hand away from her arm and took a step back to get a better view of the complete expanse of her colossal proportions. “You don’t?”

“No I don’t. (gasp, pant) This is by far the biggest I have been in my life and I’ve never felt sexier (huff) or more like womanly and feminine.”

“Really?”

She nodded. “I want us to explore our (pant) sexuality more deeply. Life’s too short to have meaningless (gasp) normal sex. Life is too (gasp, huff) short to spend it caring about what other (pant) people think. I want to really find out what makes you tick. I want to get (gasp) bigger.”

He stared at her.

How much had she had to drink?

He cleared his throat. “You do?”

“What are you brain dead now?” She smirked and shrugged. “Yeah…well (pant) maybe just a little bigger.”

He stepped forward and wrapped both arms around her waist, then he let his hands fall across her more than generous backside. “How much bigger?”

Her lips were only inches away from his and they parted in a small coo of a gasp. "Will you (pant) help me gain weight?"

His heart was ready to beat out of his chest.

He could feel his cock throbbing in agony and rubbing against the denim of his pants.

Her words were hitting him like hurricane force winds and excitement was building up inside and shooting his eyebrows halfway to his hairline.

It was one thing to have fun in bed, making sexy dirty talk about her fat ass and feeding her as an act of foreplay, but this was on a whole other level. This wasn't just bedroom talk, this was real, carnal, life changing insidious desires that were far beyond his comprehension of how truly sexy a woman can be.

"How can I help?" he said.

She smiled knowingly, then spoke in a slow sensual tone that nearly brought him to his knees. "Well (pant) you could buy me lots of food, you could feed me in (gasp) bed, you could treat me like a (gasp, pant) queen and make sure I never have to (pant) lift a finger…"

"Just let you lay in bed all day?"

"Yes, (pant) lay in bed all day and just eat, all day."

Mike stepped backwards again as if the love and lust that he felt for his girlfriend was too much for him to take standing upright. He stared at her in total awe for a moment. "Who are you?"

She slowly licked her lower lip with her tongue. "Are you surprised?"

He swallowed and tried to temper his astonishment. "Pleasantly surprised."

She turned her body around and let her ass fill his pelvis. She backed into him as he reached around and cupped her breasts and rubbed himself into her like a magnet on steel. "This is (gasp) what you wanted isn't it."

His hands ran all over her magnificent curves, let his chin rest on her left shoulder and then whispered in her ear. "I didn't even know I wanted it." He grabbed her hefty hanging belly and squeezed hard. "Do you have a goal weight?"

She wiggled her hips with a happy nestling shift. "(gasp) Hmm…a goal weight? That sounds like (gasp) a fun idea."

He brought his lips to her earlobe and poked her diamond studded piercing with his tongue. "What's your goal weight babe?" he whispered.

She turned around. "I don't know, (pant) I don't want to get too big."

His face became serious and eager to please once again. "Right, of course…I mean you know, just for fun, you can always lose it later if it's too much or whatever."

"Ummm…well….It would be fun (pant) to just be a total fatty for a couple of months." Her eyes went to the ceiling. "I'll be 29 in October. (gasp) I think I would really love to be 300 pounds on my birthday."

Mike's face flushed red and it took all of his willpower not to shout to the heavens with joy. He took a breath, closed his eyes, then opened them. "Really?"

She slammed herself into him like a freight train of pillows and let his manhood grind into her chubby thigh. "Yeah, (pant, gasp) but then you better help me lose it if it does end up feeling like too much."

He nodded. “Okay deal.”

She kissed him softly and slowly on the lips then looked at him with yearning melting eyes. “This is (gasp) going to be so fun. (pant) There’s cake (pant, gasp) in the fridge, can you get it and bring it to the bedroom? (gasp, huff, pant)I need to get off my feet and I'm going to slip into something (gasp, huff) a little more comfortable.”

Chapter 15

Autumn indulged in food in ways she never had before in her life during the remaining half of the summer of 2021. It was no longer merely mindless snacking, it was now purposeful and deliberate eating that was nothing if not unholy gluttony.

"Come on babe, you gotta finish that bacon so I can take your plate and get you some ice cream," Mike said.

She rolled back in her chair and looked up at him with glazed over eyes. Sitting at her desk in front of her laptop, her breakfast plate was empty save for a thin layer of maple syrup and a lone strip of bacon.

Having already consumed her morning milkshake, an entire German pancake and 5 strips of bacon, she was stuffed to the gills to put it mildly. "Oh god, (gasp) I don't think (huff) I can handle one (pant) more bite, It usually takes me hours to eat this(hiccup) and you gave me so much bacon."

He leaned over her and gently kissed her on the side of her neck just below her chin. It was obvious that she was in some discomfort and breathing heavily from being so full. "Try and push yourself."

"(gasp) Okay, (wheeze) but then you're (pant) going to have to help (huff) me lay down (gasp) for a while. My last (hiccup) meeting is over at 11."

"Short day?"

"No, (gasp) just cleared my (pant) schedule, I'd rather be lazy (huff, wheeze) and eat in bed, and this (pant) chair is killing my back."

"Sounds like a plan." He picked up the thick, crisp baconstrip and brought it to her mouth. She ate slowly and carefully. Her breasts were heaving from the effort but she managed to get it all down.

She looked at him, her eyes soft and heavy with lust. "(gasp) Oooh, holy shit, (wheeze, pant) I'm sooo (hiccup) stuffed, I could really (huff, gasp) use a cigarette."

He turned and grabbed the bag of Sativa gummies from the edge of the desk. He took one and handed it to her. "Here, this will help your appetite, and help you relax."

"Okay, thank you baby." She plopped it between her lips then stood behind and started massaging her shoulders and rubbing the back of her neck with his thumbs. He looked down at the way her perfect body was poured into that chair.

Those daily and nightly heavy cream weight gain shakes were having more of an impact than he could've imagined.

She was getting really big.

It was fucking amazing and almost absurd.

It was late August, and she was now encased in so much fat that added blubber seemed to be fighting for space amongst her luxuriant curves. Soft folding rolls choked her womanly back and had become so large they were beginning to droop and sag from the area just below her armpits clear down to her lower waist and hips.

He drew his hands downward and felt the inviting warm softness of her art-like form, noticing with pride that both armrests of her office chair were propped up to make way for her ass. Just the feeling of her flesh against his fingertips made him weak.

He licked his lips and slowed his breath in an effort to mitigate his raging excitement.

It was like he was living in a dream.

"I'll go get your ice cream."

Later that afternoon Mike stood next to the bed and tightened the brown leather belt around his jeans. He turned towards Autumn who was still sprawled out on the mattress panting and naked, flat on her back in starfish position as the sun bounced against her shiny white skin, highlighting the faint stretch marks that had recently formed around her hips and butt.

Since when did she have that much cellulite?

"Are you sure?" he said. "I don't mind going by myself if you need to rest."

She struggled to move onto her side. "No, (gasp) I want to get out of the house and come with you. It would (pant) be fun to pick out all the stuff I really like…all the tasty snacks you're going to feed me."

She propped herself into a sitting position and flopped her legs over the side of the bed. She grabbed her Juul e-cigarette and began sucking on it like a baby's pacifier.

Mike smiled as the mattresses groaned and depressed beneath her weight. She had gotten considerably heavier during the past couple months. "Whole Foods then?"

She put the Juul back on the nightstand, arched her back and pushed her bloated belly of jiggling blubber further out onto her lap. "No, (pant) let's go to QFC, I want junk food."

My how things had changed.

He held out his hands to help her to her feet. "You got it baby."

Mike circled the car around the parking lot but the closest spot he could find was still a good hundred feet from the store entrance. He quieted the air-conditioning and turned to Autumn who was packed into the passenger seat like the overflowing goddess of indulgence that she was. Her hips were honestly too big for his car now. "You sure you don't want me to just run in? You can stay off your feet."

She smirked and released herself from her snug seat belt with a gasp. "I appreciate (pant) that baby, but I want (gasp) to do this together."

He nodded, got out and came around to her side. He opened the door for her and watched as she uncomfortably squirmed in her seat. "It's getting so hard for you to get out of this car now isn't it."

She panted with short girlie gasps and looked at him helplessly. "Mmm, (gasp) I know, but that's why I have you."

He clutched her dough-like forearms and aided her to her feet, noticing the suspension of his CRV jolting upward as she exited the vehicle. "Sorry, I couldn't park closer."

"It's okay, (gasp, pant) next time."

Beneath the fluorescent lighting of the supermarket, Mike pushed the shopping cart as Autumn walked beside.

She looked stunning in her new stretchy orange tube dress and matching cardigan and she was receiving more than her share of head-spinning looks from the male customers despite her mask.

He liked being out in public with her, though it was a rare thing since the start of the pandemic.

Knowing that his girlfriend had both a prettier face and fatter and more shapely ass than any woman they would ever come across made him feel lucky and extremely proud that she was with him.

Knowing that she loved him, knowing that he loved her.

Gone was the wandering eye that he struggled with in previous relationships. To him there was now only one woman on the planet that he wanted to look at.

There was Autumn and no one else, and The Beatles seemed to echo that thought as they sang from the grocery store's speakers, "The way she looked, was way beyond compare."

The cart was already half full with two family sized bags of potato chips, a tray of store made cheese covered mashed potatoes, 4 pints of Ben & Jerry's Chunky Monkey, along with 3 bottles of red wine and a two liter bottle of full sugar Dr. Pepper.

She placed her hand on top of his as he gripped the handle of the cart. "God, (pant) this is so much fun, I wish we would have done this sooner."

"Me too," he said as he rolled into the bakery section.

She lurched forward at the sight of a large plastic tub of chocolate dipped madeleines. "Oh my God, (pant, gasp) we're definitely getting these." She grabbed it and plopped it in the cart, then excitedly turned toward a 24 pack of thick frosted sugar cookies. "And these too."

He smiled. "You really are enjoying this aren't you baby."

She turned and looked at him coyly and arrogantly and gave her hair a subtle toss. "Not as much as you."

"I can't argue with you there."

She wiggled toward him with her arms flung out at her sides as if she was having trouble maintaining her balance. Her body was not yet used to her extra curves and it showed in the way she moved.

"It's just (gasp) that I've never done (pant) this before," she said. "I've never (huff) allowed myself to just go crazy and buy whatever I wanted without looking at calories and everything, much less actually trying to stock up on the yummiest, most fattening treats (gasp, pant) I can find."

"Liberating isn't it."

She stepped closer so that her breasts were nearly touching his lower chest. "Extremely liberating, especially knowing how much it turns you on."

"I don't know, it seems to me that you get just as turned on as I do. Or is that just my imagination?"

"A lady never tells." She gave him a long stare then turned toward a big plastic container of glazed chocolate donut holes. "Ooh, we should get more stuff like this, things that are easy for you to feed me, you know in bed."

He leaned forward against the cart. "Fuck…are you trying to kill me?"

"Always." She smiled, then wiggled towards the refrigerated display case. "We're going (pant) to need lots of cake too, maybe some (huff) frozen desserts as well."

His head collapsed in blissful agony.

He could not articulate the reasons why, but these recent developments in Autumn's attitude were severely exciting to him.

No longer did he have any concerns about her becoming too fat or too curvy. He was now obsessed with the idea that she was going to get bigger, heavily fueled by the fact that she wanted it too.

The whole thing was so beyond sexy that he would be lightheaded if he actually thought about it for too long.

"Jesus Christ," he said. "Good thing I have this shopping cart, cause I don't think I can stand up straight."

She turned and drew her eyes below his belt. She smiled. "Oh no, (pant) better save that for later."

She turned away and grabbed a full sized black forest cake and put it in the cart with a look of satisfaction on her lips. "Mmmm, (pant, gasp) I never realized how much of my brain (huff) was consumed with calorie counts and watching my weight until now. (pant, gasp) It feels so good to let that go."

"Maybe I should try it," he said.

She came forward and ran her fingers against his chest, slowly outlining the pectoral muscles beneath the bamboo fabric of his black t-shirt. "Noooo don't. (pant) I like you all lean and strong. Remember (gasp, pant) the secret to a happy relationship is making sure that your (huff) woman always gets her way."

He couldn't help but smile. "Oh really, is this a new theory of yours?"

She clung to his shoulders as if to transfer some of her weight away from her aching feet which were crammed into espadrille wedges. "It's the (pant) oldest theory (gasp) in the world."

She felt warm, and he noticed that her breathing had already become somewhat labored. "Are you getting tired?"

She rested her head gently against him. "Yeah."

"Do you trust me to get the rest? You can have the keys if you wanna get off your feet and wait in the car."

She nodded slowly. "Okay, I trust you. But be sure to get some hostess treats and poptarts, I haven't allowed myself (pant) to have that kind of stuff since forever."

"What kind of poptarts?"

She looked at him like he was the dumbest man on the planet. "Uhh! (huff, gasp) brown sugar cinnamon of course."

He smiled. "Okay babe."

She shifted her weight to one hip and crossed her arms beneath her breasts. "Don't fuck this up."

"I won't."

"And don't take (pant) too long because all this (gasp) walking has made me really hungry."

"I'll be as fast as I can."

"Good."

He took a step towards her and lowered his voice. "Make sure nobody's walking behind you to the car, there's a couple guys in here that have been like following you all around the store."

She rolled her eyes. "Whatever, (pant) it's not my fault men are such perverts."

He watched as she slowly wiggled away and marveled at how differently she moved than when they first started dating. She couldn't swing her arms the way she used to as her hips pushed them further outward. He doubted that her ass could even fit on the back of his motorcycle anymore, not to mention that her current weight would possibly cause a malfunction in the suspension.

Damn.

No woman had ever looked better walking away from him.

After pulling into the underground parking lot of their building, Autumn went straight up the elevator and collapsed into bed while Mike unloaded the groceries in three separate trips. When he was done he ran up to the bedroom to find her laying on her side with the skirt of her dress drawn up to her waist, leaving a massive dimpled thigh completely exposed.

He leaned over her and kissed the flush cheek of her face. She was very warm, as the effort of getting out of the car and hauling herself all the way up to the bedroom had left her overheated and exhausted, even with the air conditioning humming at a cool 69 degrees Fahrenheit.

He squeezed her mountainous hip and gave it a shake, then watched in awe as it continued wobbling well after releasing his hand. Her cardigan was off and her pillowy arms were looking bigger and sexier than ever. He caressed her belly which was spilling onto the bedding despite being slightly restrained by the snugness of her dress but she pushed him away before he could proceed further.

"You (pant) didn't bring me anything?" she said.

"I uh…"

"How dare you (gasp) come up here empty handed, (pant) I told you I was starving."

"Right, I was just going to ask you what you wanted."

With her head resting on the pillow she stared at him blankly. "I want cake."

"Do you want a slice or-"

"Just (huff) go get it!"

Like a bullet he was down the stairs and back up with a fork and medium sized plate with a huge slice of black forest cake on top.

He sat on the edge of the bed and brought it near her face. "I hope this is enough."

She shimmied herself up a little, propping her head up with her hand. "Doesn't really (pant) matter to me, the more I want, the more (gasp) times I get to watch you run up and down the stairs (pant) like a crazy man."

"Do you like that?"

She took a big bite. "Mmm…I(chew) like it when (chew) you bring me fattening treats. What girl (chew) doesn't love it when a hot guy brings (huff) her food?"

He crawled on top of her, lifted her dress further up her waist and began kissing her thigh.

She rolled onto her back and let her legs spread apart, although her inner thighs were still touching each other simply due to their sheer size. She continued forking more cake into her mouth and Mike could hear from her lip smacking and moans of pleasure that she was already turned on from the food alone.

Sex and food, food and sex.

Was this a permanent thing now?

Despite laying on her back, Autumn's belly had become so large that it was still protruding upward like a squishy round hill of pudding and Mike couldn't resist burying his face into it then drawing circles around her bottomless abyss of a belly button with his tongue.

Autumn squealed with delight and continued eating.

He lifted his head up and with bent knees straddled her right thigh. He gave her belly a shake and watched as she continued to stuff her face. "You're getting to be such a big lazy girl."

With her gorgeous hair pressed against the headboard and her now more prominent double chin tilted towards her breasts, she licked a smear of chocolate off her lips and paused for a moment. She had a look of breathy orgasmic bliss from ear to ear. "(huff) Enhh…chuunnnky?"

He gave her belly another shake, causing tremors and vibrations throughout not only her whole body but also the entire mattress. "Yes, maybe a little beyond chunky."

"I'll (gasp, huff) have to step on the scale tonight and see if I've reached my goal."

"You haven't checked yet?"

She went back to eating. "Ennhh…no, (chew) (chew)I want to be surprised."

"It's not even September yet, you still have plenty of time before your birthday."

"Yeah but (chew, chew) I can already tell, (huff, gasp) it's going to happen sooner."

"300 pounds is a lot of weight."

"Yes, (huff) 300 pounds (chew) would mean that I'm really really chunky."

He leaned his head closer to her face. "It would mean that you're fat."

Her nose scrunched and her lips parted as if his words had made her climax. She nearly dropped her fork. "Ohh (huff, gasp) baby, say that again."

"Fat?"

"Call me (pant) fat."

He grabbed her belly with both hands. "You are fat, and you are getting really fat, I actually can't believe how big you've gotten."

He spoke with complete honesty, but she reacted as though it was sexy dirty talk and went straight back to eating.

"Mmmm, (chew, chew) god baby don't stop."

He tilted his head again and kissed her just below the fattest part of her lower belly. Along with her hips, she had developed faint outlines of stretch marks in the undercurve area above her pussy and below her navel. "You've turned into such a lazy greedy fatass."

She convulsed in supreme comfort, wiggling her ass deep into the bed. "Ohhh (huff, gasp) God, yeah, I'm totally a fatass."

He shoved his face between her now very portly thighs and kissed her gelatinous pussy as she savored the feeling of his facial stubble against the quivering tenderness of her silky soft white skin. She didn't have any panties on. She rarely did anymore when wearing a dress. He poked his eyes toward her blissed out face, peering over her bloated tummy. "You like being called that?"

"(gasp, huff) Mmhmm."

His eyes rolled back with elation and his voice lowered to whisper. "Fuckkk…me, you are too sexy." He wanted to get her dress all the way off but she was still making love to her cake like a woman possessed.

"The (chew) softer I get, (chew, chew) the harder you get." She began eating more aggressively, scraping frosting off the plate with her fork and shoveling it between her wet lips in frantic repetitive successions. "I love (chew, chew) making you (chew) hard."

"I love making you soft."

She finished the last bite and held up her now empty plate. "More."

He clutched and massaged her right thigh with both hands. It was so mushy that he could sink his fingers deep into her pampered flesh like playdough. "Jesus that was fast, you really are a fatass."

"More!"

He took her plate and eased himself toward the side of the bed. He gazed at her tangled hair and sexy dark eyes and he felt overwhelmed by her beauty, overwhelmed by everything. "Okay baby, I'll go run and get you another big piece."

"No!"

With his feet now on the carpet, he paused and turned. "No?"

"Bring (huff, gasp) the whole (pant) cake!"

Chapter 16

A surge of euphoria rose in Mike like nothing he experienced before.

The whole cake?

Had she gone crazy, or was she really as turned on and intoxicated by her expanding body and unapologetic gluttony as he was?

Perhaps she just loved the undivided attention, and being doted on in ways she never imagined.

He wasn't going to argue or over-analyze the situation.

The cake was heavy, and he held it in his arms like a baby as he scurried back up the stairs. So dense, so rich, so much frosting and an unfathomable amount of calories, it would have been an appropriate dessert for a party of 6 and yet, there was his curvy vixen of a girlfriend wanting it all for herself.

She was now sitting on the edge of the bed naked, staring at him with the eyes of an assassin. With straining effort, she stood and approached him, never losing eye contact. She paused, biting her lower lip in such a way that turned Mike's legs into noodles.

She took the cake which was still on the plastic tray it came with and brought it to the bed without saying a word, placing it near the headboard where she had draped a light brown bathroom towel over the white sheets.

This wasn't simply the impulsive behavior of an intoxicated sex-crazed girl. This was premeditated.

On top of the mattress, she crawled on all fours with her butt sticking up and out behind her like an invitation.

She knew what she was doing.

Her ass wobbled back and forth as she dove head first into the cake.

He threw his black shirt across the room and stripped himself naked.

He crawled up behind and cradled her hips in his arms as she went on eating the decadent dessert like a hog in a trough.

She looked amazing from the back in that position. In spite of her incredible size she was still classically curvy, and her hips, thighs and ass dominated her voluptuous figure as much as they dominated his thoughts.

He thrust himself against her buttcrack and slipped effortlessly into her soaking pussy. He cupped her hips with both hands as she continued eating with savage abandon. He could explode at any moment but he held back, saving himself and enjoying the spectacle of his obese girlfriend stuffing herself as if she were a slave to food.

That was something to think about.

Obese girlfriend.

Autumn was now most certainly obese, very obese. There was no denying it, and yet the reality of that fact still felt surreal, as if he was in some sort of fantastical alternate universe.

The minutes flew by and Autumn kept on eating and eating and eating. She moaned and panted and her lips smacked as she made the most arousing sounds Mike had ever heard.

"Come on baby, keep eating, you can't stop can you," Mike said.

"(gasp)No, (chew, chew, moan) I can't, (chew, chew) I don't want to."

He shook her enormous cheeks and spanked her. "You're just in love with how big your ass is getting aren't you."

"Mmhmm, (gasp, pant, wheeze) yes, (hiccup) but (burp)I want it bigger!"

There was no way anyone could consume that much dessert all at once, but perhaps to the shock of them both, she ate until the cake was gone and the plastic tray was more or less licked clean.

Holy fuck.

She was completely out of breath, sweating, and her body was on the brink of collapsing under its own weight.

Mike helped stabilize her by cupping her hips and clutching her love handles and he shoved himself into her, back and forth as she squealed in gasping ecstasy.

This was fucking.

It was dirty, sticky, sweaty, messy, wild, selfish, and it was amazing.

Autumn had never felt so full and fat and sexy in her life and suddenly there was no past or future, no job at Oracle, no coronavirus, no fear or anxiety. There was only her and Mike and a belly so packed with cake she felt like she could explode. "Cum (pant, gasp) baby, cum (huff) for me," she moaned wearily between breaths with chocolate coated lips. "Cum like (wheeze, pant) this...fuck me (huff) from behind."

Spooning afterwards, Mike had one arm beneath her gushing torso and the other on top of where her hip dipped into the folding rolls of fat, bunching together at her waist.

She was wheezing like a pig with her ass shoved into his pelvis, quivering with burps and hiccups from being so stuffed.

"That (huff, wheeze) was (hiccup) fucking (gasp) amazing baby," she said in a dreamy yet strained voice.

He pressed himself against her warm softness. "Yes it was."

"You're (wheeze, huff) still hard."

"Wanna go again?"

"Slow (huff, wheeze) down, that was already twice buddy, and I can (gasp) hardly move." With some effort she wiggled closer against his hardness, savoring the feeling of his hands against her skin. "Aren't you curious?"

"Curious about what?"

She let out a drawn out girly and breathy sigh."How (gasp) much I weigh."

His head shot upward. "Should we go find out?"

"Mmmm, (hiccup) yeah…but (pant) I feel (gasp) so relaxed right now."

"Come on, let's get you up. My arm is asleep anyway."

After some difficult contorting, he managed to free his numb limb from beneath her swollen love handles and bloated gut. He stood next to the bed and wiggled his fingers to regain blood flow.

She clumsily rolled onto her back and took long deep heaves of air, her overstuffed belly moving slowly up and down. "Are (pant) you going to help (hiccup) me?"

He leaned forward and pulled her into a sitting position, then pulled again to get her to her feet.

This task was far more difficult than it used to be.

She exhaled a great gasp of relief then smiled. "I really (pant) like this," she said.

"What?"

She stared at him with the most deliciously sensual look in her eyes. "You (pant) being home all time, taking (huff) care of me. I've never (hiccup) allowed myself to be (gasp) taken care of like this before, (pant) ever. It makes me sad to think you'll have to go back to work."

"Yeah, makes me sad too."

He steadied her and led her into the bathroom and she stepped on the scale. The numbers fluttered and the springs squeaked.

She tilted her head toward her naked breasts. "What's (huff, burp) the damage?"

Mike looked down. "I don't think it can decide."

"Is it (hiccup) broken?"

"Don't think so. What's the limit on this thing?"

"Goes (pant) up to 350 I'm pretty sure."

"Step off for a sec."

She gave him a pouty look but did as he said.

He let the numbers go back to zero. "Okay, try again."

She sighed, bit her lip and carefully stepped back on.

His eyebrows shot up. "Oh my goodness babe."

She gasped sharply and opened her eyes wide. "What?"

"You're not gonna believe this."

"Would you (huff) hurry up! (gasp) I really don't want to be standing any longer than I have to."

"You're three hundred and nine pounds."

She stepped off and playfully punched him in the shoulder. "Shut (gasp) the fuck up!"

"That's what it says."

"No fucking way!" She turned toward the mirror and gave her hips a shake. "Okay (huff) why is this making me wet all over again?"

He came up behind and wrapped his arms around her waist. It was now getting to be a bit of a reach for him to do so. He gently kissed her pale neck before he spoke. "Because it's really hot."

She bent over slightly and wiggled her butt into his crotch. "Oh my God, (pant) I'm such a chunky fatass." She stood up straight and froze for a second, then turned around, twirling her finger in her wildly sexy hair. "Wait, (gasp) today's only the 28th right?"

He was unable to stop smiling. "Yep, almost September. Pumpkin spice latte time."

"That was (pant) the fourth of (gasp) July when I was 285?"

He thought for a moment. "Ummm, yeah, yes it was."

"Soooo, I gained what…24 pounds (pant) in less than 2 months?"

He grabbed her by the hips and pulled her close.

She was really getting wide.

"Well you have been a very greedy princess."

Her lips parted as she bounced her belly against him. "Ohhhh, (huff) god baby I'm (pant) such a pig!"

He bent forward and kissed her on the stomach, still aghast by how incredibly big it had become and how much cake was packed inside. "You are the sexiest woman I have ever seen."

She smiled. "I better be."

"You are."

"Holy shit, (pant) I can't believe how fucking huge this thing is." She took a step back and lifted her belly up with both hands, then let it drop down with a heavy jiggle. "Ooohh…I don't (huff, wheeze) feel so good. I can't believe (gasp) I ate the (hiccup)whole (pant) thing."

"Let's get you back in bed. It's not good for you to be on your feet for this long."

She nodded sheepishly. "Yeah, (pant) be gentle with me, and maybe get me another edible and...ooooh... (pant) something to drink."

"Okay baby."

In the following days and weeks Autumn continued to indulge her growing appetite without a qualm, yet she didn't pull off a feat such as eating an entire cake in bed while being fucked from behind.

Mike kept hinting that she might need to set a new goal, as she prematurely passed the 300 mark well before her birthday, but she seemed reluctant to do so.

Although she found gaining weight exhilarating and wildly sexy, the reality of being over 300 pounds was proving to be more difficult than she initially realized.

She was constantly out of breath, often overheated and she developed nagging pains in her feet and lower back from carrying around so much more weight than her delicate frame was designed for.

Her belly made it difficult to paint her toenails and even zipping up her fancy boots had become a challenging chore and because she gained so much weight in her lower half, taking a bath had become a tight squeeze for her hips, so much so that there were a handful of times when she had nearly gotten stuck, and needed Mike's help just to get out.

These problems became more glaring as Mike gradually began to ease back into work in September of 2021, and wasn't around as much to dote on her every need.

"Oh God (huff) baby, (gasp) I think that this is just too much weight," she said as she wiggled into the living room. "I think I (pant) felt a lot more comfortable when I was in the 280 range."

Mike set his coffee down and looked at her from the couch. She was dressed in skimpy loungewear that was clearly too small. Her boobs and belly were causing her gray top to ride up her torso leaving her massive gut exposed and spilling over her elastic boyshorts.

"Ohhh no!" he said with an exaggerated whine. "But you look soooo hot."

She collapsed on the sofa next to him and placed both hands on the bare skin of her belly. "Oooff, (pant) I still sometimes wish I could take all this and put it in my boobs."

He leaned towards her and tenderly kissed the upper part of her left breast. "But your boobs are already so big."

She made a face of displeasure. "It's (pant) this belly that makes it so hard for me to move around, especially hard if you're going to be gone all day."

"I can get up early and make you breakfast before I head to work, every morning if you want."

"What are you gonna get up at 5?"

He smiled. "I wouldn't mind one bit."

She sighed then reached forward and grabbed one of the chocolate glazed donut holes that Mike had expertly placed in front of her on the coffee table. She plopped it in her mouth like it was a grape. "It's okay, (chew, chew) I think my body could use a break (chew) from all this eating and maybe stop with all the (huff) milkshakes and stuff. I really do not want to get diabetes, and I'd like to be able to wear jeans again."

Mike ran his fingers over the silky skin of her thigh as she finished chewing. His shoulders slumped. "But no pants are the best pants, remember?"

She wiggled her hips in her seat with the feeling of his touch."God babe (pant) don't look so sad! I'm still going to be extra curvy for you."

"Yeah I know. It's probably terrible to say but I'm sad that all this pandemic stuff is ending, sad to be away from you."

She gazed at him, looking seductive as hell. Her face was simply mesmerizing. "Well we sure had fun while it lasted, and honestly (pant) it lasted way longer than either of us thought, so there's that."

"It was fun wasn't it." He lowered his head into her lap, gave her belly a quick kiss, then looked up. "I just wish you could lay in bed all day and I could stay with you and take care of you all the time."

"Mmmmm, you and me both. I always said I'd love to have Samson's life, just be a lazy house cat." She reached forward again and grabbed another donut hole.

"Maybe someday," he said.

She looked at him with raised eyebrows before taking a bite. "Oh (chew) really?"

"Well, yeah."

"If that's (chew) what you want (chew) you're going to have to make some serious commitments." She wiggled the fingers of her left hand directly in his line of sight, emphasizing her lack of jewelry. "And I don't know if you're capable of that."

He smirked. "I might surprise you."

She leaned forward and took yet another donut hole. "Actions (chew) speak louder (chew) than words." She finished chewing then gently slid the bowl toward the edge of the low table with her perfectly pedicured foot. "Okay (pant) you need to get these things away from me, you know I can't stop eating when there's food in front of my face."

He gave her thigh a squeeze. "But I love watching you eat."

"I know you do, (pant) but I also know that you don't want me to get diabetes so please get these out of my reach before I eat them all."

He gave her a hyperbolic look of despair. "You know just how to break my heart."

Her eyes brightened and she squished her full lips together in the most adorable way. "Mmmhmm, I know exactly how." He began massaging her belly and breasts before she pushed him away. "Okay stop it, (pant) don't be needy, it's not attractive. Besides, I feel crampy and my ovaries are hurting."

"Okay baby. Let me grab you an edible so you feel better." He rose and went to the kitchen, then came back and inserted an indica gummy between her lips.

"Mmm, (chew, chew) thank you baby," she cooed. "God I'm gonna get addicted to these things.

"It's just THC and CBD, it's probably better for you than Midol."

"Yeah (chew) I guess that's true."

He watched as she finished chewing and thought about what she told him. It felt as though the world's longest and best snow day was finally beginning to melt, and soon he'd be forced to go back to school.

Chapter 17

The world seemed to normalize as summer cooled into fall.

People were traveling again, restaurants were fully open and faces were reappearing on the streets uncovered.

Autumn had stopped with all the daily milkshakes and was no longer purposefully eating to gain.

She gave up alcohol for two weeks in November and to Mike's surprise, even went down to the Anytime Fitness a few times to walk on the treadmill.

They planned to go to Oregon for Thanksgiving, but Patty canceled at the last minute due to another spike in covid cases and the onset of the new omicron variant.

Mike's mom canceled all of their holiday get-togethers as well, including Christmas, saying that it was too risky for Grandma to be around people, vaccinations or not.

Their cautiousness was curious to Mike, but also kind of a relief, as he had been nervous about how the families would react to his girlfriend's weight.

He set his backpack down and went upstairs. Autumn was in the loft, sitting in front of her desk. It was only 5 pm and it was already dark outside.

"How was work?" he said.

She rolled back in her chair and sighed. "My boss is talking about possibly sending me to Europe for a few weeks next year, assuming covid cases go down."

"Really, where?"

"The Dublin office, maybe Paris and Vienna too."

"That sounds like a lot of traveling."

"I know. I'm not counting on it though, just wait and see I guess."

"Would you even want to go?"

She took a deep breath. "Not really, it would be exhausting, although I've never been to France."

He peered at the empty plate next to her computer. "Can I get you something? There's still those eclairs in the fridge, you should eat them before they go bad."

Her eyes softened. "No thank you baby, no more carbs right now." She paused. "I was actually thinking about heading down to the gym. Want to join me?"

"Still with the gym?"

She leaned forward and placed her hands on the edge of the desk and slowly got up. After a short moment to catch her breath she gazed into his icy blue eyes. "I just need to."

He wrapped his arms around her waist then let his hands dangle against her backside. His lips drew a half-hearted smile. "Well let's just be sure to not overdo it or you're gonna be sore again."

She smirked haughtily. "I'll be fine. Don't (pant) worry, my ass isn't going anywhere."

"How do you always know exactly what I'm thinking?"

"Because I know you." She wiggled a few steps away, turned and gave her hair a subtle toss. "But stop being so grumpy, (pant) my body needs exercise too, I can't just keep gaining weight all the time."

He shrugged. "I'm not grumpy."

She put her weight on one hip and crossed her arms beneath her breasts. "Bullshit."

He walked forward and again pulled her close. He smiled. "Guess I'm just missing all the fun we had in the summer."

"I know you are, but that's lust." Looking at him directly she pressed her finger into his chest. "Lust is a temporary fleeting feeling, love on the other hand is not."

"But I love you."

She rolled her eyes then turned around and playfully bounced her butt against his jeans. "Do you love me or just my ass?"

"Both."

"Okay, I suppose that's (pant) an acceptable answer, but if that's true I need you to support me and come exercise with me, hold me accountable."

He squeezed the sides of her waist and let her gushy body fall into his strong, solid physique. "I think you've lost some weight baby," he said.

"Don't get all fixated on my weight, but yes, I've lost a little, thanks for noticing."

"You weighed yourself?"

"Maybe."

"How much did you lose?"

She pushed him away. "I'm finally under (pant) 300 pounds again and I'd like to keep it that way. I have so much more energy than I did a few months ago."

"Well that's good." His posture deflated, but he caught himself and quickly stood up straight and forced a smile. "It was sexy though, wasn't it."

"What, being over 300?"

He stepped forward, bringing his arms around to clutch her ass with both hands. His voice lowered to an intimate rumble as his lips approached her ear. "Yeah, and feeding you in bed, seeing the numbers go up on the scale, watching you get so curvy and…chunky."

Her body quivered as if his words sent shivers down her spine. “Okay stop it, you're (pant) going to turn me on with that kind of talk.”

He smiled and stepped back. “See I knew you loved it.”

“Well of course I loved it. What woman wouldn’t love being treated like a queen all the time, and getting all that affection…but we can’t do that forever.”

“Sure we can.”

With an open palm she pushed him in the chest. “Stop it…”

He sighed. “Okay okay, I know you’re right, and I support you.”

“That’s a good farm boy. Now (pant) let’s get going before I lose my motivation.”

“As you wish.”

He understood where she was coming from, and had to admit she seemed more sprightly as of late. She hadn’t lost all that much, maybe just 10 or 15 pounds, but she was breathing better, and moving better than she was in October. Her face wasn’t as puffy as it used to be and her belly wasn't quite as swollen looking, plus she had been cigarette free for 8 months and her lungs were continuing to heal.

Why then did this feel like a somewhat disheartening and confusing way to bring 2021 to close?

Why did the very idea of her losing weight feel like a dull knife to his heart?

What the fuck was wrong with him?

She said her ass wasn't going anywhere, and she was still a big girl with an incredible body.

Shouldn't he be happy?

Shouldn't he be thankful and grateful that he was so lucky to witness such a sexy and stupefying progression that was his girlfriend's growing curves?

Shouldn't he be relieved that she imposed a limit on herself before her weight became out of control and started to seriously affect her health?

Would things be different if they were married?

In February of 2022 Mike pulled into Seatac airport departures and hopped out to help Autumn shimmy out of the car and help with her bags. He stared at her next to the curb knowing it would be the last time he would see her in person for quite a while.

"I'm gonna miss you," he said.

She sighed and lifted a few strands of hair away from her eyes. "I'm gonna miss you too."

He gestured at her purple roller suitcase. "You sure you're gonna be okay getting all the way to the gate with that thing?"

"I can manage."

He gave her a long tight hug then kissed her on the lips. "Watch out for Irish guys."

She smirked. "Maybe I'll run into Damian Rice and he'll ask me to marry him."

"Tell him you're taken."

She ran her left hand through her thick soft hair. "Guess I'd have to, otherwise how would he know?"

His face turned somber. "Be safe and try not to work too hard. I love you."

"I'm scared."

"Scared of what?"

"I'm scared of being away from you for so long," she said. "What if we like, you know, start to drift apart."

His eyes danced over her body. With her sophisticated and well put together way of dressing she looked like a very beautiful and extremely curvy young woman and less like the hot and bloated sex goddess she had been, although he didn't think she was any smaller than she was in December. "I said I love you."

She took a deep breath and gave him one last kiss. "I love you too."

He stared at her for as long as he could as she walked away with her luggage rolling behind. Her black leggings showcased her oversized backside magnificently and she was already beginning to turn the heads of a group of pilots that were chatting on the sidewalk.

How the hell was she going to squeeze that butt into economy seating?

Would she have to turn sideways just to walk down the aisle of the plane?

Shit.

Walk down the aisle.

All of a sudden, everything seemed serious.

It was a shock for Mike to be alone again after spending nearly every waking minute with Autumn for so long. The apartment felt cold, dreary and sad, and the constant drizzle of Seattle rain didn't make things any better.

He went to work, went home, ate top ramen and microwavable burritos for dinner and did countless pushups and pullups just to pass the time and suppress his anxiety.

He imagined Autumn getting hit on everywhere she went in Europe, and it dawned on him fully that if he didn't put a ring on her finger there were thousands of eligible men who happily take his place and do the job for him.

But all the feeding and weight gain stuff had been such a thrilling gift that he was having trouble thinking of anything else.

The way Autumn had been talking worried him, and the more time they spent apart only fueled his concerns.

They Facetimed frequently, or as much as they could considering the time difference. She seemed to like Dublin okay, but complained about all the walking and lack of decent food.

As the days went by Mike's mind went crazy with thoughts of Autumn being deprived of her favorite desserts, meeting guys with charming Irish accents and constantly walking the Docklands.

She would soon need to go to Paris and then maybe Vienna and it would just be more of the same and by the time she returned home she'd be a significantly slimmer version of herself.

Why did these thoughts bother him so much and keep him up at night?

It was her body and he had no right to worry about what she ate or how much exercise she got.

She was not some art project of his to control. Obese, curvy or in-between she was a real lady and a gorgeous woman of the absolute highest quality and he felt like a toxic masculine pig for not wanting her to lose weight.

Before she left he had sneakily wrapped a string around her finger while she was sleeping. He needed to pop the question when she got back, and he needed to get a ring and the ring needed to be the right size.

It was time, but what if Europe ended up giving her a new outlook on life?

What if she wanted to lose more weight, would he still want to marry her?

What if she ended up slimming down to the point where the ring would just slip right off her formally chubby finger.

What if.

Laying on his back on the sofa, he lifted his phone above his face and stared at the darkened screen. He could see only vague shadows of Autumn's hair and face, but her voice came through crisp and clear. It had been a few days since they last spoke, and over two weeks had passed since dropping her off at the Airport.

"You would love it here, so much history," she said.

He fiddled with his hair, distracted by his own image in the upper right corner of his phone as always. "Over your jet lag yet?"

"Yeah, finally."

"Turn on some lights I can't see you."

"Noooo, I just woke up, I don't have any makeup on or anything."

"You don't need makeup."

She leaned in and Mike could see a hint of a smile on her face. "Ooohh, five points for that remark," she said.

"How was the flight from Dublin?"

Her eyes narrowed, smug and proud. "It was good, you're not going to believe it but they upgraded me again."

"What, first class?"

"Yep."

"How is that even possible?"

"I don't know? I've been lucky and keep getting these straight male flight attendants and I suppose I can't help but, you know…exercise my feminine powers of persuasion. It's a good thing because…and I know I haven't flown in a while but I swear to god, it's like the seating (pant) has gotten even tinier and more crammed over the pandemic or something. I think they are more like plus-size-phobic over here than they are in the states too. The hotel rooms are more compact, the doorways are narrow and even the toilet seats are smaller."

His eyes brightened. "Is the food better?"

She yawned. "Way better, there's so many options here, at least more than just pubs. Justine and I have been walking everywhere, my legs are sooo sore, but the coffee is amazing."

"Did you get some crepes, or french fries or anything?"

"Not yet, we're actually a little north of Neuilly-sur-Seine, outside the main part of the city, maybe we'll explore more of old Paris this weekend and I'll get to experience the real French cuisine."

He sat up straight and cleared his throat."What's the word on Austria?"

She sighed. "Sounds like they really want me to go."

"For how long?"

"At least another week, maybe two."

"So you don't know when you're coming back yet?"

"No, not yet." She paused for a moment. "How's Samson?"

"Samson is good, but he misses you, we both do." He brought his phone closer to his face. "Are you getting enough to eat though?"

She brought her screen close to her face. "God how many times do I have to tell you, stop worrying about what I eat or how much I eat."

"Okay, I'll stop, I'm sorry," he said. "I'm glad you're getting to explore Europe."

"Thank you."

They stared at each other in silence for several seconds. "What?" Mike said finally.

She pursed her lips together. "I have a confession to make."

"Okay."

"I may have umm, accidentally caved and umm... bought a pack of cigarettes."

"Ohh baby no!"

"I know I know...I just couldn't help it, seems like everyone smokes here."

"Bad girl."

"Don't worry, I'll quit again, just need to get through this trip." Her darkened eyes quickly shot downward. "Omigod, I need to shower and get ready for a meeting."

"Yeah and I should get to bed." He collapsed back down into a lying position. "Love you."

She blew him a kiss. "Talk to you soon."

"Bye."

The call ended and Mike set his phone on the coffee table. He closed his eyes.

Fuck, he missed her.

He missed the sweet smell of her perfumes and lotions. He missed her touch, and the feeling of her thick soft hair tangled in his fingers.

He missed her ass.

Her big juicy ass.

But it wasn't going to be quite as juicy as it used to be.

He already knew it.

She was smoking again. That would probably curb her appetite and French women don't get fat and all that stuff.

He wasn't there to cook for her, he wasn't there to buy her desserts every night, he wasn't there to feed her.

And now it seemed likely that he wouldn't see her again for at least another 3 weeks. It would be a month and a half apart if not more.

Fuck.

A month and a half was a long enough time to break habits and lose more weight.

He grabbed his phone again and scrolled through his photos.

He found the ones of Autumn at their fourth of July party from the previous year when she was still gaining and getting close to her peak.

He stared like a hungry dog.

He zoomed in.

He put his hand in his pants.

Chapter 18

After a stop at Starbucks, Mike parked in the cell phone lot and waited while the gray sky darkened into night. The woman in the Subaru Forester next to him cracked her window and lit up a smoke.

God that smell.

Since quitting he seemed able to detect the scent of cigarettes everywhere.

It was the odor of temptation and he wanted one so bad he could almost taste it.

Fuck they were hard to quit though.

He didn't want to go through that pain again no matter what and his envy of the woman soured into pity.

But once a smoker, always a smoker. At least that seemed to be the case for his girlfriend.

She wasn't going to be just his girlfriend for long though.

During his month and half alone, he looked deep inside himself and warmed to the idea of seeing her at a lighter weight.

She'd still have her otherworldly curves, her gorgeous face and perfect ass. He wondered if her ass might look even better and appear more prominent if she ended up shedding inches from her waist.

Appearances aside, there were other perks to dropping a few pounds. They could go hiking together and go on motorcycle rides again. She would have more pep in her step, more stamina in the bedroom, and most importantly she would be an overall healthier person.

Whatever happened it wasn't up to him and for maybe the first time in his life, Mike understood what it meant to be truly in love.

He recalled the bible verse from his Sunday school days as a kid.

Love is patient, love is kind. It does not envy, it does not boast, it is not proud. It does not dishonor others and it is not self-seeking.

He looked at the iced venti caramel macchiato in the cupholder. He figured Autumn would be tired and thirsty after a long flight and he didn't want to pick her up empty handed, but a part of him worried that she might now scoff at such a grossly American drink and accuse him again of trying to make her fat.

He took a deep breath and felt a calmness throughout his body, then his phone buzzed.

He pulled up to the curb at arrivals and jumped out of the car.

His heart was racing.

For what seemed like an eternity, he scoured the sea of strangers moving in and out of the terminal's automatic sliding doors and along the sidewalk and then, about a hundred feet away, sticking out like a flower among weeds there was a very attractive woman in a black dress toting a purple suitcase on wheels. With gorgeous shoulder length auburn hair and milky white skin, she was extremely well endowed, yet clearly very overweight.

She was the hottest fat girl he had ever laid eyes on, or perhaps the hottest woman he had ever seen period; an embarrassment of riches in the form of ample, plush and wobbly curves so prominent that her severely feminine walk appeared tiresome and labor intensive.

That black dress covered her like a sheet, but despite its flowy looseness, it could not disguise the lush opulence of her uncommonly generous proportions.

Autumn wasn't that wide, was she?

Weaving through the crowd she came closer until the outdoor overhead lights illuminated a face that Mike would have recognized anywhere.

Goddamn.

It was her.

They locked eyes and her pouty unhappy lips flipped into the prettiest smile in the world. She powered towards him and it looked for a second like she was making an attempt at breaking into a slow jog before thinking better of the idea; instead continuing that ultra sexy wiggle until stopping just feet away.

Time stood still and the bustling frantic noise of cars and people seemed to fade into dreamlike silence.

With her weight on one hip she stared at him and in a breathy voice said, "Could (pant) you have parked any further away?"

He erupted into an unrestrained grin. "What? You said United didn't you? This is United."

They gazed into each other's eyes as if frozen in space, then Mike lurched forward and embraced her in a most delicious hug.

With her lips near his ear she whispered, "Did you (pant) miss me?"

He squeezed her tighter and took in her familiar captivating essence. "Holy fucking god yes."

"Come on, (gasp) let's get out of here, I need a cigarette so bad I could die."

He clung to her for another few seconds, savoring the ultra-sexy sound and feeling of her heavy breathing before reluctantly releasing. He took a step back and examined her.

Despite the travel fatigue, she looked stunning as ever, but to his surprise didn't appear to be any slimmer than she was a month ago. On the contrary, and although it was difficult to tell, she seemed bigger than she was before she left, but that couldn't be.

He threw her luggage in the back, then opened the passenger door and she climbed in. Her hips were so wide they spilled over both sides of the seat and she needed to re-adjust her position several times before he could get her door closed.

Damn.

The CRV had been a bit of a tight squeeze for her for a while now, but wasn't this difficult when he had dropped her off, was it?

Once back behind the wheel he watched her struggle with her seatbelt. "You got it okay?"

She squirmed like an overgrown jellyfish, tugging on the belt and stretching it as far as she could towards the buckle which was wedged beneath the left side of her hip. "Yeah (pant) I just, (huff) fuck, (gasp) what did you do to this thing while I was gone?"

"Nothing." He leaned over to help, grabbing the latch and pulling the strap taut across her lap. "Scoot back."

"I am (pant) scooted back."

"Just try."

She gave him a look then pressed her hands against the glove compartment and wiggled and shimmied her butt around until she was shoved as far backwards as she could go.

He yanked on the seatbelt again and finally managed to click her in, although the gray polyester straps looked to be digging painfully into the fluffiness of her swelling flesh.

She fanned herself. "Fewww! (gasp) I know I've said it many times before but I think we might need a new car." She turned and noticed the expression of contentment on her boyfriend's face. "What?"

His eyes drew down, then up. "Nothing. I just like how you said, we."

She stared at him blankly and fluttered her dark eyelashes, then with straining effort, reached forward and took the Starbucks beverage from the cupholder. "This for me?"

"Yes baby. I mean, only if you want it." He put the car in drive and weaved into the left lane. "You wanna go I-5 or the fun way?"

She took a long pull from her straw then put the drink back. "The fun way, (pant) but can we pull over somewhere please?" She began digging into her purse.

"It's okay," Mike said with one hand on the wheel and the other dangling against her thigh.

"It's okay what?"

He shrugged. "You can smoke in here."

"No way (pant) I couldn't do that to you, (cough) that's just cruel."

"It's alright, trust me," he said. " I actually kind of enjoy the second hand smell."

"I don't want (cough) to be a bad influence."

He gave her a brief glance as he exited the airport. "Just have one already, I'd rather you be comfortable. I know how it is after a flight."

She sighed. "Okay." She took out her pack and lit up. "Thank you."

"Dunhills?"

She cracked her window and blew smoke into the starless night. "Yeah, London rubbed off on me. I don't know why but these seem a little classier."

"You didn't tell me you were in London."

"Yes I did, went there on a weekend when I was in Ireland, and (cough) I flew out of Heathrow remember?" She took another sip from her sugary latte.

He shrugged and turned onto a main avenue which was packed with an array of fast food places and strip malls on both sides. He gazed at her, noticing the way her breasts and belly jiggled with every bump in the road. He cleared his throat. "Are you hungry?"

"I'm starving."

His eyes widened. "I can stop wherever, what do you want to eat?"

She flicked ash out the window. "I don't care, just whatever, something that doesn't require me to get out of the car."

He scanned the surrounding neon lights, shining brightly against the night sky. "Umm, Wendy's okay?"

"Sure."

In the drive-through line, she ordered a Hot Honey Chicken Sandwich, fries and a chocolate frosty, much to Mike's astonishment.

He could feel his instincts fighting with his willpower as his fixations and obsessions over her weight came flooding back.

He longed to ask her if she wanted chicken nuggets with her meal. He longed to ask her if she wanted him to feed them to her, stuff her face, rub her belly and grab her ass. He wanted to ask her if she had gained the weight back and was over 300 pounds again; but he didn't.

After pulling out of the drive-through he parked in the lot to give her a chance to eat and relax in the comfort of a stationary vehicle. He had yet to kiss her lips since she left for Europe, and he suddenly felt like he was on a first date with an arrestingly beautiful woman that was out of his league.

"So what was your favorite place, what did you like best?" he said.

"I don't know, (chew) maybe Vienna."

"Was it like Before Sunrise?"

With her mouth full of fries, she smiled as much as she could. "Yeah I (chew) guess, (munch, chew) been a while since (chew) we watched that though so I can't remember." She finished chewing and licked her lips. "I mean I love Paris too, but Vienna was just easier, less crowded and touristy. I don't know, it was hard because I had to work all the time, and then my co-workers wanted to go out every night and I didn't have good shoes for walking so I mostly took Ubers." She bit into her chicken burger. "But (munch, chew) oh my god (chew) the bakeries in Paris were incredible."

"I can imagine."

"I have to say though, (chew) being there for so long made me appreciate America more."

"How so?"

She continued eating and talking simultaneously. "Just like, (chew, much) everything over there (chew) is so slow, lines at every restaurant, every coffee shop. I feel like the states are more progressive and accommodating towards…you know, curvier women too."

"Were you able to sleep on the plane?"

"Yes it was lovely, took an edible, had a couple glasses of champagne and I was out cold."

"Did you get first class again?"

She nodded with her mouth full. "Mmhm."

He smiled, amazed. "How do you always do that?"

"It was all (chew, munch) I could find and it's a business expense so why not? Plus there's no way I (gasp) could handle a 10 hour flight in regular seats."

"Good job baby."

"Mmm (chew, munch)...let's go, (chew) I can eat while you drive. I'm excited to see Samson and sleep in my own bed."

He merged onto the 509 freeway while Autumn continued to devour her food. When the familiar Columbia Tower dominant skyline of the emerald city came into view she had consumed the entire meal, frosty and Starbucks iced latte included.

He was in a state of mind somewhere between confusion and euphoria. The way she looked, the things she said and the way she ate told him her days of gaining weight were far from over and the mere thought of that sent a wave of mad passion down his spine.

Finally back home together in their apartment, Autumn kissed Samson's furry little head and then set him down on the sofa. She turned towards Mike in the kitchen, stretched her arms out wide and sauntered his way.

She smiled with a heavy layer of seduction beaming from her eyes. "You know (pant) what I missed most of all though?"

Mike let her fall into his grasp. He kissed her neck and brought his smirking mouth to her ear. "My dick?" he whispered.

With her head resting on his shoulder, she whispered back, "No, you're big fluffy German pancakes."

He let her belly and breasts squish into him and his knees began to tremble as his temperature rose. "Didn't they have stuff like that over there?"

"Not as good as the ones you make."

"I'll be sure and make you that for breakfast then."

She pushed him in the chest and took a few steps back. "No, I want one now for dessert." She turned, bent over to grab her cigarettes from the coffee table then gazed at him, haughty and sublime. She lifted her ankle-length dress all the way up to her waist to reveal her dimpled thighs, naked ass and absent panties. "Big and fluffy like my butt."

Mike was speechless, and for a moment he wondered if he was dreaming. He couldn't contain his raging urges for a second longer and lurched forward and kissed her lips. Her pack of Dunhills fell to the floor as he cupped her softened jawline and let his tongue dance against her's, relishing in the warm pleasing taste he so sorely missed.

After making out with the unbridled candidness of teenage lovers, Autumn finally came up for air and peered into the intense focus of his eyes. "I'm sorry baby but (pant) I've been a bad girl."

"How so?"

"I think I gained some weight in Europe. (gasp) Everything we did there revolved around food and when we were not out in restaurants, I was stuck in my hotel room just like binging on kraphens and cream puffs in the middle of the night just to fight off the boredom."

He squeezed her ass with both hands. "Oh god baby, you're going to kill me."

She smiled. "What, (gasp) am I too sexy for you?"

"You are way too sexy, but please don't stop."

She peered up at him. "Does my ass feel bigger?"

"I wasn't going to say anything, I mean…you know, didn't want to be rude."

"I honestly didn't mean to, (gasp) but I was so lonely for you and I just couldn't seem to stop eating. It made me feel closer to you."

"Why didn't you tell me?"

She sighed and clawed her fingers beneath his white t-shirt. "Oooh…I almost sent you some selfies of my stuffed belly, (huff) but then I decided it would be more fun to surprise you."

"You get off on teasing me don't you?"

"Only as much as you get off on teasing me." She smiled, released herself from his groping clutches then bent over again to pick her pack of smokes off the floor. With a deliberate fling of her hair she again stood up straight and stared at him. She placed her fingers on his chin, lifting his jaw shut. "You better get started on my dessert you lazy bum, (gasp) I won't be long."

She turned away and wiggled towards the coat rack and his jaw again fell open.

When she returned from the balcony there was a lit vanilla scented candle next to a glass of red wine on the coffee table.

She removed her jacket and tossed it on the sofa. "Oooh, what's this?"

In the kitchen, Mike wiped his hands on a dish rag then hurried towards her.

His eyes burned with an adorable nervousness that Autumn found irresistible.

She gazed at him inquisitively. "Why do you have to look so handsome all the time?"

"I um…I'm not very good at this," he said, reaching into the right front pocket of his jeans."

"Michael?"

"I had planned to um, do this later, but I just can't wait a second longer."

He dropped to one knee, holding a little velvet box in his hand. He opened it with trembling fingers and looked straight into her eyes. "Autumn Murrell, will you be my wife?"

Her nose scrunched and her hands flew to the sides of her cheeks. She stayed silent for a moment. "Are you serious right now?"

"Dead serious."

Mike could almost see the defensive walls that had surrounded her heart for so long come crashing down in the form of a single tear rolling down her face.

She turned away to hide her eyes, waving her arms in a fit of emotion. She then looked back at him and burst into a giggling smile.

"Yes Mike," she said. "I would love to be your wife."

"Will you marry me?"

She kicked his shoe. "Yes!"

Mike stood and Autumn threw herself into him.

He took the ring and brought it to her outstretched finger.

He slipped it on. It was a perfect fit.

"It's beautiful," she said with a sniffle.

"So are you."

Chapter 19

Neither Mike nor Autumn had interest in a big expensive wedding. The pandemic changed them in many ways, and like so many others, they had grown accustomed to the more antisocial existence that had become the new normal for the past two years. Besides, covid-19 was dying an excruciatingly slow death, as even in April of 2022, people were still testing positive for the virus at alarming rates.

"I really don't (pant) want to get a fat face baby," Autumn said, looking at her phone.

Mike handed her a glass of wine then sat next to her on the sofa. He gently touched her cheek with the back of his hand. "You don't have a fat face, you have the most beautiful face I have ever seen, and that is not an exaggeration."

She looked at him expressionless. "I've been researching Kybella."

He grabbed the remote and put the TV on mute. "What's that?"

She tilted her head up and inspected her neck with her hand. "It's (pant) just a natural way to remove some of this, permanently kill the fat cells like under my chin."

"You don't need that."

She took a sip of her wine. "But just the (gasp) idea of a wedding is giving me an anxiety attack, and there will be pictures."

He gazed at her as she sat with her legs tucked beneath her butt. She was wearing only black panties and a white camisole.

She wasn't saying anything about her weight specifically, but it didn't seem like she was getting any smaller.

Knowing exactly what she looked like when she was three hundred and nine pounds back in late August of 2021, he estimated she was over 310 at her peak in September.

She said she was under 300 in December, and seemed to be about the same when she left for Europe. When she returned from Europe in March she looked almost as big as ever, maybe 305 or more.

Now, after being home for a month and falling right back into many of her habits, he estimated she was more than that, perhaps a new all time high but he didn't know for sure and he wasn't going to ask.

It was hard to guess her weight sometimes because she didn't look like a typical 300 pound woman. When fully dressed, her trendy and tasteful sense of style gave her the appearance of a picture-perfect voluptuous goddess, a plus-size socialite; but when naked or in her underwear as she was now, she looked indisputably obese, perhaps morbidly so.

This however could not be said of her face, as her chubbiness still mostly avoided that area. It may have simply been her genetics, natural beauty and idyllic bone structure, as she retained the high cheekbones and delicate jawline that never failed to turn the heads of both men and women alike, and the only notable facial development was the softening slope of her neck and cutely budding double chin.

"Your face already looks so perfect," he said without a hint of falsity.

Her lips turned sultry and she untucked her legs and shifted her hips towards him. "But I'll be 30 this year, (gasp) and this way I can have a fat ass, without getting like chubby cheeks you know."

He smiled, his pants feeling tighter. "If this is wedding anxiety, I'd be fine if we just went to the courthouse, signed the papers and went away somewhere, just the two of us."

"We can't elope, your mom would kill me." She put her phone down and reached out her arm in the direction of the chocolate cheesecake that he had placed on the coffee table earlier.

"She'd get over it, she's the one who canceled Christmas two years in a row," he said, grabbing her the slice and handing it to her with a fork.

She paused and took a bite. "Mmm…I think (chew) we should apply online, (chew) get the certificate and just have a small ceremony somewhere fun."

"That's important to you, a ceremony?"

"Not really, (pant) but it would mean a lot to my dad."

"To walk you down the aisle?"

"Yeah." After a gulp of wine she took another bite of cake. "I just (chew, chew) don't know how I'm gonna fit into a wedding dress."

"Nobody looks better in dresses than you do."

She pointed her fork at him. "That's what you think, but what about your parents? They haven't really seen me in so long."

"Let's not wait though." He gently ran his fingers through the ends of her hair. "I don't want to be one of those couples that's just engaged for years."

"I agree with that." She scraped more cake off her plate and shoved another forkful between her lips. "Mmm…I (chew, chew) actually kind of like the idea of doing it with the (chew) corona stuff still going on, it's a good excuse for us not to have to invite a bunch of people, and I could really use a vacation."

"How do you feel about Hawaii?"

She licked her mouth slowly with her tongue before she spoke. "For the wedding?"

"For a small ceremony," he said. "If people don't want to fly, they don't need to come. If they want, they can buy their own tickets."

"Hawaii would be amazing, (gasp) but maybe somewhere other than Maui."

"Right, the boyfriend who didn't want to take you out to dinner."

She rolled her eyes and continued eating. "Don't (chew) remind me."

"You'd love the Big Island, it's less touristy."

"(chew)I wouldn't (chew, chew) be opposed to that, but you know I'm going to need to fly first class."

He scooted closer and began caressing her hip like it was some sort of supernatural piece of art. He kissed her thigh, then looked up and wiped a dab of saliva away from the corner of his mouth. "Maybe we could just buy three seats, have a row all to ourselves and cuddle up by the window."

She took another sip of wine, then handed him the empty glass. “Don’t be cheap.”

“Buying three seats isn’t cheap.” He stood, then headed towards the kitchen to replenish her wine. “Plus we need to keep looking for a house right?”

“We’ll be fine, don’t worry about money.”

He returned and gave her back her glass, again now two-thirds full of Apothic Dark Red. His brows tightened. “Did you sell your Zoom stock or something?”

She rolled her eyes. “Yes, a long time ago.”

Sitting back down, he crossed his boot over his knee and draped his arm over the back edge of the couch. “You do want a house right?”

“There’s no need for us to live in the city other than your job.” She slurped her berry flavored wine like it was water then went back to working on her cheesecake. “(chew)I don’t know, (chew, chew) it's just that I always pictured that when I was married I would live in a house. (gasp) It just sucks that the market is so crazy right now.”

"There's an old Chinese saying that says the best time to plant a tree is 50 years ago, the second best time is right now."

"Okay Confucius," she said, handing him her empty plate. "What's the best time to order dinner for your soon to be wife?"

"Umm, what, or…when?"

"(gasp)30 minutes ago."

He put her plate on the coffee table. "You hungry already baby?"

"What's (gasp) the (hiccup) second best time to order dinner?"

He smiled and stood. "I'll grab my phone."

Part 2

Chapter 20

Mike looked at the bookshelf in the living room of the modern suburban house. He scanned the little framed pictures and polaroids of the homeowners as if he didn't live there. The photos told a story.

On the far left was Autumn in her senior year of high school, looking cute and skinny and innocent as ever. Her brown eyes were bright and clear, so full of hopes and dreams and possibilities. Next was a photo of her in India during her college days. She wore an orange head scarf and a black shirt that hung loose over lithe shoulders, highlighting a pronounced collar bone.

There was one of her and Tabitha at a kickboxing class back in 2017, both girls toned and fit, and both roughly the same size. As the photos progressed in time mostly from left to right it was easy to see the changes, the softening jawline, the fuller face and fleshier arms.

There was one of her with her old T-Mobile co-workers at a formal dinner, her perfect hourglass figure showcased beautifully in a shimmering crimson dress; there was one where she was on the ski slopes of Snoqualmie pass when she had bangs and copper highlights, and then he himself quite literally entered the pictures.

A selfie of him and Autumn at a Black Flag concert at the Neptune Theater early on in their relationship, another on the ferry on their way to the San Juan Islands, and one from the New Year's Eve party at Tabitha's apartment in the final hours of 2019. He remembered being amazed by how thick she looked that night, but compared to the wedding photos at the Mauna Kea Resort in Hawaii on the opposite side of the TV, she was a stick.

"Babe I need your help!" she yelled from the master bathroom.

He turned, headed to the kitchen and put his mug of coffee on the counter.

It was Thanksgiving Day, and thus far 2022 had been a very busy year.

Since their engagement, covid cases had gone down and containment regulations dissipated. Autumn had an actual in-person meeting with her boss for the first time, which resulted with her receiving a promotion.

Funny how that works.

They had gone house hunting frequently during the spring and summer and after much deliberation settled on a single story 2 bedroom place in the Seattle suburb of Kirkland. It wasn't cheap, and it took a little help from both their parents to make a decent down payment, but considering Autumn's growing six figure salary, it was within their price range.

He went down the hall, through the ivory white double doors of the master bedroom and into the adjacent bathroom where he found his wife in front of the mirror as usual.

"Yes dear, what is it?" he said.

He soaked her in. It never failed to amaze him with how good she could look in a dress.

Fucking hell, that was his wife.

Applying eyeliner, she was sitting on one of the bench-like bar stools that would normally go in the kitchen with the others.

She used to stand during her beautification routines. When she started putting on weight, she'd often curl her lashes with her belly resting on the countertop, but as she got heavier, chairs moved into bathrooms and makeup was now done only while seated.

With a black pencil in hand, she pointed toward the small bong between the sinks. "Can (gasp) you do the thing for me?"

He raised his brows. "Again?"

"It's (pant) hard with nails, and you always do it better anyway."

"Just take it easy if you're having wine with it," he said.

There was a half empty glass on the granite slab counter next to an ashtray.

"I know (gasp) but I need it for my back pain, plus what better (pant) time to get the munchies, and I need to do it now so I'm not too loopy when the people come."

Autumn said as she carefully lined the corner of her eye. "(gasp)I'm so looking forward to just (pant) sitting, and eating." She put the pencil down and reached towards her husband.

He helped her up and let her body press against him. "Mmm, that's my girl."

Fuck she felt good.

In the months leading up to and following the wedding she had continued to slowly pile on the pounds. Mike didn't think it was a conscious thing, but he also knew that she knew exactly what turned him on, and didn't doubt she enjoyed teasing him.

He also knew that she was becoming increasingly lazy, and some of her more self indulgent habits were getting worse or were morphing into other habits.

What he didn't know was how much she weighed. The last time he asked her to step on the scale she acted offended and gave him a speech about how he shouldn't get caught up in numbers.

But damn she was uber thick.

What was she, 320, 330, 335 pounds?

Could she even be more than that?

Since returning from her European work trip eight months ago, it was getting harder for him to tell, but he knew she was often heavier than she looked, and she looked pretty heavy.

She wiggled her tits into his lower chest and placed her hand on the growing hardness poking tight beneath his gray slacks. "Is (pant) your penis gonna be able to make it all the way through dinner?"

He buried his nose in her hair. Her smell intoxicated him. He cupped her breast. "I'm sure he'll manage somehow."

She smiled, released herself from his grasp and stepped backwards. She stretched her arms to her sides, displaying herself in her dress. "Okay, what (gasp) do you think, (pant) this one or the yellow one?"

He looked at her starry eyed. It was a curve hugging black sheath that clung to her hips so tightly it almost looked wet before falling loose at her ankles. It was sleeveless, and the slender straps did nothing to hide the wobbly girth of her arms or the deepening cleavage between heaving breasts. "Oh that's a tough decision."

She spun around to show the back. "Be honest."

He blinked.

Jesus fucking Christ.

It was backless and cut a large U-shape of exposed white skin from her shoulders to her butt. She now had multiple rolls of fat that dripped in downward slopes starting below her armpits until disappearing beneath the taut fabric squeezing against her sides.

Damn, that ass.

He had no idea a woman's backside could be so huge, so wide; yet still so full and ripe and plump all at the same time.

She was bigger than ever, no doubt about it.

So big, so out of shape, but so proportionate and well put together it was just stupid.

What would her parents think now?

When he and Autumn went down to Oregon to tell them the news of their engagement, the look on Patty's face still burned in his mind, as did the passive aggressive comments she made during the little Hawaiian wedding reception back in June.

His eyes bulged and he had to remind himself to breathe as he came to the realization that just one of his wife's butt cheeks was bigger than his entire ass. He cleared his throat. "It's not too tight is it?"

She turned and faced him again. "No, (huff) I don't think so. (pant) Do you think it's a little too much boob for family?"

He leaned against the counter because the sight of her was too sexy to take standing. He looked her up and down again and swallowed. "I think they'll just have to deal with it. You look amazing."

"Okay well wipe the drool off your face and help me." She gestured toward the bong.

He loaded it up with the damp pungent buds from the clear plastic container on the counter. When he finished he handed it to her, now seated on the toilet. She brought it to her mouth as he lit it with a cigar torch.

She coughed and filled the room with smoke.

He turned the fan on.

She took long wheezing breaths as she recovered then looked up at him. "What (cough) time is it?"

"It's a little after 4, probably an hour before they get here. We should clean all this shit up in case someone needs to use this bathroom."

She let out a few more short coughs, then gave him an adorably pouty look. "But (gasp, huff) it will be so hard for me in these shoes, (pant) and I would need your help to get them off."

He looked down at her feet. She didn't wear heels much anymore, and he knew she was going to have trouble walking around tonight. He sighed, leaned forward and kissed her on the lips. Sometimes he forgot how much he loved spoiling her and treating her like a princess. "I'm sorry baby, I'll do it, you just relax."

She gazed into his eyes for a moment then smiled. "Okay get out of here (huff) and go check on the turkey. (pant) I need to finish my makeup."

He helped her up then headed towards the door. He stopped. "Get your smoking done now though."

She turned around with a lit cigarette in her hand. "Way ahead of you." She clicked a heel into the tile floor, blew smoke into his face and smiled. "As always."

Chapter 21

Steven Murrell drove a rented Dodge Caravan across Lake Washington on the 520 floating bridge. His wife Julia was at his side, and their two kids, Noah, now 5, and Lily, now 7, were seated behind them.

“Mommy?” Lilly said.

Julia turned around. “Yes sweetie?”

“Is Auntie Autumn fat?”

Julia’s eyes widened and she shook her head. “Umm…remember it’s not polite to call anyone fat.”

The child scrunched her nose. “But she is fat isn’t she.”

“She’s a grownup dear, and she’s your Auntie and we’re going to be guests in her house so you need to be polite okay?”

Lily gave a look of confusion. "But she didn't used to be fat, like when I was little."

"Sometimes people change," Julia said, "but we are not going to use that word tonight, some people really don't like it and they could get hurt feelings."

Lily shrugged and lifted her hands to her sides with her palms facing up. "But Bana always said that Auntie Autumn was pretty."

Julia smirked and rolled her eyes at the same time. "Well yes, Auntie Autumn is pretty."

Now Lily looked really confused. "You can be fat, annnd pretty?"

Julia sighed. "Put your headphones back on honey, we'll be there soon."

Julia faced forward and sat in silence for a moment, savoring the peaceful quietness of the drive with both her children once again comfortably glued to their tablets. She peered out the window at the serene fall landscape; the rolling hills of evergreens dotted with the orange gold of half barren maples and jagged snow capped mountains in the distance, signaling the coming winter.

Goodness it was pretty here.

Pretty.

It seemed everybody always had to make comments about how beautiful Julia's sister-in-law was, even her own daughter.

She turned the heater up a few notches then looked at her husband. "Do you think Autumn had some work done?"

With one hand on the wheel, Steven gave her a quick glance. "How do you mean?"

"Fat and pretty?" Julia said, repeating her daughter's words. "I don't know like on her face."

Steven adjusted his Tom Ford spectacles. "Uhh… she's too young for botox right?"

"No like lipo. I mean come on, you were just as shocked as I was at the wedding, you saw how big she was. How can you be that big and still have a face that looks like that, and still have, you know, like a figure."

He shook his head. "I doubt my sister would do that, she's not the type."

"She's changed, like a lot."

"I think covid changed everyone."

Julia looked at him like he was crazy. "Oh please, we didn't all gain a hundred pounds."

"Now you're just exaggerating."

"Am I? I thought I was being conservative. What do you think she is 250, 270, maybe even more than that?"

"No way." Steven slowed the vehicle, exiting the freeway. "I'm sure she'll lose it soon enough. She told me she quit smoking, people gain weight when they quit."

"I didn't know she smoked."

"She was more rebellious than I was," Steven said.

Julia got quiet for a moment, then smirked. "Maybe I should give her some diet tips."

"She's not stupid. She's probably lost some weight already. She's always been pretty good at keeping herself in shape."

"Maybe when she was 24, or I guess even pre-pandemic."

Steven stopped at a red light and adjusted his glasses again. "Well, like I said, I think covid changed everyone."

Mike opened the solid mahogany front door of his house. He watched as Steven, Julia, and the kids came across the wet leaf covered lawn and up to the short concrete steps that led to the porch. He smiled. "Hello hello, welcome. Watch your step."

With a casserole dish in her hands, Julia admired the lush quaint surroundings. "Oh my gosh, I forgot how beautiful it is here, love your house!"

Mike looked down at her. She was significantly slimmer than she was when he first met her 3 years ago, and based on her stylish boots and form fitting sweater dress, she was eager to show off. "Thank you," he said, " and thanks so much for making the trip up. Where's Bana and Boppa?"

"They were right behind us," Steven said as he entered the house, followed by his family. "Your parents aren't coming Mike?"

Mike closed the door to shield away the cold then took the dish from Julia and walked it towards the kitchen. "Nah, they're all at my sister's with my brother in law's family. We'll see them for Christmas, although we've been saying that for the last two years and it still hasn't happened."

Steven chuckled. "I know right, it's been nuts."

Mike took a quick peek in the oven then looked at Steven. "How's the Air B and B?"

Steven shimmied out of his puffy Patagonia jacket and hung it on the coat rack behind the front door. "It's good, Jules loves Seattle, and it's been fun for the kids to spend so much time with my mom and dad. It's big enough we could've had Thanksgiving there."

Mike smiled. "No way, we wanna show off the house."

"I know I know," Steven said.

Mike's smile faded as he drifted off in thought.

Show off the house or show off what the pandemic had done to Autumn?

Suddenly he felt nervous about the whole thing, much like he did before the wedding.

He looked out the window at the driveway as a BMW X3 pulled in behind the Caravan. "Here they are."

He turned to Steven and then to Julia who was in the living room with the kids. “Get warm and make yourselves at home, plenty of snacks to hold you over, I'll see if they need a hand. We got Disney Plus and stuff in the spare room if the kids wanna watch something.”

“Where's Autumn?” Julia said.

Mike made his way towards the door. “Probably in the bathroom, I’m sure she’ll be out in a sec.”

After helping Patty with a foil covered plate of sweet potato pie, and getting everyone situated inside, Mike closed the front door again as the sky quickly darkened.

“This is so lovely,” Patty said. “It smells delicious in here.”

There was a vegetable platter with ranch dip on the coffee table along with a plate of Brie, crackers and castelvetrano olives. On an end table in the corner, one of Autumn’s laptops softly played a Harry Connick Junior song from one of her playlists.

Julia examined the living room. “I love what you’ve done with this bookcase, oh and the fireplace.”

Gary eyed the TV showing the Patriots and Vikings football game on mute, then looked at Mike. "Where's pumpkin?"

The scent of sweet perfume preceded her, but on cue, with a slow click-clack of heels Autumn emerged from the hallway.

She looked stupid hot.

Her dress was designed to be comfortable and casual, but with the extreme generosity of her space-eating hourglass figure, it looked lavish and extravagant.

With eighty percent of her weight, surely well over 300 girly pounds on the balls of her feet, her walk was wobbly, wiggly and sultry to say the least, yet at the same time it was not clumsy, but rather elegant and polished, in spite of her size or perhaps because of it.

The heels changed her posture and altered her shape. They arched her spine, thrusting her boobs forward and shoulders back, effectively cinching her waist and making her already shelf-like butt stick out even further. With her feet close together and a glass of red wine in her right hand, she smiled. "Hello everyone."

There was a faint gasp throughout the room, as everyone stared in shock at her appearance. Whatever tricks she had been up to in the bathroom had somehow rendered her more beautiful than Mike thought possible and his nervousness about her family's reaction to her weight faded as he became overwhelmed with lust.

She had thrown on her brand new black cashmere cardigan which covered her pillowy arms and matched her dress like a shawl, but with only one button fastened over her buxom chest, it did not hide the inches of cleavage displayed between her tits. The cardigan was skin-tight and it seemed she had already outgrown it, or perhaps it was the wrong size to begin with.

After a brief silence, Steven said, "Jeez sis, you make us all look a bit underdressed, as usual."

Julia looked perplexed, like she couldn't process what she was seeing.

Autumn had gotten fat, far beyond chunky and chubby, but for reasons she couldn't explain, Julia still envied her beauty, her curves, her style. The dress and heels may have tightened her up and sucked her in certain places, but they could not disguise how flat out big she had become, specifically in her hips and booty.

"Umm, did you change your hair or something?" Julia said.

Autumn shifted her weight to one hip and brought her free hand to the ends of her soft auburn tresses. "I got it done yesterday. (pant) You like it?"

"Looks amazing.".

Autumn turned toward Gary. "Hi daddy." She stepped forward and gave him a warm and very squishy hug. "So (pant) glad you could make it."

Gary grinned and held his daughter but he looked surprised by how much of her there was to hold. "Umm, me too."

Autumn then looked at Patty. "Hi mom."

Patty's eyes went down, then slowly up again. Autumn had gained even more weight since the wedding. A lot more by her estimation, and the wedding was only 5 months ago. She forced a smile, although her eyes were still large with amazement. "Oh, umm, hi dear. Happy Thanksgiving."

They hugged, then Lily toddled out of the spare room. "Bana and Boppa!" She squealed as if she hadn't seen them less than an hour before. After a quick pat on the back from grandpa, Lily turned toward Autumn with squinting eyes. "Who are you?"

Autumn, visibly surprised, bent down towards her. "Oh (pant) don't be silly I'm your Aunt."

Lily scrunched her nose. "Wait, yooou're my Auntie Autumn?"

Autumn gave Lily's shoulder a loving squeeze. "Yes of course, (pant) don't you remember when you were in Hawaii? Did you find Mr. Samson the friendly kitty cat yet?"

Sensing the potential awkwardness of the situation, Mike tried to direct attention elsewhere. "Please sit, get comfortable, help yourselves to hors d'oeuvres, turkey will be done in a few minutes. Can I get you a glass of wine Patty?"

Autumn stood up straight and looked at her mom. "Mike (gasp) sort of turned into Julia Child over the pandemic."

Patty looked at her daughter again, then turned to her newly christened son-in-law. "Sure Mike, I think I would like a glass."

Mike had been up early, working hard all day on preparing a spread worthy of impressing his new family. There were all the usual Thanksgiving staples, but he also baked homemade butterflake rolls, cornbread with honey, bacon wrapped sausages, along with pumpkin and cherry pies for dessert.

Gary finished chewing and wiped his mouth with a cloth napkin. "Mike I have to say, the turkey was done perfectly."

Mike, seated next to his wife, smiled. "It was just six hours in the oven, and a whole lot of basting, injected it with homemade garlic butter too."

Patty looked at her daughter from across the table. "Autumn, did you do any of the cooking?"

"No, (pant) it's all this guy," Autumn said as she nudged her husband with her elbow. " I just get to be the (gasp) taste tester."

Mike reached his left hand under the table and gave her thigh a squeeze while maintaining eye contact with Patty. "She's too busy working all the time, this is a much needed four day weekend for her."

Steven finished chewing. "These are the best mashed potatoes I've ever had."

Julia nodded. "I second that, but oh my goodness, so many calories. That's why we only have them once a year."

"Mike makes me (pant) mashed potatoes all the time," Autumn said as she spread a heap of butter over a flaky roll. "Anytime I ask him."

Mike smiled and savored the feeling of Autumn's cushy hip gently pressing into his side. She wasn't sitting especially close, but her butt had become so wide that it expanded beyond the limits of normally spaced chairs.

He noticed the way her belly filled up her lap and was brushing against the table with the slightest movement forward, which was quite frequent as she was constantly leaning in to shove another fork-full of rich gravy drenched food into her eagerly awaiting mouth.

Her appetite amazed him.

20 minutes into dinner and Autumn was stuffed to the gills, simple movements were cumbersome and strenuous, she was already too big for her seat, her dress squeezed painfully into her inflated feminine bulges, ample folds of fat smothered her overworked organs and still, despite all that, she continued cramming calories between her lips with no signs of slowing down, nor self-conscious or perhaps even awareness of how much she was eating.

Before she took that second bong hit, he had been wondering if she would try to show some restraint in front of her family, but based on the way she was stuffing her face it seemed her hunger was something she could no longer control, unless of course she was trying to prove some perverse point to her parents.

"I'm so glad you all came," he said. "Nice to be able to travel again without masks on all the time yeah?"

"Well Gary and I still wear them when we can, just as a precaution," Patty said.

Steven looked at her surprised. "Really? Are there still cases in Oregon?"

"You do hear about people testing positive sometimes, but it's just our age, and Gary is still a bit in the danger zone, can't be too careful," Patty said.

Steven pressed his glasses tight to the bridge of his nose. "You guys aren't even that old. It's so stupid. It's all the non-vaxers that ruin it for everyone."

Julia drained her wine and rolled her eyes. "I don't think age is much of a factor. It's more the people that are very inactive or obese, those are only people that are actually dying from this thing."

"Smokers too," Gary said after he finished chewing.

A lump formed in Mike's throat.

Smokers?

People that are inactive or obese?

He placed his hand on his wife's thigh again, apprehensive as to how she might react, and curious about what she must be thinking, offended, concerned or indifferent. So far she looked unfazed, more interested in getting butterflake rolls into her belly.

"That's why I started doing the flexitarian diet," Julia said.

Gary put his fork down. "What the hell is that?"

"Gary, watch your language," Patty said.

Julia smiled. "It's plant based, with whole grains only." She pointed her fork towards her plate which was still mostly full of food. "This will be my cheat day."

Autumn took a heaping bite of stuffing. "Mmm… (chew)seems like (chew) every month they come up (pant) with a new diet."

Julia raised her eyebrows. "Have you tried it?"

Autumn arched her back and adjusted her hips in her chair. Her eyelashes fluttered as she looked at Julia expressionless. "No. (gasp) I'm actually starting to get more and more like, anti-diet culture."

Julia leaned forward. "What do you mean?"

"I think it's all propaganda," Autumn said. "It's marketing, the whole thing. Society is always trying to tell us that we're not skinny enough, we need to be stick-thin in order to be healthy and they make billions of dollars by exploiting people's insecurities, especially women."

"Well, I don't see what's wrong with it," Julia said. "I know I have a lot more energy since I've lost weight."

Autumn shoveled more food between her luscious shimmering lips. "I'm (chew, munch) not saying I haven't fallen victim to it, (chew, chew) I was constantly on whatever the latest diet was in my early twenties," she said, "but now I just don't have time and I think life's too short to worry about (gasp) something as shallow as a (hiccup, wheeze) number on a scale."

Julia glared at her. "Try having two kids and see how much time you have."

Autumn stared back then downed the rest of her wine with a haughty look on her face, arching her back again and pressing her boobs forward.

Patty cleared her throat. "Diets have certainly changed a lot since I was young. I remember when every magazine had to have an article about how to lose inches in your hips, now it seems that everyone wants bigger hips, I just don't understand it."

"I know," Julia said, "And then there's the whole body positivity, love yourself at any size movement."

"I think it's because Americans are fatter than ever now," Steven said, either forgetting that his sister was in the room, or forgetting she was now a fat person herself. "If everyone's butt is getting bigger, then just say that big butts are beautiful and it's okay. If exercise is too hard for you, just accept yourself and keep ordering doordash without getting off the couch."

Autumn leaned back and brought her napkin to her mouth so she could let out a burp as discreetly as possible. "Better to (gasp) love yourself than to be constantly striving to (pant) meet some unobtainable standard of beauty generated by a bunch of women competing against themselves."

Steven peered across the table, suddenly feeling embarrassed for his sister and ashamed of his last remark.

There was a brief yet awkward silence then Mike held up the bottle of Pinot. "More wine anyone?"

"Yes please," Autumn said as she stared at Julia blankly. "Pass the mashed potatoes (pant) too."

After dinner and when she was finally finished eating Autumn wearily staggered into the living room and dropped onto the sofa with a heavy thud. Her mother Patty sat down next to her after Gary went off to mingle with the grandkids.

"Are you okay dear? You seem winded," Patty said.

Autumn leaned back into the cushion and sprawled out lazily with her knees apart, looking like she wasn't going to move again anytime soon. She turned her head towards her mother, slow and lethargic. "What? (pant) I'm not winded mom (gasp) I'm just breathing."

Patty watched her daughter's grossly overstuffed belly move up and down with each labored breath. Autumn had taken her cardigan off and her figure was now on full display, and in her seated position, every fold, roll, bulge, crease and dimpled mass of spreading flab was completely visible, whether beneath the fabric of her dress or not.

Patty was stunned and appalled by just how much bigger Autumn's body was than it used to be, especially up close. So much bigger everywhere it was like she had become a different person.

She leaned over and put her hand on Autumn's forehead. "You're not getting sick are you, you feel a little warm."

"Mom, (pant) seriously, I'm fine. I just need to (gasp) sit and relax for a second." She tilted her head toward Mike who was in the kitchen with Steven. "Baby (gasp) can you grab me some more wine?"

"Red or white?" Mike said.

Autumn sat up a little so her voice would carry across the room. "Let me (pant) try the chard."

Patty raised her eyebrows. "Wow I guess chivalry is alive and well. Nice to see a man that knows his way around a kitchen." She looked at Mike as he grabbed a bottle of Sonoma county reserve then turned to her daughter, knowing this would likely be her third or fourth glass. "Does he always wait on you like this? You didn't re-aggravate your knee did you?"

Autumn sighed and sank back into the couch, letting her arms hang limp at her sides as if too heavy to lift.

She had eaten way too much again, way too quickly and felt bloated.

Her inner thighs rubbed together with budding perspiration, her belly was getting squeezed by the tightness in her dress and her bra dug into her back fat and upper love handles and yet somehow, all of these things added up to her feeling wickedly sexy and sinfully intoxicated by her own deliciousness, boob sweat, heartburn and all. She turned to her mother. "No, (huff) my knee is fine, why?"

"You just don't seem very light on your feet these days."

Autumn rolled her eyes. "(gasp) I'm wearing heels and my hips are killing me from sitting so long in those hard dining room chairs."

"Hey, those were a wedding gift."

"They're too small (huff) and not very comfy."

Patty's eyes darted from Autumn's flush cheeks and double chin, to her dimpled and pillowy white arms to her hips, which were so wide they nearly took up the entire couch cushion. "Are you getting enough exercise, how is your weight?"

The two women paused for a moment as Mike showed up with a wine glass filled two thirds full. "Here you go babe," he said, handing it to Autumn. "Can I get you something Patty?"

Patty peered up at him and gave a fake smile that wouldn't fool a soul. "No thank you I'm fine."

Mike nodded and looked at them curiously. He could tell they were in the middle of something and seemed best for him not to interfere. He gave his wife a quick look of encouragement before rejoining his brother-in-law in the kitchen.

Autumn took a long sip of her chardonnay then glared at Patty. "What about my weight mom?"

"I know the pandemic was difficult for all of us," Patty said.

"What are you (pant) trying to say?"

Patty shifted her knees so she could face Autumn more directly. "Well I mean your body has obviously changed a lot in the last couple years, are you working towards trying to shed some of the corona weight? Are you getting any exercise?"

Autumn took a deep breath and gave her a heavy eye roll. "Oh god mom, (gasp) why is this even an issue for you? (huff, pant) Why do you always need to make a comment about someone's weight every time I see you?"

"I'm just concerned that's all, you know that there's nothing more important than your health."

Autumn tried to wiggle her hips into a more comfortable position but it was difficult to move. "Oh really?" she said sarcastically. (pant) Health is important? (huff) Thank you for the information I had no idea."

Patty's eyebrows slanted. "I've just never known you to be such a big eater. Are you unhappy, are you stressed?"

"Mom please (pant) I'm a 30 year old woman. I can take care of myself. But I am happy, very happy."

"I'm just not used to seeing you like this," Patty said.

"Like what?"

"Seeing you so, so much…bigger."

Autumn brought her wine to her lips and subtracted another inch. "Stop it. (huff, gasp) I know I gained weight but I'm not that big. Not that it matters anyway. How much I weigh is nobody's business but mine."

"Mom and sis?" Steven said from across the room.

Patty froze for a second then turned toward her son. "Yes?"

"Wanna go see if Boppa and the kids are ready for pie?"

"Pie already? I'm still so full from dinner," Patty said.

Autumn, eager to get away, looked at her husband, then at her brother. "Dessert sounds good, (huff) I'll go get them." She put her wine on the end table then spread her legs apart, rocked herself forward in an attempt to get up. Patty noticed the way she now needed to put both hands on her knees to lift herself into a standing position.

The effort notwithstanding, (pun intended) Autumn took a deep breath and with an arched back lurched upwards, only to find herself sinking back into the sofa a second later.

Mike could see from the kitchen that she was too stuffed, tipsy, tired, stoned, and too much of a princess to go through the effort of getting up under her own power, and he was by her side in an instant, relishing moments like this.

"Whoah whoa whoa, hang on honey let me me help you," he said, and with both hands helped her to her feet. "You shouldn't try and exert yourself like that right after dinner."

Autumn stared into his eyes and let her belly and breasts press gently against his pelvis and stomach. "(gasp)Thank you (huff) baby."

Patty glared at them. "Are you sure you didn't re-aggravate your knee?"

Hours later, right after all the family had left and gone back to their rented place in North Seattle, Autumn sat down on the stool in their spacious master bathroom.

"Oh (huff, pant) my god," she said between gasps. "feet…(gasp)killing me." She was still a little high and somewhere between tipsy and drunk. She was holding her phone, scrolling through the photos her mom sent. "Uhhh, (gasp) god I look fucking gigantic in these pictures! (huff)

These angles are terrible. (hiccup, burb)Am I really that much (pant) bigger than Julia?"

Mike put his hands on her shoulders, leaned in and kissed her on the forehead. "You are stunning. You were wonderful tonight. It's late in the evening…"

Ignoring her husband's singing, she put her phone down on the edge of the bathtub then placed both hands on her belly. "Oooh, (pant) I'm sooo (hiccup) stuffed. I should not have had..oooh..(gasp) that last piece of pie, (pant) and you gave me way too much ice cream."

He walked behind her and continued massaging her shoulders and neck from the back. He looked down and smiled as he felt her body react to his touch. "You ate a lot tonight."

"Mmm…you noticed?"

"Of course I did."

She leaned forward in her seat so she could unfasten her heels, giving her husband a spectacular view of her hips. "Enhh, (gasp) ehh, (huff) little help?"

He pried his eyes away, came around to the front of her stool then kneeled at her feet. He clasped her foot and shapely calf with both hands, then unfastened the strap around the soft skin of her delicate, yet slightly swollen ankle.

She moaned with delight. "Ooohh…It's just so hard (gasp, pant) with my belly and boobs (huff) always in the way you know?"

Mike smiled and after pulling off the second shoe, tossed it to the side next to the other. "I'll bet that feels better."

"(gasp)Mmhmm." She gestured toward the pack of Dunhills on the counter. "Can (pant) you just reach my…"

He sprang up, grabbed her a cigarette, placed it between her lips and lit it for her.

"Phewww! (gasp, huff) Thank you baby," she said, filling the room with smoke. " God I thought (cough) they'd never leave."

He turned on the fan, leaned against the counter and shrugged. "I thought it went well didn't you?"

She took another long drag, making it look deliciously satisfying. "It was fine, (cough) family is family I suppose."

"Was your mom giving you a hard time about something?"

She pointed her cigarette toward the cupboards. "Can you load up the thing, (pant) I really need to decompress."

"Yeah sure."

"My mom (huff) thinks I'm too fat."

He bent down and took out the paraphernalia. "Why do you think that?"

"I can just tell, (gasp, huff) I know how (hiccup) she is, so old-fashioned." She grimaced, adjusted her bra strap and put her hand on her belly. "Oooff, (pant) I'm so full baby, I need you to help me get this off so (huff) I can breathe."

"Yeah yeah of course." He put the bong down..

After the clumsy, breathy, sweaty and jiggly ordeal of her husband peeling off her dress and unsnapping her bra, she sat down on the stool.

She picked up her smoldering cigarette from the ashtray and said, “Do you think (pant) I’m too fat?”

He stared at her like a dead fish, awestruck by her nakedness. “Do you really need to ask me that?” He took a step toward her. “I think you’re perfect, and I can prove it.” He turned his body to the side, displaying his erection currently pitching a huge tent in his gray slacks.

She puffed on her smoke and smiled. “Like what (pant) you see huh?” She curled her toes around the wooden frame of her stool, arched her back and pushed her tummy out. “You know baby (gasp) that this is by far the biggest I have ever been.”

He gulped. “Umm, bigger than you were last year?”

She lowered her voice to a sultry purr, her speech altered from the wine. “I think so baby. (pant) I know you haven't said anything recently, but I’ve gained some weight since the wedding.” She made a pouty face with her lips and stared at him for a long moment. “Ooopsi.”

“How do you know?”

“I can just tell. (gasp) I can tell by how much my ass jiggles when I walk, (huff, pant) and by how heavy it feels. I've gone up a few cup sizes too, don't pretend you haven't noticed."

He swallowed as his heart rate accelerated. He felt emboldened by her drunkenness, and he wanted to take advantage of it the best he could. "I guess we better see exactly how much you've gained." He looked into her eyes and smiled. "Or do you really think life's too short to worry about something as shallow as a number on a scale."

She smiled back, then took another long and provocative drag off her cigarette. "Maybe I am shallow, (huff) and I want to find out."

He quickly went into the cupboards beneath the two bathroom sinks, pulled out the scale and put it on the floor. He reached his hand toward her. "Help the lady to her feet?"

She looked at him blank faced for a second, then rolled her eyes and giggled quietly. "Wow, someone is getting a little excited." She put out her cigarette then held out her hands.

The scale sounded like it might break when she stepped on, and Mike kneeled down to get a reading.

"Shit," he said.

"What?"

"It just says error."

"Oh god! (gasp, huff) How high does this scale go up to?"

"350."

Her hands clasped her face. "Oh god! (huff) Fuck me!"

He stood and smiled. He grabbed her by the waist and pulled her close. "Fuck you is right," he whispered.

She fell into him, pushing him into the counter.

She kissed him on the lips, then gazed into his eyes. "Holy shit (gasp, wheeze) I've gotten so fucking fat baby." She put one hand on her naked belly and let it squish against his belt. "(huff, gasp) I honestly can't believe this is really my body sometimes, but then the actual reality hits me (pant) and I get really horny for you."

He put his chin on her shoulder and held her close and tight, one hand on her ass and the other groping her love handles. "My poor baby has gotten too big for her scale."

She nodded meekly, still pressing him into the counter. "You'll have to get me a new one. Or maybe it's just a sign that I really need to (gasp) lose some weight."

"No no baby, I'll get a new scale tomorrow morning, first thing."

She pursed her lips for a moment, then said, "After you (pant) make me breakfast."

He smiled. "Okay second thing."

"Get one that (pant) goes up to 400, no, 500." She tilted her head back so she could see his face. "Or do you think that's too much?"

"Baby, even if you weigh 700 pounds I'm still going to be madly in love with you and chasing you all around the house until the day I die."

She raised an eyebrow. "Not going to be much of a chase (pant) if I let myself get that big."

He paused and cleared his throat. "Did it piss you off, when they were talking about the corona stuff, saying that it's the obese smokers that die and stuff?"

She rolled her eyes. "It pisses me off that companies like Pfizer and Moderna have instilled so much fear into people to make money, (pant, huff) and everyone just rolls over and goes with it." She brushed some hair away from her face and looked up at him. "But honestly (gasp) a lot of that obesity talk and stuff turned me on, and it… ooоohh…made me really want a cigarette."

He pulled her close again and gave her ass another squeeze. "You're turning into such a bad girl, and I love you for it."

"Mmmm…you need to stop (pant) getting sidetracked and finish getting the thingy ready for me."

"I'm sorry baby you're just so fucking distracting."

She turned around, wiggled to the toilet and sat down. "Ooohhh, (gasp) it's getting a little tight in here, god my hips…ehh, (huff) always in the way."

He finished loading the bong and handed it to her. "Maybe I'll get us a new toilet, and widen this area out a little."

"Yeah, (pant) I need more room."

She brought the mouthpiece to her lips and he lit the stem. She inhaled deeply, then coughed.

It was still weird for him, seeing his wife develop such a taste for Amsterdam's finest over the past year, but he supposed it was his fault for buying her edibles in the first place, not that he was complaining.

It mellowed her out and made her so relaxed and what's wrong with that?

He glanced at the bong, clutched tightly in her feminine fingers, he looked at the smoldering cherry, still half green. "Let me try some of that."

Her eyes shot into his. "Are you sure?"

He nodded.

She handed it to him and he blazed up as memories of his college days came hazily back.

She watched him cough and his eyes water. She smiled and held out her hand. "Now take me (pant) to bed Spicoli."

Chapter 22

Mike and Autumn spent the last remaining month of 2022 in a state of romantic bliss that only comes with the passions and lustful exuberance of a young married couple in love.

Mike bought a My Weigh XL bathroom scale with capabilities up to 700 pounds and called it an early Christmas present. On Black Friday, (the same day he bought it) it was revealed that Autumn was 363 pounds. Her reaction to this shrill and strident truth, this reality that she had eaten herself deep into obesity, surprised him.

Her reaction was no reaction.

She didn't seem shocked or concerned.

She just looked at him with doe eyes and her lip tucked beneath her teeth.

Was she really okay with it?

Maybe she was high.

At 363 she was far beyond the point where she could simply change a few habits, get a little exercise and get back into some sort of reasonable shape. She could hardly walk around for more than a few minutes without getting out of breath or complaining of knee and foot pain; and it seemed unlikely she would conjure the motivation or discipline to push herself into any type of regular workout routine anytime soon.

She didn't have the time anyway. They no longer lived in an apartment building right above a gym, and the 8 or 9 hours she spent at work in front of her laptop drained most of her energy.

Whatever time she had away from work she wanted to spend with her husband, and she loved the way he loved her and made her feel so wanted and so sexy. The way he touched, worshiped and adored her body, the way he fed and waited on her so attentively, and with such admiration, appreciation and affection.

New weight continued to cling to her ever-softening figure. Over the holiday season she ate in quantities that Mike found staggering when compared to what she consumed when they first started dating.

He didn't have to try anymore.

She didn't need his encouragement.

She seemed to be loving it as much as he did and was teasing him and tempting him constantly.

All through December she would send him pictures of herself with a full, bloated belly after a huge lunch during the weekdays, and brag through texts about how much she ate, how much she was snacking and how she needed belly rubs and kisses, and how she couldn't wait for him to get home because she wanted to step on the scale for him.

Once again, everything was foreplay, every aspect of both their lives revolved around food and sex.

Her attitude was changing, her body was changing, and at Christmas dinner at Mike's parents house, people were noticing.

While most of the women were having their after-dinner coffee and dessert around the kitchen table, Mike and his dad John slipped into the living room to catch some of the football game, Rams versus Broncos.

"Looks like Autumn's sure been enjoying married life," John said. "Seems like she's having trouble putting the fork down."

Mike turned up the volume on the TV and walked further away from the kitchen. "Excuse me?"

John took a sip from his bottle of winter ale. "It happens with women after they tie the knot sometimes."

Remote in hand, Mike crossed his arms and sighed. He had known a conversation like this was coming, and he was surprised it hadn't come sooner, but he dreaded it nonetheless, especially because it was with his father a few beers deep. "Are you trying to give me advice?"

John looked across the room. He watched Autumn reach for another shortbread thumbprint cookie while chatting away with his wife Debbie and his daughter Megan. "Hey, I've been married 35 years, don't you think I might have a few useful tips to share about women?"

"Okay, what do you know about women dad?"

John shrugged and lowered his voice. "I know that you've got to get a gym membership and start exercising together. You can't just tell a woman she's getting fat, in fact never ever do that. What you can do is suggest working out as a couple, then lead by example and she'll take the hint." He took another swig of beer. "Otherwise these girls you know, they'll just keep getting bigger if you let em."

Mike was flabbergasted by the words that were coming out of his father's mouth. He wasn't sure what he was expecting to hear but it definitely wasn't that.

John glanced at his wife then leaned toward Mike. "You know your mom struggled with her weight quite a bit in the years after you and your sister were born."

"I uh…I didn't know that."

"She used to be a jogger when we started dating, but after the wedding and the kids…all that stopped and the pounds kinda crept up on her. You know how I handled it?"

Mike sighed and rolled his eyes. "How did you handle it dad?"

"I didn't say anything about it, I didn't criticize her at all I just bought us both some new running shoes, told her I was getting some for myself but got a discount if I got her a pair too."

"Wow dad, that is very clever of you."

"Okay knock it off you little punk." He gave his son a playful shove in the shoulder. "Seriously though, remember what I told you." He turned and made a gesture towards Autumn and then in a whisper said, "It's not healthy for her to be carrying around so much extra weight like that."

Mike looked at his wife. His dad may have been corny and a tad politically incorrect but he wasn't wrong.

Autumn had gained an unfathomable amount of weight in the past few years, but there she was, as real as the day was long, sitting 20 feet in front of him, so fat that even his usually respectful and tight-lipped father, (his father that always adored Autumn's beauty almost as much as he did) had to voice his concerns.

And yet it was these awkward moments with family members, the shock on their faces, the scolding tones, passive aggressive remarks or disapproving comments that seemed to excite Mike and turn him on, if only because they served as confirmation that he wasn't dreaming.

By the end of December, the end of 2022, Autumn weighed in at an incredible 375 pounds. As erotic as it was to see the numbers go up on the scale, with the new year looming even she had to know she couldn't go on like this for much longer.

The weeks continued to pass however and she became all the more entrenched in the habits she had formed during the pandemic.

Work took over, life took over, and her occasional bursts of motivation to quit smoking, maybe eat a little less and get physically active were often forgotten as soon as she became hungry again, or as soon as her husband returned home from work with takeout food, or as soon as he squeezed her arms, kissed her belly or buried his face between her growing tits.

He'd bring her food, let her eat, sometimes feed her, rip her clothes off and satisfy the fuck out of her, always making her feel like the sexiest woman on the planet not despite the extra poundage but because of it, and consequently, by March of 2023 her weight was at an all time high, again.

Mike started the dishwasher then turned to her in the living room. "You doing alright, need something?"

It was a Saturday afternoon and Autumn was sprawled out comfortably on the sofa.

With knees bent and her calves tucked under her thighs beneath a blanket, she looked at him pouty-faced. "Uhhh, (gasp) I need a cigarette but I don't want to get up."

She tossed the blanket off her legs, sat up straight then began to slowly scoot herself forward.

It wasn't easy.

It was only 2 pm and she had already nearly eaten herself into a food coma.

Having slept in until 11, she had her usual weekend brunch in bed, prepared and delivered by her husband. Today it was waffles with berries and whipped cream along with 4 strips of bacon, hash browns and scrambled eggs; sides which had become mainstays that always accompanied whatever she was having for breakfast on a given day.

After the late morning meal she had transferred herself over to the living room and camped out on the sofa, letting only an hour or so pass before she began going through her phone in search of new and interesting restaurants to try on doordash.

Online food delivery was getting too easy, too convenient, and it was common for her to order something delicious via doordash several times per week, sometimes even multiple times per day as Mike often took the car to work.

Although it was one of her usual favorites, she had settled on Ezell's famous fried chicken, and after grazing on several tender strips, a couple of drumsticks, two breasts, two big juicy thighs, a few rolls and two sides of mac and cheese over consecutive episodes of The Office, she was stuffed and uncomfortably bloated.

Mike, still in the kitchen, watched as she struggled to move. "Baby what are you doing?" He scurried towards her.

She was wearing only panties and a t-shirt.

There was so much fat in her thighs that they pressed together like pillows all the way to her knees, or at least to where her legs bent, as her patellas were now so buried in blubber they appeared nonexistent.

"You shouldn't try and overexert yourself like that, let me help," he said.

She gazed up at him and rolled her eyes, but let him hoist her to her feet with both hands. "Okay (pant) but you really need to stop doing this all the time."

He pulled her close and let her belly ooze into his pelvis. "But I love doing it."

"I know (gasp) but it's teaching me to be lazy and I'm afraid I'll get too used to it. It's like my whole body goes limp when you're around."

"So what?" he said in a lustful whisper. "I'll help you anytime, day or night. You are a queen, and you should be treated like a queen."

"Well I don't need (huff) your help to get up you know."

He smiled. "I know baby, It's just fun for me." He put his hand around her waist, quickly snuck behind her then sat down on the sofa, pulling her onto his lap in one fluid movement. Her ass was so soft and warm and squishy and her hips looked to spread out at least three or maybe even four times wider than his own. She felt so heavy, so wonderful, so big and gushy all over. He could've let her sit on his lap all day if he didn't feel like he was getting crushed.

"Hey! (gasp, huff) What are you doing?" she said breathlessly.

He pressed his face into the center of her back and caressed her belly with his hands. He kicked her dainty little feet off the coffee table and let all of her weight sink into him. "I just need to hold you for a second, this is like medicine for me."

She turned her head. "Ooohh, am I (pant) squishing you?"

He stared at her pink panties and the way her beautiful ass cheeks were sucking them into her deepening buttcrack. "Yes baby, I don't think I can get you off me."

She wiggled her hips. "Oh you poor boy."

"You like squishing me with your fat ass don't you."

She leaned backward, pinning his torso against the back cushion. She wiggled her hips again. "A real lady (pant) would never admit to something like that."

He held her hips and despite his enjoyment of the moment, he grimaced from the pressure of her ass pushing downward onto his slender masculine thighs. "Fair enough."

She paused, reveling in the power she had over him then said, "Okay now you (gasp) can help me up." She scooted forward a little and placed her feet back on the floor.

"So you do need my help?" He put his hands on the doughy white skin of her butt cheeks and shoved her forward with all his strength.

She stood up straight and after a toss of her hair turned toward him. "I just know (pant) how much you like to feel important."

He stood. "We're going outside yeah?"

"Yeah but…eh (gasp) I don't want to put my pants back on." She gave her panties a tug. "I really need to do more shopping."

"Well you really shouldn't be smoking in the bathroom unless it's freezing out." He grabbed the fleece blanket from the sofa. "Just cover yourself in this." He gave it to her and watched as she begrudgingly wrapped it around her immense hips. "No pants are the best pants remember."

She wiggled her foot into her fluffy Ugg slippers while holding the blanket tight to her waist. "If only I could (pant) dress like this all the time."

"You can if you want."

She rolled her eyes and held out her hand so Mike could help keep her balance while she navigated around the coffee table. "Come on, (pant) I'm not that lazy."

Outside on the back porch she sat down in a bowl shaped Papasan chair, her hips filling it to its capacity despite its large size.

Mike grabbed the silver case that was left on the low patio table, took out a cigarette, placed it between her lips and lit it.

"I really need to (gasp) get some exercise," she said after blowing smoke into the air. "My ankles have never felt this weak before."

He stood next to her and took a puff on his disposable THC vape pen, a habit he had picked up after Thanksgiving. He was all too familiar with addiction, as it was something he struggled with personally in his early 20's; and while he still abstained from alcohol, he justified the cannabis to himself so long as he kept it to disposables and edibles, despite his wife having no such qualms. "If it clears up maybe we could go for a walk around the block."

She looked up at the fascia wood of the awning that covered the patio, then gazed toward the small lawn that made up most of their backyard as the soft rain continued its calming pitter-patter from above. "Yeah I think that would be a good idea." She took a drag on her smoke. "I just wish (cough) I had the energy."

He bent down and took one of her half-smoked pre-rolls from the table. "Try this one again."

She took it and pinched it between the fingers of her left hand, her cigarette in her right. "Is this the euphoria?"

"That's what you told me yesterday."

She placed it between her lips and Mike lit it with his zippo. She made a face and coughed. "Oooh (cough,

cough) it's strong, burns too hot." Drawing her other hand to her mouth, she took a quick puff on her cigarette then began slowly bending her knees up and down, stretching her quads and ankle muscles. "God my legs (cough) feel so sore." She looked up at her husband. "(gasp) Is it too early for wine?"

He smiled. "It's Saturday baby, you worked hard all week and you can have wine anytime you want."

She hit the joint again. "Uhhh, (cough) don't tempt me."

He crouched down in front of her and gently massaged her thigh. He gazed into her eyes. The sparse and casual makeup she wore looked perfect, and Mike would be damned if she didn't look every bit as beautiful as she did when she was 27.

Her face still mesmerized him and radiated intense beauty, perhaps even more so than ever before.

Her cheeks had become puffier over the years, but the Kybella procedure she did before the wedding help maintain the delicate definition in her jaw-line, giving her face an appearance that didn't match the amount of weight she carried in her body at all, and yet somehow, it fit her perfectly and looked natural.

He gazed longingly at her legs and hips as with that huge blanket wrapped around she looked gigantic. "You're the one who's tempting me."

She took another drag off her cigarette. "We should (pant) probably start thinking about (cough) what we're doing for dinner."

He smiled inwardly, but looked at her blankly. "I was thinking of ordering pizza, and maybe making some cinnamon rolls for dessert or something."

Her eyebrows perked up. "Mmmm, the kind you made last time with the (pant) cream cheese frosting?"

"If that's what you want, I'll make it."

"So just stay in and be lazy all day?"

He smiled, for real this time, then stood and took a puff on his vape. "Why not? The weather sucks." He stepped forward and gave her fluffy arm a squeeze.

"Maybe we can get in a little, um…nap time too."

She smirked. "If you're lucky."

He took a longer pull on his vape and looked down at her.

Fucking hell.

He needed to know how much she weighed.

Whether she realized it or not, he knew she had to be creeping ever closer towards a milestone that to him would be nothing less than mind-blowing.

The more he thought about it, the more obsessed he became with it.

It was a tricky thing though. When she was in certain moods she seemed to get as excited about a weigh in as he did, but lately those moods were sporadic and difficult to predict or get a read on.

It was a subject that had to be approached delicately.

He soaked her in with his eyes again.

Damn, she was so big, so curvy, so sexy.

Too big, too curvy, and way too sexy.

Fuck it.

He cleared his throat. "Maybe we could get you on the scale?"

"No no stop it." She waved her cigarette at him and blushed. He was the only person on earth that could make her blush like that. "I really don't want to think about that right now, (pant) and I still feel weird about it sometimes, especially because I'm always like way way heavier than I look."

His disappointment didn't show. "Yeah, of course baby."

She took another drag on her cigarette before extinguishing it in the ashtray on the table in front of her. "I really need to (cough) quit smoking again soon."

He quickly pulled another Dunhill out of her cigarette case. "Here I got ya." He placed it in her mouth and lit it.

She sucked in her cheeks, exhaled then coughed. "(cough)Thank you."

"Of course baby."

When she finished her second cigarette and the rest of her joint, she put her hands on her fleece covered knees, and looked at her husband. "Okay (gasp, pant) so whenever I'm sitting (burp) in this chair, I definitely need your help."

Mike raised his left brow. This was a new development. “Yeah you sink pretty low in that one, comfy though yeah?”

She rocked forward and let him hoist her to her feet. “Ennhh, (gasp) yeah.”

The blanket fell and Mike picked it up and re-wrapped her dimpled legs and wobbling hips.

“Ooohh, (pant) thank you,” she cooed.

He took her by the hand. “Of course baby, now let's get you inside so you can get off your feet. I’ll pour you a glass of Pinot, sound good?” He pulled the sliding glass door open wide so she could enter first.

“Yes, (gasp) that sounds perfect.”

As the days went on, Autumn continued to excel at her job and her job continued to demand all of her mental capacity. In the evenings and weekends she wanted nothing more than to turn her brain off, relax, indulge in a little greenery, a little wine, plop in front of the TV and eat.

Whether she was willing to step on the scale or not, it seemed obvious to Mike, she was still gaining.

Chapter 23

In the beginning of 2023 Autumn and Sydney started having monthly girl nights, usually ordering lots of food and drinking way too much wine, sometimes to the point where Sydney would end up spending the night in the guest bedroom.

By summertime, with the two friends progressively feeding off each other's habits, their drunken get-togethers had turned into a weekly routine.

"Oh my god, (pant) thanks again for breakfast Mike," Sydney said, "That was beyond delicious. (huff) I don't think I need to eat again for a week." She slid her chair back and stood up next to the round kitchen table.

It was a beautiful Saturday morning in June, and the girls had just finished their omelets and French crepes with whipped cream and fresh strawberries.

Mike shoved the Kitchen-Aid mixer against the wall then looked at Sydney from the other side of the counter.

She had changed.

Her dark brown hair was longer, now falling below her shoulders, her glasses had been replaced by contacts and her punk-rocker wardrobe had morphed into stretchy athleisure that seemed to now be the style for every woman in America.

She'd changed in other ways too.

He remembered thinking that she was at least 50 pounds heavier than Autumn when he first met her at that softball game on Capitol Hill.

Damn. That was 4 years ago.

Autumn was well under 200 pounds back then, but like his wife, the covid years had done a number on Sydney's figure.

She was bigger all over, and now had to be over 300 pounds by Mike's estimation, and these more frequent slumber parties weren't doing her waistline any favors.

He watched as she tugged on her lululemons and pulled down on her top. She was totally stuffed from breakfast and her clothing looked ready to burst at the seams.

Holy fuck she was fat.

"It was my pleasure," he said. "You girls ever gonna invite Tabitha over?"

"Uhhh, she's always on a diet and she's no fun anymore, ever since Derek broke up with her," Sydney said, patting her huge gut. "She gets up at 6 every morning and goes to the gym. Who even does that?"

Autumn, still seated at the table, fanned herself with her hand. "God (pant) I can't even imagine."

Sydney wrapped her finger around the ends of her hair and made a pouty face. "She makes us feel judged."

Mike looked at her curiously. "Oh, really?" He had been delightfully amused by the developing closeness between the two women.

Sydney had always been fat, and he liked that Autumn had a fat friend; an eating and drinking buddy who wouldn't make her feel self-conscious about her size or appetite in the slightest.

It was obvious why they enjoyed hanging out together. It was a big excuse to eat lots of food as perhaps the company of a like-minded peer helped normalize what could only be described as binge eating or flat out gluttony.

Autumn scooted her chair back with a dull screech against the oak flooring. She spread her legs apart and put her hands on her knees. She rocked forward, then back. She gave Sydney a quick glance. "Oooff, (gasp) can you give me a hand please."

Sydney smiled and helped get Autumn to her feet. "Oh man you look more full than even me."

Autumn, slightly out of breath, looked at Sydney. "Mmm, (huff, gasp) I know. It feels so good. (pant) Mike makes the best breakfasts I just (hiccup) couldn't stop eating."

Sydney's eyes narrowed as a devious smile formed on her lips. Having been inspired by Autumn and the seemingly perfect relationship she had with Mike, Sydney now had a steady boyfriend of her own, who for once in her life loved and adored her body not in spite of her size but because of it.

She knew from all her late night wine-fueled talks with her best friend, all about how Mike appreciated her curves and weight gain, and Sydney thought she had a pretty good grasp as to why he enjoyed cooking for them so much.

"He really does, doesn't he," she said to Autumn in a whisper. She turned to Mike in the kitchen as he continued to do dishes. "You're a great cook Mike! (huff) You're gonna turn us into a couple of blimps."

Mike turned and looked at them standing next to each other.

They already were a couple of blimps.

Together they looked to him like the ultimate example of excess, instant gratification, privilege, sloth and indulgence; in other words the modern American woman in a so-called post-covid world. They also both looked incredibly sexy.

Sydney was broader at the shoulders and top heavy compared to the curvier and more classically feminine cello-like figure of Autumn.

Wearing comfy loungewear of pale pink waffle knit leggings and a matching short sleeve top, Autumn's thighs were bigger than Sydney's, her ass was bigger and much rounder, but her waist was smaller, her tits were smaller and her arms, (despite their girthy plushness) were smaller and more delicate.

Fuck he felt lucky to be married to a woman so blessed in the looks department.

He smiled. "I will cook for you ladies, anytime."

The girls giggled then Autumn put her hands on Sydney's shoulders and looked her in the eye. "You know you can (pant) shower here if you ever need to."

"I know,(huff) I just want to get home while Kegan is gone so I can nurse this hangover."

"He went on a hike?"

Sydney nodded. "Yeah." She smiled, and in an attempt to mimic her boyfriend's voice said, "I know we're missing out on all the fun and beautiful nature."

Autumn laughed. "(huff)I'm sure he's not complaining." She glanced at her husband still working away in the kitchen, his pull-up bar installed in the doorway behind him next to his mountain bike hanging in the laundry room. She turned back to Sydney. "(gasp) I love how the men in our lives are always (pant) being all active and healthy and we're over here just (hiccup, gasp)stuffing our faces…(burp, gasp) oooh… (hiccup)" With a look of discomfort she leaned towards the table took a quick sip of her bloody mary. "You sure you don't (hiccup) want one of these?"

"I'm okay, thank you though. I love you." Sydney gave Autumn a very fluffy and boobalicious hug.

"Love you too," Autumn said.

Sydney headed towards the door. "Bye Mike, until next time. Bye Samson, wherever you are."

Mike smiled. "Bye Syd."

He dried his hands then went to his wife. He stood behind her, put his arms around her waist and watched as Sydney's Toyota Corolla pulled out of their driveway. "She seems happy," he said.

Autumn wiggled her ass against his jeans. "Yeah, (pant) Kegan is good for her I think." She turned towards the living room. The coffee table was covered in high-end pizza boxes and two empty bottles of cheap wine. "Oh god, (pant) we drank way too much last night."

"Yeah sorry I didn't get a chance to clean that up yet. Looks like you girls had fun though. You were out cold when I got back."

"We're so old and lame, (huff) Sydney and I can barely make it past midnight anymore."

Mike fondled the soft overlapping rolls of pudge on his wife's sides then down to the massive curves of her flaring hips.

When did her love handles get so hugely thick?

He placed his chin on her shoulder. "You feel like doing anything today?"

She playfully bumped her butt into his crotch again then wiggled a couple steps towards the table and grabbed her bloody Mary. Just a twitch of hips could send her whole body jiggling for seconds. "Uh, (gasp) I'm going to finish this outside, have a smoke, and then I am (pant) ready for nap time."

Mike moved his eyebrows up and down. "Nap time, or…naapp time?"

"Nap time."

"Which one is that again?"

She came towards him and pointed her finger into his chest. "(huff)You know maybe if you smoked real weed (gasp) you wouldn't be so horny all the time."

He grabbed her by the hips and pulled her close. His voice lowered to a deep and sexy growl. "Impossible. Not when I'm waking up to you every morning, not when you're teasing me all around the house and being so fucking sexy all the time."

"I'm not even (pant) doing anything." She smiled and rolled her eyes. "(pant) Come outside with me." She started walking towards the back sliding doors, although it was more of a jiggly waddle than a walk. "I can't get out of that (huff) stupid chair without you, remember?"

After finishing her drink and her smokes, he helped her into bed, but by the time her head hit the pillow she was out of breath and exhausted.

"You okay baby? You need to just rest and let that food digest for a bit?"

Laying on her side, she nodded weakly. "Yeah, (gasp) I think so."

He pulled the comforter off her hip, climbed on the end of the bed and straddled his knees over her lower legs and calves. He gazed down at her amazing body, her upper thigh now wider than his own torso, her belly spilling onto the mattress and covering her pelvis like an apron of lard.

She had become so big she made the king sized bed they bought right before the wedding look more like the old queen sized mattress they had back in their Belltown and Capitol Hill apartments.

He placed his hand on her hip and gave it gentle nudge, then watched as it jiggled and wobbled back and forth for seconds afterwards. He jiggled her again, then rubbed his erect penis against her thigh, despite both of them still wearing pants. "God you are so beautiful."

With her head on the pillow and her eyes closed she said, "Stop it, ehh…(pant) you're so annoying."

He continued to slowly dry hump her hip, then put one hand on her ass and the other on her belly and squeezed. She had so much belly to grab now, and Mike couldn't get over it. "I can't help it."

She yawned, arching her back and shoving her butt backwards towards the edge of the bed in the process. "(yawn)Oh my god. (gasp) Why don't you go workout or go on a bike ride for like an hour, (huff) then come back and maybe I'll be ready for you."

He leaned in and kissed her upper arm, just beneath the hem of her sleeve. "Is that what you want?"

She gave her hips a wiggle. "Well (pant) you can lay here with me but I have a feeling you won't be able to keep your hands under control. (gasp) You'll end up turning me on and then I won't get any beauty rest."

He lifted himself up with his knees still mounted over her legs. She had slept in until 10, got up just to eat a huge breakfast, and now she needed her rest again. He climbed out of bed and covered her with the satin sheet and down comforter. He gave her a kiss on the cheek. "Okay sleeping beauty."

He looked at her and smiled. She was getting so lazy.

So beautifully and wonderfully lazy.

As the summer progressed it occurred to Mike that Autumn wasn't nearly as willing to get out and do things as she used to be. He could blame it on the coronavirus rendering humans into societies of shut-ins, but he knew deep down, it was due to her size.

Her lifestyle had somehow become even more sedentary. She was smoking weed daily, drinking wine nightly, always snacking and whether she was aware of it or not, the pounds kept piling on.

Mike sometimes wondered if she was in a bit of denial as to how big she was actually getting.

Was that why she didn't want to step on the scale?

Maybe she just didn't care.

Her husband loved her curves so why not keep eating?

Also, perhaps her weight didn't seem like it was a problem because she stopped putting herself in situations where it might become a problem. All the things they did early on in the courting phase of their relationship were now things to be avoided.

Join a co-ed softball league again?

No thank you.

Go out to T-mobile park and catch an afternoon Mariners game?

What if she couldn't squeeze into the seats?

What if there were stairs?

Go to the movies?

Seats.

Restaurant?

Seats.

Motorcycle ride?

Seat.

The Seattle Art Museum?

That's a lot of walking.

Gun range?

A lot of standing.

Stay home, watch Netflix and order doordash?

Yes please.

She was usually hungry and exhausted anyway.

It was as if her lifestyle had reverted back to the way it was when she had her knee and ankle injury.

It was in October of 2023 however, when some big shots from London came to visit Oracle's Seattle offices, and Autumn needed to be at work in person for an entire week.

With only one car it was decided she would drive herself to work and Mike would suit up in his rain gear and take the motorcycle. Not long after the wedding, they had upgraded to a roomier 2019 Nissan Pathfinder, as Autumn had sort of outgrown the old Honda-CRV.

Mike watched as his wife stood in the master bathroom and stuffed the last of the cheese danish between her lips.

"I'm sorry you don't have time to have a real breakfast baby," he said.

She was wearing a form-fitting wine colored sweater dress, and she looked impossibly gorgeous and impossibly thick.

"It's (munch, chew) okay, I just (chew) need to go." She took one last puff on her cigarette before stabbing it out in the ashtray on the counter. Giving him an arousing whiff of Chanel perfume, she wiggled past and towards the bedroom. "Can you grab (huff, cough) my laptop bag?"

He turned off the bathroom fan and followed her, grabbing the leather business tote on his way out. "Got it."

He opened the door to the garage for her and then he opened the garage door itself and then the car door. He held her hand as she stepped up to get in the vehicle. It was only recently that he was coming to know that the simple logistics of having an ultra-curvy wife prosed a multitude of struggles if not for his constant attention.

It took a lot of effort, but he supposed anything or anyone worth possessing and keeping took effort. He would call it work to keep her happy, but he enjoyed every second and took great pleasure in making Autumn's life as easy as possible, and in turn, she kept him on his toes and made him want to always do his best for her.

With her knees wedged between the steering wheel and seat, she wiggled and jiggled her butt around, fighting to get situated. "Did (huff, gasp) you adjust (pant) this yet?"

He nodded, still holding the door open. "It should be good." Although he was 6 inches taller, because of her girth she actually needed the seat further back than he did.

With her leg stretched towards the brake pedal she started the car, bounced and shimmied a few more times then tilted the wheel up a notch so that her thighs had adequate room. "Okay." She yanked on the seatbelt, and had to lift her right butt cheek up just to get it buckled. "God (gasp, pant) this seatbelt feels way snugger than last time I drove, oooohh…(cough) I can (huff) barely move, is it pinched or something?"

The diagonal strap was tight to her chest, squishing her boobs and when she tried to lean forward more than a few inches, it ran out of slack. Mike hid his amusement and shrugged. "Should be the same as always."

She gave him a look. "Uhh, (gasp) whatever. I definitely need Starbucks."

He smiled in spite of her displeasure. "Okay, all the way in?"

She gave her hips one more scoot towards the center of the vehicle. "(huff)I think so."

He shoved the door closed and she rolled down her window. He looked at her and smiled. "Good luck today, love you."

She took a cigarette out of her purse and placed it between her crimson lips. He whipped out his zippo from his pocket, leaned in and lit it for her.

She took a quick drag then blew smoke towards the windshield. "Love (pant) you too."

He gave her a long wet kiss on the lips but his head jolted back when she gave the window a short pulse upward.

She smiled. "Don't mess up my lipstick."

He smiled back and watched her drive away in the bleak grayness of morning.

He had never seen her more tired than after that first Monday.

It was such a basic and normal thing, going into work, but for Autumn it was something she had only done a handful of times in the past several years.

Her body wasn't used to it, wasn't ready for it, and she had changed considerably since the last time she went into the office nearly a year and a half ago.

"I (chew, chew)swear to god," she said after a bite of lasagna, "My boss looks (chew, munch) at me like I'm a juicy piece of meat or something. (gasp) He actually gets red-faced and tongue-tied just talking to me, it's super awkward."

He turned away from the Monday Night Football game and looked at her, sitting on the opposite side of the couch. "Probably just not used to being around a beautiful woman."

Holding her plate in her lap, she looked down at her food and stabbed it with her fork. "Do you (pant) seriously think that's it?"

"I have no doubt."

She took a bite. "Is that why (chew, chew) I had like 6 guys (munch, chew)) with British accents ask me out to lunch today?"

He sighed. He could only imagine how his co-workers would react if they saw someone who looked like his wife suddenly show up at the office. It's not everyday that you see a woman that hot, with those proportions wiggling around in a skintight dress; unless of course you're married to her. "Well yeah, but there's also the fact that they admire your intelligence, respect your opinion and value your input and your boss skills."

She rolled her eyes. "Oh yeah I'm sure."

"What are you saying I'm wrong? Give yourself some credit, you know you're more than a pretty face."

"Yeah (gasp) I'm a lot more than a pretty face." She took a few more bites of food, finished chewing then sighed deeply. "Two of the (huff) women from London didn't recognize me at first."

He put his fork back on his plate. "That's weird."

"Yeah (pant) I know and (chew, chew)) they were like rude to me."

"Do they out rank you?"

"No."

He smiled. "Then just fire them."

She shoved another forkful of cheesy pasta in her mouth. "(chew, chew)Uhh, I'm too exhausted (chew, munch) to think about work right now. (gasp, huff) I just want to finish eating and then take a salt bath. (huff) I forgot how tiring it is (pant) running around the office all day." Her voice slowed and her lips parted as she began taking long and deliberate breaths of air. She scrunched her nose and pressed her hand into her hip. "My (huff, pant) entire body (gasp) hurts."

He put his plate down, got up and came towards her. He went behind the sofa and began gently rubbing her neck and shoulders. He looked down and watched as she continued to make quick work of the oversized rectangle of lasagna he had given her, her belly and breasts slowly heaving in and out as she ate. "I'm sorry baby, you'll get through it, and next week it will all be back to normal."

She was even more tired on Tuesday than she was on Monday.

Too tired, too much knee and hip pain.

She had turned 31 that month. It wasn't normal for a woman as young as she was to feel so completely drained of energy and achy all the time.

It had gotten so bad that she took an extra couple of hours during lunch, having made a last minute same day appointment at the holistic doctor's office just across the street from work, near Pike Place Market.

She had been there before as she developed an appreciation for homeopathy during the past year or so, believing with more conviction than ever that doctors of modern medicine demonized fat and seemed to have one cure for everything which was always to simply lose weight.

Foot pain?

Lose weight.

Back pain?

Lose weight.

Tired all the time?

Eat less, exercise more, lose weight.

To her it was all bullshit designed to feed off the propaganda of billion dollar corporations and make a profit, telling women they needed to be skinny in order to be thought of as beautiful, which in her experience, couldn't be further from the truth.

This holistic doctor on the other hand was kind, caring and thoughtful. She asked real questions that made sense to Autumn and she never brought up weight as a potential issue. Instead, based on the information Autumn provided, she gave her a list of foods to avoid and a list of foods that would be healthy and beneficial to a woman of Autumn's age and body type. Not that she was going to take all the advice seriously or literally, it just made her feel better to have some peace of mind.

The first thing she did when she got home was unsnap her bra and strip herself free of the painfully uncomfortable confines of her skirt and collapse on the sofa.

Mike had ordered Chinese food and she ate pot-stickers, sweet and sour chicken, and chow mein straight from the cartons, only getting up to go to the bathroom, have a smoke, take a bath and go to sleep.

She didn't have the energy or desire to deal with the doctor stuff just yet, nor to tell her husband about it, and when he offered her cake and ice cream in bed, she accepted without thinking.

The following morning, she reached her breaking point.

She rolled over and turned the alarm off on her phone for the third time, then heaved her corpulent legs over the side of the bed. Her face contorted in pain. "Ohh, (gasp, huff) ehhh, fuck."

Mike, already up and dressed, came to her aid. "Are you okay?"

Her eyes were puffy and tired, and she gave a worried look. "Can you (gasp) get the bong and bring it here?" Her voice sounded very weary, breathy and weak.

"You sure?"

On Sunday she had announced that she wasn't going to show up at work under the influence of THC, but the expression on her face told him not to argue and he did as she asked.

Still seated on the edge of the mattress, she smoked and coughed with harrowing wheezes, then she put the bong on the nightstand and took a drink of water from her half-full Essentia bottle.

She looked around the room then peered up at her husband. "Baby, (gasp) I don't think I can (cough, cough) make it outside right now."

His gaze swept over her.

Jesus Christ she was really fat.

Dressed in a purple baby-doll nighty, her belly was protruding onto her lap, covering the upper half of her thighs and inching ever closer towards her knees.

Her gut had become noticeably more massive in recent months, and she had developed a double-belly, the upper half more narrow and round as it curved out beneath her breasts like a support pillow, and the lower half, divided at the navel, was wider, flabbier and more spare-tire-like; and together they folded over themselves with nowhere to go but forward.

He could tell she needed a cigarette. "Can you make it to the bathroom?" he said.

Her eyes pleaded at him. "Yeah (huff) but I'm not going to sit on that stool right now. Can you just bring the ashtray in here, please? I'll burn some (cough) sage or something later."

He sighed. "Okay."

After filling the room with smoke, Autumn carefully scooted back in the bed so she could lean against her pillows, although just doing that was a struggle. "I don't know babe, (cough) I think I need to make some serious lifestyle changes." She held her hand in front of her face and squinted. "Look how (gasp) swollen my fingers are."

Crouching beside the bed, he clasped his palms around her right hand after she transferred the cigarette to her left. He massaged the area beneath her knuckle with his thumbs. Her hand was very soft, but it seemed obvious to him that it was chubby, not swollen. "It's probably the atmospheric changes or something, yesterday was the first sunny day in a month."

She grimaced and fiddled with her wedding band. "I think my ring (pant) is cutting off my (cough) circulation."

"Do you need to take it off?"

"I don't (gasp) think I can."

"I'll get some lotion or something."

After some oil and careful pulling, Mike was able to slip the diamond studded band off her finger. It was strange that while doing so, he felt as if a huge weight was lifted from his shoulders.

She did some work on her phone, finished her cigarette then laid down on her side, her eyes facing the wall.

Mike climbed in bed and spooned her, wrapping his right arm around her thickening waist which was only partially covered by her nighty. Her breathing was labored and her breasts and belly expanded and contracted considerably with each elongated gasp.

After a period of silence she cleared her throat. "Maybe (gasp) I need to cut out wheat. (cough) Oatmeal is gluten-free right?"

Oatmeal?

Gluten-free?

What the hell was she talking about?

He pressed his face into the back of her head and cuddled up close. He was the big spoon but in comparison to her he was small. She was bigger than him everywhere now, and while that should seem obvious he was still surprised by how much higher her hips and even her back, towered above him. "Umm, yeah, but I doubt that wheat is the reason your hands are swollen."

"It's not just my hands. (pant) My feet hurt so bad last night (cough) I almost cried."

"You sure you have to go into the office today?"

"(gasp)I don't think I can, (huff) I'm in too much pain."

She shifted her body, and just the slight movement added length to her husband's cock. She wasn't wearing panties and her butt was exposed.

Her ass was so perfect, Mike sometimes felt that if he did nothing more than just look at it for the rest of his life he would die a happy man. He noticed there was some new cellulite on her upper thighs and new stretch marks on her rounded mountain of a hip.

He dangled his fingers over her back rolls, mesmerized by the very sight. "You should take an edible."

"Then I (gasp) really won't be able to focus." She laid still for a moment. "Maybe I'll just take half of one."

He got up and went to the walk-in-closet, when he returned he came to her side of the bed and handed her a gummy. "It's only 10 milligrams."

She propped her head up with her left hand. "Ennhh…you (gasp) think I should just eat the whole thing?"

"You already had a bong hit yo, and you're in pain."

"Okay yo." She put it in her mouth.

He glanced at his phone then sat near the foot of the bed. It was strange that she hadn't asked for coffee and something to eat yet as she usually needed both in the morning before she was ready to even talk. He stared at her for a few seconds before he spoke. "Are you hungry? Why were you asking about oatmeal?"

She sighed. "Because I (pant) went and got a check-up yesterday."

He gazed at her, but her ass was so huge it blocked his view of her head, now resting back on the pillow. "You did?"

"Yeah, (gasp) I just needed to figure out (pant) why I have absolutely no energy."

"What'd he say?"

"She. The doctor is a she."

He climbed back in bed and spooned her again. "Did you go to the clinic?"

"Eeww no way. (gasp) I just went to the natural medicine place near work. I think I have a lot of inflammation, and she gave me (gasp) a list of foods to avoid.

"What do you mean you have inflammation?"

"Come on you've seen how puffy I've been looking in pictures lately, my entire face is like inflamed, I just hadn't noticed it was so bad in my hands until now. I'm supposed to cut out caffeine and wheat and (huff) a bunch of other things."

"How do they come up with these lists?"

She sighed again. “It has to do with body-type, (pant) ethnicity, where you live, what you do for a living and things like that.”

“What body type are you?”

She yawned dreamily. “I thought I was (yawn) an hourglass but she said I was a pear.”

He nestled closer into the warm softness of her back and clung on tighter to her belly. “Baby that is not a real doctor, you can’t take what these holistic places say seriously.”

She lifted her head up. “Oh my god, (pant) yes you can. I’ll take what they say way more seriously than a fucking quote, regular doctor, (cough, cough) they’re good for birth control and prescriptions but not much else.”

“Why didn’t you tell me you went for a check up?”

“It was such a last minute thing. (gasp) But I don’t know, won’t it, you know, make you sad if I need to give up wheat? You love to bake so much.”

Mike didn’t know what to think. He had never been so physically attracted to someone than he was to her at that moment.

She was just so sexy.

She was so sexy that he suspected if he actually thought how sexy she was for too long, his whole body might explode.

It was her weight gain, her added fat, her over-abundance of curves and divine feminine laziness that turned him on and fascinated him infinitely, but her health was clearly suffering because of it. It was a draw in the metaphorical chess game between his brain and his dick.

He clasped her ankle lovingly and chose his words carefully. "Baby, you really need to learn how to let some-one other than yourself take care of you." "That's what being married is, that's the reason for going through life with a partner. I take care of you, just like you take care of me."

She laid still for a moment. "A partner that loves you (huff) right?"

He climbed on top of her thigh and kissed the side of her belly. "A husband who adores you."

She tilted her head up. "And loves you."

"Yes, and loves you, very much." He glanced at his phone again, then got out of bed. "Can I get you anything? What's your plan you know it's almost 7."

"I can cancel my meetings." She stretched her arm toward the nightstand. "Can you get me my phone?"

He unplugged it and handed it to her. "You're staying home then?"

She nodded. "I feel like (cough) shit. Every muscle hurts, I'm not going anywhere. (cough, cough) If you look in my laptop bag there is the list from the doctor's office. (gasp) Maybe you could pick up groceries on your way home. (huff) We really need to start eating healthier."

He sighed and looked down at her. "Okay, but please don't lose this beautiful ass." He leaned in and gave her hip a squeeze.

"Oh my god, (cough) get out of here already."

"I can take a personal day. Are you sure you're going to be okay on your own?"

"Yeah I just (gasp) want to go back to sleep, you should go."

"You haven't even eaten anything."

She lifted her head and gave him that blank-faced fluttery eyelashes look that he always found to be as intimidating as it was sexy. "Do (huff) not micromanage me."

His face turned somber. "Okay. Call me if you need something."

When Mike returned home that evening he was surprised to find that his wife was still in bed just as he had left her.

Her nightstand however, looked different.

The ashtray he brought her was now full of butts, and next to it was two empty boxes of something from The Cheesecake Factory along with a crumpled up paper bag.

He kneeled at the edge of the bed and brushed a few strands of auburn hair away from her face. "How are you feeling?"

She blinked a few times. "Mmmm…(gasp)better I think."

He put his hand on her forehead. "Do you think you're getting sick?"

"No. (yawn) I think I just needed rest."

"Glad you found some food."

She scrunched her nose. "Eew, (pant) throw that stuff away. I told myself a hundred times that I wasn't going to order doordash today and look at what I (cough) end up doing. This is my problem."

"It's okay baby you still need to eat."

"Did you get the groceries?"

"Yes."

With the entire bed squeaking and groaning beneath her weight, she rolled onto her side and was confronted with the sight and smell of her spent Camels. "Ewew, (gasp) please get rid of this ashtray. I'm not having any more cigarettes for the rest of the day." She held out her arm and let her husband assist her into a sitting position. She gazed up at him, frowning. "I'll try to (gasp) get up and (pant) and take a bath while you cook dinner. You got salmon right?"

"Yeah."

"Can we have salmon and quinoa, maybe a kale salad?"

Mike shrugged. "Sure."

"Oh my god, (pant) if I asked you to bake me cookies you'd already be in the kitchen."

He blushed at her keen ability to see through him. "Well, cookies are more fun than kale and quinoa."

"Yes but we need to eat healthier. (pant) You know you still eat like a teenager and you're practically a middle-aged man at this point."

Said the girl who just doordashed half the menu at The Cheesecake Factory.

"I am not middle-aged," he said. He grabbed both of her wrists and rocked her forward, then hoisted her to her feet.

She came close, wedging him between herself and the bedroom wall. "Yes you are, (gasp) just because you somehow still have abs doesn't mean you aren't getting older." She pointed at his temple and smirked. "(pant) Look I can even see a few sparkly grays."

His knees weakened as her belly and breasts brushed against him. "What? Come on, I'm still a very young 34, I don't have no grays."

She rolled her eyes. "Yeah and (pant) I don't have a fat ass."

He put his hands on the bare skin of her hips and looked down at her. "You better not turn me on right now."

"You better not turn me on. (huff) I need to take a bath and you need to cook dinner, remember?"

"You make me forget what I'm doing."

She rolled her eyes again then fanned herself with her hand. "Ooooh…okay (gasp) now I'm tired of standing." She shimmied to her right and began slowly wiggling towards the door. She stopped, turned around and looked at him. "By the way umm, (huff) we don't have any plans this Friday right?"

"You would know better than me. Why?"

"My boss is taking a few of us out to dinner. (gasp) It would be nice if you came, I want to show you off."

He took a few steps toward her. "Yeah, of course I'll come. I'm not letting you out of the house until you put that ring back on."

She smiled. "Okay funny guy. (huff) Now where did I put my cigarettes?"

Chapter 24

Richard was in awe of what had happened to Autumn during the pandemic. To see her go from the ultra-curvy smoke-show she had been when he first interviewed her in January of 2020, to the wobbly and morbidly obese seductress she was now, was more arousing and amusing to him than anything he had ever seen. He had no idea that a woman gaining so much weight like that could be so attractive.

He stared as she slowly wiggled her way across the lobby and towards the table.

The soft lighting of the high-end steakhouse seemed to give her an angelic glow. Wearing no jacket, her sleeveless dress squeezed every curve, roll and bulge on her body and its muted yellow color brought out the redness in her gorgeous hair and left him breathless.

Dear god.

Those arms, those hips, that rack.

"Autumn, glad you could make it," he said.

Standing before him she fanned herself with her hand and took a few deep breaths. With her ruby lips, glossy bronze blush and effortless dark eye shadow, she looked even more beautiful up close. More beautiful still with the houseboats of Lake Union shining through the dark rain shimmered windows behind her.

"Well, (huff, gasp) Canlis is hard to say no to Richard. "She smiled and gestured to the man standing to her right. "This (pant) is my husband Mike. Mike, this is my boss, Richard."

Mike grinned and shook Richard's hand. "Nice to meet you finally."

Richard gazed up at Mike and his heart sank. He supposed it was inevitable that Autumn's husband would be absurdly handsome, so good-looking that Richard felt foolish for having ambitions of infidelity with his most precious protege. Despite his wealth and position of power, and with only a simple introduction to go by, Richard knew he would never be able to compete with a guy like Mike.

"The pleasure is mine. Please, sit down," Richard said before sitting himself.

There were a dozen or so people seated around the table and after getting situated, making a few more introductions and brief small talk, Mike noticed the look of discomfort on his wife's face. "Are you okay?"

"Yeah, (pant) better now that I'm off my feet," she said. "Could definitely use a drink, you're driving by the way."

He smiled and unfolded his cloth napkin. "No problem." The rain had been heavy enough that morning that Mike left his motorcycle at home and carpooled with his wife.

Autumn eyed the steaming bowl of bread and its various sides of butters and olive oils, ironically placed directly in front of her. "Oh god, (gasp) that looks so good right now, (pant) I wish I could have some."

Justine looked on from across the table. "Are you doing the low carb thing?"

"No, (huff) I'm just trying to give up gluten for a while," Autumn said. "I've been very low energy (pant) lately so I want to see what happens if I try something different."

Justine nodded. "Makes sense. I gave up caffeine last year and I actually have more energy now than I did before." Like Richard, Justine was also amazed by how much Autumn had blown up over the years. It was staggering how big she had become, and Justine thought that for Autumn, this anti-gluten thing was a long time coming.

"That's great," Autumn said, still eyeing the bread.

She ordered bacon wrapped scallops, and a twelve ounce filet mignon with a side of sautéed brussels sprouts. Despite dinner being a work expense Mike was so disgusted by some of the prices that he simply went with a cheeseburger and fries.

"God…mmm(chew, chew) this is so delicious," Autumn said after a bite of the juicy and tender steak. "You (gasp) need to try this babe."

Mike cut a piece from her plate and put it in his mouth. "Yeah that's really good. Wanna try a bite of my burger?" It was only after the words left his tongue that he realized that she wouldn't be able to have any.

Autumn smiled. "Mmm…I thought (pant) you'd never ask."

Surprised, he handed her the burger and she took a big bite.

"Mmm, (chew, chew) this is (chew) amazing." She held it with both hands, and then took yet another large bite before finally giving it back to her husband.

Mike looked at her with a twinkle in his eye but restrained from commenting.

As the evening progressed Autumn consumed everything on her plate, then proceeded to mindlessly graze away on her husband's fries, and then, after her third glass of Malbec, she dove into the bread whole-heartedly.

Justine raised her eyebrows as she witnessed the way Autumn was smothering herbal butter on piece after piece of bread before shoving them into her mouth, one after the other like they were going out of style.

What the hell happened to her?

How in the world could she let herself go like this?

She was so fat it was kind of unbelievable to Justine, and no less cringy to see her continue to eat her way towards oblivion.

Justine looked up and made a quick eye-exchange with Mike, both of them seeing the same thing and both deciding not to draw attention to it.

"(huff)Shit," Autumn said, entering the house from the garage. "So (hiccup, gasp) much for (wheeze) giving up wheat. God why the fuck (pant) do I always end up eating too much whenever we go (cough) out."

Holding her hand to keep her steady, Mike guided his wife to the sofa where she dropped like stone. She was tipsy and so stuffed that she was wheezing, sweating and struggling to get enough oxygen into her compromised lungs.

Once she started on the bread during the dinner she had been unable to stop, and when she had eaten almost a total of two loaves, she flagged down the server and asked for an order of lobster ravioli before summoning both a slice of cheesecake and a bowl of bread pudding from the dessert menu.

"Don't beat yourself up about it," Mike said. "Giving up gluten is insane anyway."

"How (huff, gasp) do you mean?"

"Do you seriously want to voluntarily make yourself live in a world without baguettes, croutons, pasta, pie, cake and nearly every other food on the planet?"

"I just (gasp, cough) wanted to try it (huff) for a while, I wasn't going to do it forever."

He crouched, placed his hands on her knees and looked her in the eye. "Do you know what it was that first made me really fall in love with you?"

"I might (pant) have a few guesses."

"When we got coffee at Victrola right after I moved to the hill. I said something about how there was so many gluten-free people these days and you rolled your eyes and told me that you didn't give into trends that easily."

"Really?" She arched her brows. "So it was (gasp) that important to you?"

"I don't know. Maybe I just loved how you've always been your own person, so wonderfully different compared to all the other girls."

She scooted herself forward a little, pushing her belly out right in front of his face. "You just (huff, pant) needed to know I could eat wheat because you probably wanted my (hiccup) butt to get bigger."

He smiled then gave her belly a kiss. He then sunk his fingers into her massive love handles and gazed upward. "You think you've got me so figured out don't you."

"I know you (gasp) better than you know yourself." Her lips pushed into a devious smirk. "Aren't you going to make me my (pant) German pancake?"

He stood. "You serious?"

"When am I (gasp) not serious?" She grabbed the end of his silk tie and pulled. "Come here." She brought him close and made him kiss her on the mouth. "I want you and I (huff) want you to weigh me tonight, (hiccup) but it wouldn't make sense for me to step on the scale without having my...oooh (gasp) dessert first."

His heart raced, as he felt a burning lust rising up within him.

Dessert?

She'd already had two desserts.

She already had two desserts, a huge dinner, and an entire basket of bread only a couple days after announcing she was going to cut gluten from the vast richness of her decadent diet.

There was something about the way she could blatantly change her mind so unapologetically that made her seem acutely feminine, and it turned him on relentlessly. "I love you, so much."

Her intoxicated eyes beamed at him. "Now (huff, wheeze) get your adorable little (hiccup) butt in the kitchen."

He couldn't wipe the smile off his face if he tried, nor did he have the ability to say no to her. She did need to lose weight, she did need to eat less and get more physically active, but if it was tough love she required Mike knew he wasn't the person to give it. He would sooner turn in his proverbial man card than deny his beautiful wife any of her favorite treats or vices.

"As you wish," he said.

Autumn stabbed the last piece of pancake with her fork, then smeared it around on her plate, soaking up all remaining maple syrup and took a bite. She peered up at her husband with glossy weary eyes. "Oh (ooof, gasp) god. (hiccup) I think I'm ready to pass out."

Mike took her empty plate and put it on the coffee table. "No, not yet baby, please."

"First you need to get me off this couch. I don't think I can, (huff, wheeze) move right now." She adjusted her position and teetered forward, but remained seated, as her ass was simply too heavy to be lifted off the sofa under her own power. "Oh (gasp, wheeze) god, I'm not even (cough, huff) joking, I seriously can't get up."

Mike grabbed her by the wrists and assisted her to her feet. "This is what I'm here for. I'm here to make everything easy for you."

She squished her belly and breasts into him. "Fuck (pant) that is so hot."

"What?"

"Just…just the thought (gasp, pant) of being so dependent on you, being so chunky that I'm completely at your mercy. I've never let myself (pant) just completely surrender to another person before."

He held her in his arms and brought his mouth closer to her ear. "We're dependent on each other. Maybe that's what love is in a way, our happiness depends on us being together."

"Come, (huff, pant) just help me to the scale so I can go lay down."

In the bathroom, she sat on the wicker stool as Mike prepared the scale.

When it was ready she leaned forward and stood, as the stool was still high enough for her to get up on her own. "Oooofff, (gasp) I can tell already this is going to be a lot. (pant, cough) I can't even remember the last time I was able to squeeze my ass into pants."

She stepped on and he kneeled on the tile floor to read the numbers. "Four hundred forty-three pounds," he said.

Autumn's knees flinched. "400 what?"

"443.68 pounds."

"Ummm…why does this keep happening?" She bit her lip and stepped backwards off the scale. Almost losing her balance, she peered down at her husband, looking as if she had just seen a ghost. Her breathing accelerated to the point where she began fanning herself with her hand causing her entire body to jiggle with rippling waves of excess blubber. "Oooh, (gasp, huff, wheeze) well, ummm, oh my… (pant, gasp) oops."

Mike stood, and pulled her close. 443 meant she had put on over 60 pounds in less than a year. He was flabbergasted, as her weight had crept up more subtly this time around. She still had that same bottom heavy hourglass shape, it was just bigger in every direction.

It was official.

His wife was over 400 pounds and it felt surreal and dreamlike. Not only was she over 400 but she was already nearly halfway to 500. "Fucking hell princess," he said.

"Ohh, (huff) Ohh(pant, gasp) god I'm such a big sexy fatass."

"Let's get you off your feet."

She nodded meekly.

Her butt slammed into the bed with so much force that Mike worried for the frame. She was sweating and completely winded.

"Help me (huff, gasp) get this off," she said, raising her arms towards her husband.

After he peeled off her dress and unsnapped her now K-cup bra, she laid down on her side with a bouncy thud that shook the entire room. "Hand me (huff, wheeze) my toy, too tired to do anything else."

Mike, so full of raging lusty hormones, gave her the vibrator, stripped himself naked in 3 seconds flat and climbed into bed, spooning her backside as if pulled by an electro-magnet.

The vibrator had become more of a frequent thing in recent months, as with Autumn's increasing bulk and limited stamina, sex was more difficult than it used to be, though ironically, the extra weight also seemed to make her constantly horny.

He ran his hand over her side, following the severely feminine contour of where her massive gelatinous hip met her girly waist of plush love handles and folding rolls of pale back fat. "I love this part of you," he said.

"Oooh,(pant) yeah me too," she cooed, wiggling her butt against his fully erect penis. "I(gasp) want you to (pant, huff) grab my belly and cum on my ass."

He rubbed himself against her, slowly and rhythmically. "You like that idea huh?"

"What?"

He squeezed her upper belly, then cupped her breast with his hand. "Being totally at my mercy."

She quivered from his touch and pressed the vibrator deeper between her thighs. "Mmhmm, (gasp, pant) yes baby. It (huff) turns me on a lot."

"You don't need to have energy all the time anyway. I can be your energy."

"Yeah, (gasp) because I like my lifestyle too much. I don't think…ooh…(gasp, huff) I'm ready to give it up."

"Me neither."

"My ass is so fucking huge, (gasp, pant) so is my belly."

"You like that?"

"Yeah, it really does make me feel so sexy and so like (huff, gasp) provocative. I feel like such a (pant) girly princess."

His fingers dug into her pillowy rolls and he slammed his pelvis into her rear end more forcefully. "You are a girly princess."

"I'm such (gasp) a fat ass," she cooed in a breathy gasp. "I'm like (huff) Miss Piggy and you're Kermit."

He kissed the back of her neck, then began nibbling on her ear. "You're Mrs. Piggy. Just need to get your ring resized."

She moaned with bursts of pleasure as she adjusted the vibrator's cadence. "Or I can (gasp) just wear it around my neck…in case (gasp, pant, wheeze) I keep getting fatter."

He unloaded on her as her moans surrendered into orgasmic gasps of rapture.

Fucking Hell.

Chapter 25

In the following weeks Autumn became less critical of her opulent eating habits, but she also didn't embrace the idea of gaining any more weight or being completely at her husband's mercy as she often expressed during moments of intimacy and passion.

Knowing she was well over 400 pounds weighed on her in more ways than one.

Without so many words it was decided if she wasn't able or willing to drastically decrease her daily calorie intake, if she was going to be this curvy goddess of such immense proportions, then she would need to force herself to get some sort of exercise.

They bought a top-of-the-line NordicTrack treadmill in November of 2023 and had it placed in the guest bedroom.

She swore she would use it at least 15 minutes a day, just to maintain some strength in her lungs and legs; but haughty proclamations of 15 minutes a day quickly turned into more reality based ideals of 10 minutes every other day, and as time went on it became clear to Mike that she was lucky to step on the machine more than once in a given week.

He didn't pressure her either way.

They had Thanksgiving with Mike's side of the family, and got through it without too much of an ordeal over Autumn's weight, aside from a few issues involving the inadequate sizes of chairs and looks of disgust and disbelief from some relatives seeing her in person for the first time in years; as well as Mike having to go through another awkward chat with his dad. Thank god his fat Aunt Cindy was there to soften the focus from his wife.

In December with a Christmas dinner in Oregon looming, Autumn seemed to find a miraculous burst of motivation to get into a real exercise routine.

Mike stepped by the open doorway and was overwhelmed by the sight of his wife plowing away on her treadmill, still such a rare and stunning display of pampered and exorbitant beauty. She was wearing a spaghetti strap tank top and skin tight athletic shorts, skimpy enough to not fully cover her basketball sized butt cheeks.

He watched her from behind. Her hips were wider than the machine itself and each of her gargantuan dimpled thighs lumbered forward in short, heavy and wobbly strides while her hands clung tightly to the sidebars as if needing them to remain upright.

She was going at an extremely slow pace, and it was only a handful of seconds later that she brought it to a stop, and turned around.

"Jesus, (pant, gasp, wheeze) how long have you (gasp, pant) been standing there?" she said, picking a wedgie out of her butt.

He leaned against the door's frame and smirked. "Sorry, I couldn't help myself, just watching you walk is mesmerizing."

She fanned herself with her hand and after several quick gasps for air, stuck her tongue out at him. "You're such a (gasp) pervert."

"Is this 3 days in a row now?"

"What (huff, gasp) are you keeping track?"

He smiled and shook his head. "No, I just live here. How far did you walk?"

She exhaled deeply, then turned to check the treadmill's console. "Uhh, (pant) point one nine miles I guess." She gave him a look of defeat. "Damn (gasp, huff) I thought I went further than that."

"Feeling good?"

She stared at him, expressionless. "Yeah, (gasp, pant) I think better than the way I felt when I did this (huff) a couple days ago. I could barely go 2 minutes without wanting to die." She grabbed her bottle of Smartwater from the treadmill's cup holder, then carefully stepped off with a wave of jiggles, then lowered her hips into the davenport that was placed against the wall of the guest room. Her face was flush and she was still struggling to catch her breath. "Not that I (gasp, cough) don't want to die right now."

"Why are you pushing yourself so hard?"

She relaxed her posture, leaning backwards and letting her legs spread out wide to make room for her belly. "I don't (pant) know." Her head tilted downward and she ran her hand over her thigh. She sighed, took a drink of water then looked up at Mike. "I'm (gasp, pant) embarrassed to admit it but I'm nervous about (huff) seeing my parents."

He tucked his thumbs into the pockets of his Levis and shrugged. "Why?"

"I'm nervous (gasp, pant) about them seeing me this big."

"What? That's not like you. You've never worried about that stuff before."

She tossed her water bottle aside and balled her hands into fists. "I've never been this (huff, gasp) big before. (gasp, wheeze) I've never even so much as imagined I could ever even get this big, (gasp) let alone actually be this big in real life." Her eyes slanted. "I mean (gasp) I seriously can't even walk for more than (huff)a few minutes anymore."

He stepped forward and kneeled at her feet. “Hey hey hey, it’s alright.” He gently caressed the outer part of her thigh and gazed at her lovingly. “If you want to get more physically active you can’t expect to get there overnight.”

She placed her hand, slightly wet with sweat, over his. “Yeah I know, you're right. (gasp) Being consistent has (pant) always been the hard part for me.”

He looked her up and down. She was enormous beyond words. Her shirt failed to cover the entirety of her belly and she looked thoroughly encased in rolls upon rolls of fat from her neck to her calves. Her thighs were now literally the diameter of bed pillows, so massive and swollen that they lifted her belly upward until it oozed into her cantaloupe-sized tits like over-inflated balloons fighting for territory.

“Don’t beat yourself up. I’ll protect you when we go see your mom,” he said.

“Okay, (gasp) but help me stay on track with the treadmill. I’d like to be able to actually walk around my parents house this Christmas without (huff) feeling like I’m going to pass out.”

He gave her a lukewarm nod. "Alright baby. I'll do my best to keep you on track." He smiled. "Or should I say, on NordicTrack."

She fluttered her eyelashes at him, expressionless.

Autumn's fears about seeing her family at Christmas dinner ended up being moot, as sadly in December of 2023, on the first day of winter, her father Gary passed away from a heart attack at the age of 62.

The joy of the season was instantly destroyed and preparations for a holiday feast were replaced with tears, mournful phone calls and later, funeral arrangements.

It was a terrible time for Autumn and a horrible way to bring the year to a close.

Exercising once again became the furthest thing from her mind as the reality set in that her dad would never meet her kids, should she ever choose to have any. He would never be there to console her, as he had been her entire life, and her Mom would now be alone for the foreseeable future.

As the year progressed, Autumn sank into an anxiety fueled depression.

Sometimes she would stay in bed for an entire week, gorging on fast food and petting the Samson with a blank look on her face, only getting up to use the bathroom, smoke, or take a shower.

The treadmill began to collect dust and her eating habits ballooned into mindless comfort binges that sometimes lasted all day and late into the night.

It wasn't eating to gain weight or to feel sexy anymore, it was eating to self-soothe, ease stress and escape.

Eventually, winter turned to spring and spring into summer, and the grieving process for her dad took its 5 stage course and things began to feel somewhat normal again, but all that snacking and binging she had been doing during the first half of the year had left her bigger and more out of shape than ever.

It seemed to Mike that it was her increased consumption levels of THC and alcohol that kept her numb to the realities of what was happening to her.

She had taken up dabbing, often doing it first thing in the morning to nurse the excesses of the night before. Her tolerance had become high enough she was able to do this and still perform well at her job, but it was a practice and habit that prevented her from ever having a true moment of clarity.

The wine clouded her judgments in the evenings and the cannabis blurred her perceptions in the mornings and throughout her days. She still got the munchies, or so it appeared as her appetite was always ravenous and she was eating constantly.

By July of 2024, she was a hot mess and looked significantly heavier than she did in January.

"God, (gasp, wheeze) everyday I walk past the treadmill, (huff) and everyday I tell myself I'm going to start using it again (gasp) but I never do," Autumn said as she toddled past the guest bedroom after having a cigarette on the back patio.

Holding her hand, Mike helped guide her back towards the living room. "Look baby, if you want to use it, use it. Otherwise stop berating yourself for not doing something you don't really want to do anyway."

She plopped down onto the sofa, causing it to make a tremendous sound of deflation. She was so huge now that he feared it was only a matter of time before the couch gave out under her weight, and he planned to get a bigger sturdier one very soon.

"It's easier (huff, gasp) for me to workout when you're not home (pant) I think." She bit her lip then looked up at her husband. "Don't you need to go (pant, huff) for a bike ride or something?"

"Do you want me to?"

"Maybe." She arched her back and adjusted the straps of her low-cut black camisole. "I don't know, (gasp, pant) it's just that you're so healthy and here I am with my big fat tits and ass, (gasp, cough) still smoking cigarettes. It's like impossible for me not to feel(gasp) judged when you're around."

He sat next to her in the narrow space between her hip and the armrest of the sofa. He put his hand on the warm cushiness of her upper chest and felt the tiny chains of the gold necklace that held her wedding band, then let his fingers slowly dangle over her heaving breasts. "Come on, you know I'm not like that, I would never judge you. You know I love the contrast between us. I'm always hard and you're always soft."

She rolled her eyes. "I know, (huff) but you get what I'm saying. It's embarrassing for me to be all sweaty and out of breath (gasp) and so out-of-shape on the treadmill, knowing that you're (huff, cough) still probably getting off from staring at my butt. (gasp)It makes it hard to focus."

He leaned in and kissed her upper arm. It was now so big and fat that it was developing rolls of its own and beginning to sag at the elbow. "Okay babe, I'll give you some space to do your thing."

"Thank you." She smiled, reached down and tickled the side of his waist. "You need to keep an (gasp, huff) eye on these love handles anyway."

He shot to his feet and faced her with his hands investigating his lower back. "What? I don't have any love handles."

She gave him a haughty smirk. "Hey, (gasp) what do they say? If you can (pant) pinch an inch?"

"That's it, I'm going for a long bike ride."

"You better, (pant) need you to stay sexy for me."

He looked at her with an eyebrow raised. "So it's just all about looks with you is that it?"

She bent forward and cupped her boobs with both hands. "I might (pant) like the contrast too."

He grinned and leaned in to kiss her. "You bad girl."

"Shut up (pant, gasp) and get out of here," she said, pushing him away.

As soon as Mike was out the door and on his bike, Autumn grabbed her phone and opened her Pizza Hut App.

She was being honest when she told him she felt judged when he was around, but it had less to do with the embarrassment of him seeing her wheeze away on the treadmill than it had to do with him witnessing one of her true eating binges.

She was well aware that he would probably love to watch her make a total pig of herself, but there was something nice about completely letting loose and eating the way she wanted, away from the observing eye of another person, even if it was her curve chasing feeder of a husband.

It was Sunday, and having consumed one of his big breakfasts of bacon, eggs, fruit and blueberry pancakes just hours prior, she shouldn't have been hungry, but she was.

She felt starving, and the thought of warm endless slices of pizza all to herself made her mouth water.

She ordered The Big Dinner Box, which included two stuffed-crust pizzas, cheesy breadsticks and buffalo wings. It was enough food for a kids soccer party, but she tacked on an oven baked bowl of chicken alfredo pasta, two ultimate chocolate chip cookies and a two liter bottle of Sierra Mist for good measure.

Having secret fast food gorging sessions was something she had started doing after her dad died, as it seemed to temporarily fill the void he left in her heart; and large quantities of melty cheeses, toasty breads and warm gooey desserts never failed to comfort her and make her feel cozy and safe, like everything was going to be okay.

When the food finally arrived, she dove straight in, wary of the time and the knowledge that her husband would be back soon. She started with the pepperoni, then moved on to some breadsticks, then to the Hawaiian chicken pizza, then a few wings, then to the pasta and the cookies, then back to the pepperoni.

Samson stared down at her from atop the bookshelf.

She looked up at him with her mouth full.

Oh God.

Can a girl ever just pig out alone without being watched by a boy?

She ignored him and went back to eating.

It was ironic that everything was so delicious to her, as cheap highly processed chain restaurant food like Pizza Hut, was something she wouldn't have been caught dead eating a few years ago, but things had changed. Now she enjoyed that highly refined, addictive assembly line taste so far as to download an App.

She ate fast and robotically, with little wasted movements as all of her energy focused on getting as much food into her stomach as quickly as possible while keeping one eye on her episode of Friends.

Her smorgasbord of a feast disappeared steadily and before she knew what happened she looked down and found there was nothing left except a lone slice of the Hawaiian pizza, two breadsticks and half of one of the giant cookies.

She gasped and reclined back on the sofa. She was a little winded, and she placed her hands on her expanding belly and felt the way it moved slowly in and out each time she strained to inhale air into her overworked lungs.

She felt so heavy, so bloated, and so horny.

God, why was she like this?

Why did she have to stuff herself to the point of not being able to move and why did it make her feel so sexual and girly?

Her vibrator was all the way in the bedroom, but she didn't want to do any more walking than she had to in the state she was in, besides; the idea of her husband coming home suddenly now excited her.

She scooted herself forward and took a drink of the Sierra Mist straight from the bottle. She looked back at the pizza.

Just one more slice, and maybe some more of the cookie, then she had to somehow get off the couch and get the pizza box and all the evidence into the trash and recycle bins which were all the way over in the garage.

She let out a burp, took a deep breath, and went back to eating.

"Home honey I'm high!" Mike said as he wheeled his bicycle through the front door of the house with a burst of fresh air and mid-summer sunshine.

Autumn stood in the kitchen, next to the door to the garage just as it clicked shut. She looked startled and was breathing heavily. "Oh, (gasp) hey baby."

He leaned his bike against the end table next to the couch and took his helmet off. "What were you doing in the garage?"

She gazed at him and tried to catch her breath.

Damn he looked good with his tangled helmet hair, white t-shirt and REI athletic shorts.

Despite her jokes about love handles, the reality was that her husband had miraculously maintained his 30 inch waist and washboard abs, which were features she admittedly found pleasing about him.

She slowly wiggled towards him, the wood flooring creaking loudly with each step.

"Umm, (huff, gasp) nothing." She stopped walking and shifted her weight to one hip. "I was just about (gasp, hiccup) to lay down in bed, you should (gasp, burp) come with me and tell me about your bike ride."

Mike looked at her. Her face was flush and glossy with sweat, but it appeared as though she had reapplied some lipstick and touched up her makeup. She looked bloated, but at her incredible size it was hard to tell.

That being said, he had never seen her look so huge before. Her skimpy top and matching black leggings squeezed her like a sausage casing, and rolls of fat flowed out of her at every hem and edge of her stylish, yet under-sized outfit.

He took her by the shoulders and pulled her close. "Baby you're so out of breath, and you're warm. I told you not to push yourself too hard on that thing."

She gently rubbed her body against him, hoping he would smell the breath mint she just ate and her freshly administered perfume instead of the remnants of thousands of calories of Pizza Hut. "Oh, uh (gasp) yeah, (huff) might be time for me to take a few days off (hiccup) from the treadmill."

Mike's legs trembled. Even after all these years she could still give him that wonderfully weak feeling in his knees like only a woman can. With her voluminous hair tied back in a messy ponytail, the pouty part in her full lips and the penetrating gaze of her ethereal eyes; she looked so hot and so damn attractive he literally could hardly stand it.

"That's a good idea, give those shapely quads a break," he said, placing his hand on her massive trunk-like thigh.

Jesus.

Just one of her legs looked like it was as big as he was.

He smiled. "Are you hungry for lunch yet? We haven't had pizza in a few days, plus you deserve a post workout reward right?"

Her eyes wandered as she nervously played with her hair. "Sure baby, (gasp, pant) you can order me a pizza.

But (hiccup) ooohh…(gasp) get a good one, don't just (hiccup) order Pizza Hut or some crap."

"Why do you have the hiccups?"

"I don't…oooh (hiccup) I was just thirsty (gasp, pant) so I had some Sierra Mist."

"Oh…okay."

"Just (gasp, pant) help me to bed first please. (hiccup) I'm really horny for you and (gasp, huff) I need to get off my feet."

He cracked a smile and turned towards his bike. "I should take a quick shower."

She grabbed his forearm and pulled him back, then in a sensual coo said, "No. (gasp) I like your sweat. (burp) We will (pant) shower together afterwards." She pressed her tits into his lower chest.

His eyes went wide and his mind went blank.

Chapter 26

Like the season that shared her name, Autumn had a peculiar and inexhaustible influence on the mind of taste and flavor and sensuality. She could draw from any poet, some failed attempt at description, or some lines of feeling that could never do her justice.

Kegan slid open the back door of the house and stepped outside. With a bottle of Howards Blend stout in hand, he zipped up his jacket. "Damn, fall is definitely in the air."

Mike closed the lid of his Weber gas grill and turned towards him. "Yep, days are getting shorter. You cold?"

It was an early October Saturday evening and the smoky forest fire atmosphere of an indian summer had finally changed to the crisp clean air one expects of the fall season along with the turning colors of the Pacific Northwest foliage. Kegan and Sydney had come over to Mike and Autumn's house for a night of barbecuing and board games, which was a routine fast becoming a monthly tradition.

"Nah I'm good," Kegan said after a sip of beer. "Just seems like it was only a week ago when it was too hot to sleep."

Mike removed the THC vape pen from his coat pocket and took a few puffs. "Time goes faster, the older you get."

Kegan sat down in one of the white plastic chairs that surrounded the outdoor coffee table. He stared down at the cement pavers for a moment then took another swig of his local micro-brew. "That is so true. Sometimes I'm shocked when I look at my girlfriend and she's like a hundred pounds fatter than when I met her, then I realize that was like over two years ago."

Mike turned toward him with an eyebrow raised. "Don't you mean fiancée?"

"Right that's what I meant."

Mike leaned against a wooden post that helped support the gazebo style awning that covered the patio. "Are you nervous about getting married?"

"Maybe a little. Were you?"

Mike tilted his head and almost laughed. "I was fucking terrified bro. Had to kinda like…turn my brain off and just do it before I lost my nerve. The idea of me being responsible for another person's happiness, or the idea of just committing to one woman for the rest of my life was always scary for me.

Kegan sat up straight. "Really, even with Autumn?" He immediately felt silly for mentioning his friend's wife. He was madly in love with Sydney, but he thought Autumn was the most beautiful woman he had ever seen and he couldn't imagine anyone having second thoughts about marrying her. "Sorry man I didn't mean it like that, I'm just surprised. You guys are pretty much our inspiration. You two are exactly the kind of couple we would like to be."

Mike gave him a sly smirk. "Why is that?"

"A lot of reasons," Kegan said, his knee bouncing with anxious energy. "But I mean you know…what we were talking about a couple weeks ago."

Mike gazed into the window of the house then back at Kegan. "You mean the weight gain." He took a step closer. "It's okay, like I said before, we're totally comfortable with it, you can talk about it if you want. No point in dancing around the obvious, we get enough of that at family gatherings."

Kegan's knee became still. "Same here by the way. I mean it's fair game, no offense will be taken on our end either. It's just that you're like the only guy I can actually talk about this stuff with in person, you know what I mean?"

"I know exactly what you mean."

Kegan took another pull from his beer with a quick tilt of his hand. "How did you do it?"

"How did I do it?"

"Yeah." Kegan stood up and lowered his voice. "Like how did you get her to gain all that weight without her getting freaked out and stuff?"

"Is Sydney getting freaked out?"

"Yeah. I mean she does sometimes but not all the time."

"That's normal, and it's inevitable," Mike said after a long slow drag from his weed pen. He smiled. "If I had a nickel for every time Autumn vowed to lose weight and then changed her mind, I'd be a…I'd have a lot of nickels."

Kegan sat back down in his chair and drained the remaining contents of his beverage. "How do you deal with it though?"

Mike stared at him for a moment. Kegan was a good looking kid, lean and athletic with scraggly brown hair half covered in a beanie, sparse tattoos and a coffee shop beard. He was 4 years younger, and there was a sweetness about him that was hard not to like, and in him Mike saw perhaps a more innocent version of himself. He also saw that all too familiar look in his eyes, like he had the weight of the entire world resting on his shoulders.

"I was gonna have a cigar," Mike said, "You want one?"

"Uh, yeah sure."

Mike stepped forward and took the empty bottle from Kegan's hand. "Another beer?"

Kegan smiled. "Why not?"

"I'll be right back, sit tight."

He returned moments later through the sliding door with a couple of stogies in his hand and a beer and a Rockstar energy drink tucked beneath his arm. He set the drinks down on the table then handed Kegan a cigar.

Kegan brought it to his nose. "Damn, it smells like shit."

Mike dug in his pocket and handed him a stainless steel guillotine cutter and a tiny butane torch. "That's how you know it's good."

After lighting up and filling the brisk night air with rich creamy smoke Kegan said, "How are the girls doing in there?"

Mike finished firing up his own stogy. "It's funny seeing them both on that big new sofa together, they make that thing look like a tiny loveseat." He went to check on the racks of baby back ribs that were slow cooking on the grill. "But they're having a good time, eating cheesecake and chatting up a storm, watching one of those bachelorette type shows I think."

Kegan carefully set his cigar on the glass ashtray in front of him. "Ah son of a bitch, they turned the game off already?" He reached in his pocket and popped the cap off his beer with a bottle opener that was attached to his keychain. "The last thing Syd needs is more wedding ideas."

Mike closed the grill then sat down in the chair across from Kegan. He cracked open his Rockstar and took a sip. "So what are you worried about exactly? Like give me an example of a time when Sydney freaked out about her weight."

"When she hit 400."

Mike leaned backward. "Did she hit 400?"

"Chyea, a few months ago. Can't you tell?"

Mike put his Red Wing boots up on the low table and took a couple of puffs on his cigar. "I don't know… once they get to a certain size it's like, they're just fat you know?"

"Yeah but I think after 400, there's a big difference in mobility and stuff." His expression turned somber. "Sydney's really slowed down a lot this year."

"So what happened, were you doing a weigh-in or something?"

"It was a doctor's check up."

Mike leaned forward and put his boots back on the ground. "Fuck, that's the worst."

"I know and it's so confusing," Kegan said. "One minute I'm like feeding her in bed and she's being all sexy and telling me how she can't wait to get fatter, and then the next minute she's getting hysterical over not being able to find clothes that fit and shit. When she found out she was over 400, she blamed me. I felt sick about it for weeks." He paused and took a sip of beer, looking slightly ashamed, as if he had shared too much. He cleared his throat. "It's amazing how their emotions become your emotions, or is that just me being too sensitive?"

Mike shook his head. "No you're not being too sensitive. You're in touch with her feelings and I think you need to be like that in order to survive in any relationship. But girls are tricky. They're delicate and beautiful right?

And like anything that's delicate and beautiful, you need to proceed with caution, and handle it with care."

Kegan set his beer on the table. He leaned towards Mike and began speaking in a sort of loud whisper. "I just get too fucking excited and it makes me all crazy and impatient. I don't know why I can't just be thankful. Seriously man, never in a million years did I ever think she would actually get this big."

"That's the rub right there, what do you call it, it's like a paradox." Mike puffed on his cigar several times then smiled. "The fatter she gets the more dependent on you she feels, the more tied to you she feels and that can be a good thing or a bad thing, depending on how safe and secure you make her feel in the relationship." He leaned forward. "It's complicated cause it's like, I think when girls gain weight, they can either feel…deliciously feminine and sexy, or they can feel just frumpy and out of shape, right?"

"Right," Kegan said, hanging on Mike's every word like he was some world renowned marriage counselor.

"But so much of how they feel and how they view themselves has to do with the way you treat them," Mike said. "When they're in a relationship at least… it's different when they're single but you know what I mean." He took a big swig of his drink. "It goes both ways right? You feel a certain confidence because you know that she loves you and believes in you."

"So you're saying things get easier after you get married?"

Mike put his drink down and nodded. "Things get a lot easier, because then you've proven you're committed to her, and she feels totally safe with you and she'll relax and get more comfortable." He took a short puff on his cigar and let the smoke slowly dissipate from his mouth in a milky haze. He looked at Kegan and smiled. "Remember how like when you were single it seemed like the hottest women you'd meet were always married?"

Kegan shrugged. "Yeah because the hot ones don't stay on the market long."

"Is that really the reason though? I think it has more to do with what I'm saying. They get married, they blossom and gain weight, they fill out, get curvier, sexier and more beautiful all because they know they're now safe. They know someone worships the ground they walk on at home and they carry themselves that way." He turned towards the sliding glass door then looked back at Kegan. "Girls that feel safe don't go on crash diets, or hire personal trainers, they spend time with their husbands." He reached in his pocket and took a quick drag from his vape pen while holding his cigar in his other hand. "I don't know I might be full of shit."

Kegan shook his head. "No man that makes so much sense it kinda blows my mind." He took a drink. "So that's how you did it with Autumn?"

"With her I was just true to myself, true to my heart and I treated her with respect and she demanded nothing less."

Kegan went silent for a moment then he cleared his throat nervously. "She um, wasn't even fat when you met her right? Did you like…did she want to gain weight or something…or I guess I'm just curious how it actually happened if you don't mind me asking."

Mike let out a deep sigh. "It happened with baby steps. One day at a time, one pound at a time just like anything else. She had gained some weight right before we started dating, then you know with a little wining and dining, she put on a few more pounds."

Kegan brought his stogy to his mouth then coughed. "Was she like upset about it?"

"I think a little at first, but she was always pretty unapologetic about her body. Thing was, I just fucking loved the way the extra weight looked on her so much that she started to like it too. Unless I just unleashed something in her that was already there."

"Fuckin a, that's the best."

Mike shrugged. "I don't know. What can I say girls like to eat. Maybe they just need to know it's okay or something." He gazed into the back yard for a moment, noticing the quiet stillness of the night sky. He took a long drag of his dank, hand rolled corona and looked at Kegan. "Anyway that was all good, but there was a limit to it because she was starting to get back into working out after hitting 180 pounds or so, and she thought that was too much weight for her." He leaned backward and let out a short chuckle of astonishment. "Holy shit I forgot about that."

"Things change man." Kegan took a sip of beer. "So, wait, then what happened after that? How'd you get over that hurdle?"

Mike laughed. "Then covid happened and all the gyms closed."

"Oh shit!"

"Maybe it was fate," Mike said with a smile. He paused and peered downward for a moment as a gray ribbon of smoke lingered around his head like a halo. He looked at Kegan. "That's when it truly started I guess. And you know…we were getting more and more comfortable with each other. I think the pandemic made us get really close, more adventurous in the bedroom, more willing to express what we wanted."

Kegan's eyes widened. "So that was when she started to get fat?"

"Well yeah, you remember it was shelter-in-place," Mike said. "Seemed like every girl I knew gained weight during that time, and with Autumn just sitting on her butt all day, and me being me…she ended up gaining a lot, and it sort of snowballed from there."

"Past the point of no return."

"I guess you could say that."

"But she was okay with it? Like what was she thinking?"

Mike gave him a crooked smile. "Just because I'm married doesn't mean I understand how women think. I'm still not exactly sure how she feels about her weight."

"Really?"

"Yeah, like a lot of the time I get the feeling that deep down, maybe she wants to lose weight. I remember after she hit 300 pounds, she got all uptight and told me she wanted to get back down into the 280's because she was starting to get winded just from walking around the house and stuff." He puffed on his cigar and sighed.

"But she must like it. Sydney always goes on and on about how cool and confident Autumn is."

"When she loves it, she loves it, but when she doesn't, she doesn't. It depends what kind of mood she's in, you know what I'm saying?"

"Yeah I get it. Has she tried to lose weight recently?"

"It's hard to tell, I don't know if she can at this point. She keeps talking about wanting to get healthier but I'm always finding secret candy wrappers and empty fast food bags and pizza boxes in the trash and in the car and stuff."

"Do you call her out on it?"

Mike smiled. "Of course not."

"Did she ever get into gaining on purpose and shit?"

Mike nodded with raised brows. "She did. I still think that was the main reason why she blew up so much. If she didn't really enjoy it herself, and didn't go through that whole gaining on purpose period…" He looked at his cigar and the way it was slowly burning towards its band of red and gold foil, brightly shimmering beneath the soft overhead lights. "She still would've gained, but it would have been much more gradual and I'm sure she would have leveled off or hit a plateau somewhere in the 200 range or something." He took a drag and released a perfect smoke ring from his mouth. "It was never that easy or simple though. Since the beginning it was more like a roller-coaster of mixed emotions, for both of us really."

“How so?”

“Sometimes she was really into it, then sometimes she’d have these freak out moments like you were saying with Sydney. Then the next week she’d be really into it again. So much of it though was just that she developed these habits and routines during covid, eating take out everyday, no exercise and you know…10 pounds here, 5 pounds there, it starts to add up pretty quick.” He took a sip of his energy drink then looked Kegan directly in the eye. “I think that for a long time she didn’t realize how big she was actually getting. Not sure if she realizes how big she is now, come to think of it.”

Kegan scooted forward in his seat. “Does she not weigh herself?”

“It's rare these days, she’s sort of against scales, until she’s not.”

“Sydney can be like that too.” Kegan puffed on his stogy, then gave Mike a long stare. “So?”

“What?”

“When was the last time you got her on the scale?”

"Like a year ago. Exactly a year ago actually, October 2023. Shit I guess you don't forget about these things."

"Damn, been that long huh?"

"You can't push it."

"No you can't," Kegan said with a slow shake of his head. "How much was she?"

"Four hundred and forty three pounds."

"Dayam." Kegan's eyes got big and he flicked a good inch of ash into the tray in front of him. "And that was a year ago. How much do you think she is now?"

Mike looked at him, expressionless. "How much do you think?"

After a nip from his beer, Kegan tilted his head towards the ceiling of the open air canopy. "God it feels so weird to be talking about this with you."

Mike smirked. "We can't fucking help ourselves can we."

"No we fucking can't," Kegan said chuckling. He paused and his brows tightened. "If she was 443…I'd say that by now she's probably umm…getting close…"

"Yeah probably. Maybe more."

Kegan took off his beanie and stood up."Really? Over 50 pounds in a year?" He looked over his shoulder and lowered his voice. "I can't even...it's fucking epic."

"Is it though? I worry it's getting to be too much sometimes."

Kegan sat back down. "Yeah, that's kind of the dilemma, the elephant in the room."

"We bought that treadmill to help her stay somewhat healthy and more mobile, but she's so fat now she can barely use it, can't even get on it anymore without my help. There's a lot of times when I feel like I should try and help her lose weight, but then she asks me for a bowl of ice cream and suddenly I'm hard as a fucking rock and powerless to say no. I used to have to really work hard to convince her to eat more, now she's always hungry and she'll eat whatever I put in front of her. Sometimes I wonder if she's lost her mind…and then I think that if she did lose her mind, it's most definitely my fault."

"It's fucked up because that's part of what makes it so hot." Kegan leaned back in his chair. "Maybe we're just a couple of misogynistic assholes."

"Nah bro we're not assholes." Mike smiled then took a long pull from his weed pen and coughed. "My whole life, everything I ever wanted to do was something I wasn't supposed to do. I wanted to get drunk everyday and try every drug I could find in my early 20's, but you're not supposed to do that." He closed his eyes and shook his head slowly. "My girlfriend gained weight and instead of being all concerned and distraught like you're quote-unquote supposed to be, I loved it so much that I encouraged it until I became fucking addicted to it like I get addicted to everything else I like."

Kegan was surprised. Mike had never been so open and willing to divulge so much personal information with him before."You're not the only one man. A beautiful woman who eats a lot and gains weight really is the hottest thing in the world." He exhaled in awe from the images his own words conjured in his young and lustful brain. "Were you always into thick girls?"

Mike looked at him. "No not really, at least not consciously." He shrugged. " I mean we all like a little extra T and A, but I always thought I'd end up with a girl like one of my sister's friends from high school. You know, sophisticated…kinda outdoorsy, pretty, and…thin." He took a quick breath through his nose, relishing in the decidedly pleasant aroma of peppery tobacco from the cigars and maple bourbon barbecue sauce from the grill. "But what made it so hot was that Autumn was that type of girl. She was like a super hot version of one of my sister's friends. She was exactly the type of girl everyone probably thought I'd end up with. The only difference is that Autumn gained weight, and just kept on gaining. Honestly, that was what pushed me over the edge and got me to marry her."

Kegan nodded. "I never thought I would end up with a girl like Sydney. But man, once you get a taste, you can never go back."

"When did it change for you? Like when did you know you were into…this."

"I don't know, early on in the pandemic I was bored out of mind and fucking around a lot on instagram, I umm…stumbled on some plus size models, one thing led to another and I got totally hooked." He lifted his arms in the air. "Why is it so fucking sexy to see a hot chick gain weight anyway?"

"There's a lot of reasons, but maybe it's best not to analyze it, just enjoy it."

"It's so hot and it never gets old."

"I know and it only gets progressively hotter and more exciting."

"Thank god for you and Autumn man," Kegan said. "I'm so glad Sydney has a friend like her."

"I'm glad she has a friend like Syd."

Kegan got quiet and peered downward. "You know, despite Syd freaking out about 400 pounds, we've been umm, we've been documenting some of her progress online. She's been raking in pretty good money too, like quit her job type money." He looked at Mike and cleared his throat. "Autumn ever think about doing something like that?"

Mike looked at him, stone faced. "No. To each their own but, we can barely go to a grocery store without someone trying to follow us home."

"Yeah I hear you." Kegan watched as Mike's gaze drew towards the bottle in his hand. His eyes were dark like tempered steel, and he had never seen them look so tired or bloodshot before. "How long ago did you quit drinking?"

Mike took another hit from his disposable pen, blowing streams of THC vapors into the cool stagnant air. "Almost ten years."

"Congratulations."

Mike held the vape pen up. "Thanks, but now I can't stop sucking on this thing."

Kegan sat silent for a moment, looking straight ahead. "I am addicted to watching my girl gain weight."

Mike's mouth twisted in amusement as he grabbed his Rockstar. "Me too. Here's to addiction."

Their beverages touched and Kegan slurped down the last of his stout. "This all stays, just between you and me right?"

Mike gave him his best Robert DeNiro style nod and said, "What, this thing of ours?" He took a puff on his cigar."Never rat on your friends, and always keep your mouth shut."

Kegan smiled and responded in a Brooklyn accent. "Are you being a fucking wise guy wit me?"

Chapter 27

Sydney downed the rest of her wine in one big gulp, then scraped the last of the vanilla buttercream off her plate and plopped it in her mouth. "Okay (chew) I don't know what they put in this, (chew) but this is the freaking best tasting cheesecake I have ever had."

Autumn put her fork on her empty dessert dish, then muted the obnoxious TV commercial. "I know, it is way too delicious, (gasp) I can't stop eating." Her woozy eyes dropped with a lustful yearning towards the foil tray on the coffee table next to the bottles of Trader Joe's wine. What was a towering and extremely decadent Black Forest cheesecake, was now two-thirds gone. 10 inches in diameter, it would have easily served 8 people, but for girls like her and Sydney, it was just another snack before dinner. "We might (huff, gasp) as well finish it at this point."

Sydney smiled and wiggled her hips around in her seat with greedy anticipation amplified by alcohol and marijuana. "Yes we definitely should, (pant) I could eat this all day. There is no such thing as too much cheesecake." Holding her plate, she watched Autumn struggle to move her luscious body closer to the coffee table. "Can you reach?"

Scooting towards the edge of the couch with a short spurt, Autumn lifted her arm but the cake was still over a foot away. "Yeah (gasp, huff) I think." She took a few deep breaths, scooched forward some more but couldn't quite get close enough. It was her belly and boobs and hips and thighs that were in the way, and she felt too heavy and bloated to maneuver her body further. She slumped in exhaustion and turned towards her friend. "Can (gasp) you get it? I (pant, huff) think I'm just too… oooh…(hiccup) full right now."

Sydney lazily uncurled her legs with squeaks of jostled leather and foam and put her plate down. "Oooff, (pant) I got you girl." Pushing against the armrest to her right, she leaned forward and grabbed the round tray, then cut the remaining cheesecake in half with a serving knife and carefully placed a heaping piece on Autumn's plate. She did the same for herself and when she finally got resituated on the sofa, she was slightly winded. "Where (gasp) is this from again?"

After taking a huge bite, Autumn leaned against the back cushion as the rich combination of chocolate and cherries sent her blissfully back into a version of heaven. "Mmmm…(chew, chew)It's a company in New York called (chew) Happy Wife Happy Life." She pointed at the cake with her fork and looked at Sydney while batting her long dark lashes and licking her full pouty lips. "I make Mike (gasp) order them for me every couple of weeks or so, or just whenever I'm feeling… a little extra naughty."

Lost in her friend's eyes, Sydney swallowed. She sometimes found Autumn's facial features to be so stunningly seductive and arousing, it made her question her own heterosexuality. She looked down at her cake and pushed her wavy brunette locks behind her sporadically studded ear. "It's pretty boujee, how much is it?"

"You don't wanna know." Autumn took another big bite and ate slowly for a moment. "They're (chew) like sixty (chew) bucks per cake."

"Oh damn."

When Autumn finished chewing her mouth curved into a sly smile. "I bet (gasp) Kegan would buy you (pant) ten of these things if you asked him."

Sydney giggled and filled her fork with fluffy white cream then shoved it between her lips. "You're (chew) probably right."

Autumn's eyes were fixated on Sydney's belly. It seemed the more she looked at it, the more she couldn't stop looking at it. Despite being significantly lighter than herself, she was amazed by how massive Sydney had become.

Together they were wedged on the three-cushion sofa like a quart in a pint glass. Autumn's right hip squished against Sydney's left and their thighs were touching almost all the way to their knees.

They had tried to dress for comfort, but with their tremendous girth it seemed even the largest sizes of all remotely fashionable clothing would inevitably end up being tight on them. Sydney in her pink velour pajama bottoms and a sexy short sleeve t-shirt that looked more like a crop top; and Autumn in a stretchy cream colored maxi skirt and a matching camisole with spaghetti straps, that, along with her black bra, sank so deeply into her fleshy shoulders that they almost disappeared.

Combined, the girls were nearly a half a ton of sumptuous overly-extravagant beauty. Past the point of being merely tipsy, having already consumed a bottle and a half of wine between the two of them, as well as a bowl or two of purple kush, they were the epitome of excess and indulgence.

Autumn drew her gaze from Sydney's belly up to her magnificent breasts and the good six inches of cleavage displayed above the low v-cut of her black shirt. Pointing with her fork she said, "Especially (huff) if you're wearing that top."

Sydney gave her tits a shake with a shimmy of her shoulders. "I love how we (pant) can get them to do whatever we want." She took another bite of cake. "Sometimes (chew, chew) I feel bad. I told Kegan I liked his (chew) abs and now he's constantly doing situps and crunches so he can keep his six-pack while I just sit on my fat ass, (hiccup) stuff my face and watch."

Autumn laughed, causing a chain reaction of jiggling, rippling all the way down her body to the sofa itself. "Mmm… (cough)dinner and a show."

"You don't think we're like manipulating them do you?"

"No, (pant) men just (chew, chew) think with their dicks," Autumn said as she continued to robotically shovel cake in her mouth. "But (chew, chew) guys are supposed to have six-packs anyway, (chew) and think about all the waxing (gasp) and makeup and things we put ourselves through to look beautiful. (hiccup) A hundred sit ups is like the least they can do if you ask me."

"God I love how you think."

After plopping the last piece of cake in her mouth, Autumn exchanged her empty plate for her still half-full glass of wine with mild difficulty. "Women (chew, chew) are always apologizing (chew) for eating too much, (gasp) talking too much, drinking too much, taking up too much space and it honestly makes me sick just thinking about it."

She took a sip from her glass. "Do you (gasp) think men ever feel the need to apologize (cough) for any of that?"

Sydney finished chewing and said, "Hell no."

"So why (gasp) should we? I swear to god we're like (pant) brought up to think we need to be perfect all the time. (gasp, wheeze) It's like we're trained to feel guilty for asking for what we want and it's bullshit."

Sydney took another bite. "So you're (chew, chew) saying I can eat like a total lard ass if I want to?"

"Oh (gasp, pant) I think you know the (hiccup) answer to that," Autumn said before another sip of wine. After a brief silence and a glance at the TV, she turned toward Sydney who was staring at her as if starstruck by her favorite celebrity. "What?"

Sydney's eyes went up and down, absorbing Autumn's extraordinary beauty like a sponge. Her hair was gorgeous, falling just past her shoulders in textured layers and warm copper highlights. Her body had widened out so much, but Sydney was astounded by how perfect the sinfully excessive weight continued to suit her.

Her ass was significantly larger than the couch cushion, and her skirt rode halfway up her thigh and tugged tight against milky white flesh like a second skin. She was so well-endowed and well-formed that it was like her hips needed to be as wide and expansive as they were if only to make room for the vast thickness of her thighs which tapered into doughy knees like two rounded triangles of blubber.

"Nothing, (gasp, burp) I'm just a little obsessed with like your shape," Sydney said after putting her plate down. "I wish I had your legs and your butt, I feel like my belly is…oooff… growing too disproportionately."

Autumn rolled her eyes. "Stop (pant) comparing yourself, (gasp) just be true to who you are. I could… oooh…easily say (gasp) that my ass is growing too disproportionately, (wheeze) but I learned to actually really like it." She leaned over and put her hand on Sydney's shirt, just below her tits. "Ooohhh…you have an amazing belly, (gasp) I just love how soft and fluffy it is."

Sydney leaned back and let her stomach swell onto her lap like a beach ball of lard. She peered down and held it with both hands. "Ohhhh, (gasp) It's getting massive, pretty soon I'm not even going to be able to reach far enough to lift it."

"Mmm, (pant) that's so hot." Autumn smiled and gave her friend's belly a shake. Although crammed full of cake and wine, it still felt as soft and malleable as pudding, and it was exhilarating to touch.

Sydney tugged on her shirt but it immediately rode back up past her belly button. "This (gasp) is like the last outfit I have left that can actually contain me…well sort of."

"We should…oooh… do an (cough, gasp) online shopping day soon." Autumn adjusted her posture, grimacing from the effort.

"Yes, you need to tell me how you do it (pant) cause I suck at buying clothes without trying them on first."

Autumn placed her hand on the bare skin of her upper chest, just below her neck and made another face of discomfort. "I'm (hiccup) still hit (gasp, wheeze) and miss, (pant) but it's a…oooh…(burp) necessary skill. Ohh, (huff, wheeze) excuse me."

Sydney looked at Autumn. The flawless pale skin of her face had turned rosy, and a bead of perspiration trickled down her forehead. Her breathing had been audible throughout the evening, but it had now transformed into deep slow gasps, like she was struggling to get enough oxygen. "Are you okay?"

Autumn slurped the last of her wine like it was water, then fought with her thick folding belly to lean forward and set her glass down. She brushed a long tendril of auburn hair away from her face, then placed her chubby French tipped fingers back on her chest directly over her wedding band, still attached to her gold necklace. "Yeah, (gasp, wheeze) it's just (hiccup) I feel like my heart is beating really (huff, gasp) fast all of a sudden. (gasp, wheeze) It's okay, (pant) it happens sometimes."

"Breathe through your nose," Sydney said with tepid concern. "Maybe you (pant) should try standing up for a minute."

Autumn touched her sides. In her seated position it felt like all her rolls were squeezing her tiny ribcage and pinching her stomach in a vice grip of fat. She nodded sheepishly. "Yeah, (gasp) maybe that's a…ooohh… (huff) good idea."

With her elastic skirt stretching tight to her hips, she spread her legs apart and placed her hands on her naked knees in an attempt to stand. She had never felt so full and heavy in her life.

God, how much had she eaten today?

A big oven baked German pancake, bacon, and a 3 egg cheese and herb French omelet for breakfast.

Oh yeah and a croissant. Or was it two croissants? There was that pumpkin spice latte her husband made with steamed half and half from their espresso machine, and then there was the burger, fries and chocolate milk-shake from Five Guys for lunch.

Wait.

Did she end up eating most of Mike's fries again too?

Oooff, maybe that was what did it.

Why hell couldn't she control herself?

Why did she always end up eating not only her own orders of food but Mike's as well?

Of course there was also that family sized bag of Lays potato chips she had been mindlessly grazing on all afternoon.

But she didn't finish the whole bag did she?

There was that tub of vanilla ice cream as well. She did eat all of that because she remembered scraping the sides of the carton with her spoon when she was watching that Scandinavian cooking show right before her nap.

Holy shit.

She did eat all of that in one sitting, and then she still ate that little pre-dinner snack of baked ziti right before Kegan and Sydney came over, not to mention the three big slices of cheesecake and several glasses of wine she just consumed.

Damit.

Maybe she was overdoing it.

No wonder her gut was hurting so much.

She tried once more to rise to her feet, but she just couldn't budge.

Sydney was observing her and said, "Do you need help?"

Autumn tried to catch her breath and looked at her with worried eyes. "Yeah, (gasp, wheeze) I think my (gasp) butt is asleep."

"Omigod I hate when that happens." Sydney smiled, rocked herself forward and managed to get into a standing position without too much difficulty.

Again Autumn clumsily shifted her sprawling haunches closer to the edge of the leather cushion but her head jolted downward as the sturdy hardwood frame of the sofa began to creak and groan beneath her small, yet momentous movements.

"Oh shit," she said.

Sydney's eyebrows went up. "Omigod (pant) is that the couch?"

Autumn breathlessly rolled her eyes and held out her arms. "It's (huff, gasp) always making weird (cough) noises. It's fine, (gasp, wheeze) if not I'll get Mike to fix it. It's bullshit though (pant) because it was expensive and we like just got it."

Sydney shrugged then took Autumn by the hands and hoisted her up.

Autumn coughed and fanned herself, and although her heart was still racing, her ribcage and stomach instantly felt better now that she was upright. "Fewww, (cough, gasp) out of (huff, pant) breath. Not as (gasp, wheeze) easy for me to do that as it used to be."

"Oh my god, (pant) same." Sydney tried to catch her breath as well and found herself staring at Autumn in complete and utter awe. Her body was a marvel, and her otherworldly sex appeal was undeniable, even at that size.

She looked so different standing up, and seeing her full fledged, busty yet pear-shaped figure with its perfectly exaggerated proportions so up close and personal, was like seeing divinity itself in its truest form.

Her swollen belly jutted out in front of her and hung over her pelvis like a sagging fanny pack beneath her curve hugging skirt, but she still had a waist due to the colossal breadth of her round soft hips which flared out in spectacular fashion.

She was the same Autumn as always, with the same classically beautiful bottom-heavy shape she possessed when Sydney met her. She was just bigger in every direction, and although Sydney thought it perhaps an optical illusion, she now looked to be nearly as wide as she was tall with maybe two thirds of her weight lying below her navel.

"We (pant, wheeze) should go check on (pant) the boys," Autumn said. "Seems like they've been (huff) out there forever, (cough) and I need a cigarette."

Sydney nodded with an inebriated look in her eyes. "Yeah, we should. But first, (huff) I've just always wanted to do this." She smiled, stepped forward and then pressed her bulging gut into Autumn's with a lethargic thrust of her pelvis.

The floor shook beneath their weighty movements, and a frightened Samson bolted to his safe haven behind the bookshelf.

"Oooh, (gasp) Syd." Autumn's eyes went wide for a second, then she smirked and returned the gesture with a panting giggle. Sydney's gut was so big and so squishy and it felt deliciously erotic to feel her in that way, skin to skin, woman to woman. It was funny, albeit slightly disturbing to Autumn that they could touch bellies, with their heads still being so far apart. "God (gasp) it bounces (pant) so much."

Sydney flopped into her again with a titillating clap of sloshing fat against sloshing fat. "Yeah, (gasp) it's so big and jiggly, and so is yours."

Autumn gazed down at the immensity of Sydney's swollen midsection. The way it hung over her trendy pink pants and oozed out like an inner tube around her sides. Even the darkened web of stretch marks that filtered out from her frowny face navel looked beautiful to her.

No wonder Mike loved shoving his face in her own belly so much.

Bellies were hot.

Sydney's gut was flat out sexy, and Autumn didn't hold back the urge to bounce into her again."I (gasp) wonder if my (huff, gasp) belly would look like that with (gasp) an extra hundred pounds."

Sydney giggled. "I wonder if my (pant) ass would look like yours if I gained another hundred."

Autumn turned around and with a slight bend in her knees, stuck her butt out. "You (huff, gasp) think?"

Sydney's lips parted and her eyes got huge as she gazed at the perfect specimen of palatial female beauty right in front of her face. Autumn's hips spread out wider than Sydney thought possible and caused her snug skirt to ride up high enough to partially expose the dimpled blob-like orbs she had for ass cheeks. "Gawd, if only!"

Autumn stood up straight and faced her friend again, but she was now beyond exhausted from all the bouncing and standing, and she was huffing and puffing and gasping for air.

Sydney looked at her with both admiration and concern. "Okay (pant) you're breathing pretty heavy, we should probably stop."

Autumn coughed several times and put her hands on her thighs to catch her breath. "Yeah (cough, cough) but now (gasp) I have to pee. You should (gasp, pant) come with me, (huff, wheeze) bring the wine too."

"Um, okay."

After a few wheezy moments Autumn stood up straight again and then very slowly and carefully, began waddling towards the French doors of the master bedroom.

Wine in hand, Sydney followed close behind, her eyes glued on her wobbly derriere.

Autumn's ass was something else. It was still so pert and shapely that Sydney would've questioned its realness if it wasn't for the way it moved. The hips so wide she walked with a seesawing lurch accented with a gyrating jiggle. Her butt looked like a giant, doughy, upside down

Valentine's Day heart and it gave the impression that beneath her skirt it was padded with foam or inflated with some sort of magical effervescent gasses.

The floor thumped so loudly beneath Autumn's fluffy white slippers that Sydney noticed the wall mounted TV screen was shaking with each step and earthquake-like tremors were vibrating throughout the house.

Jesus. How much did she weigh anyway?

Sydney hadn't told Autumn about the videos she'd been making with Kegan and posting online. The videos where she would rub lotion on her belly right in front of the camera. Or the ones where she would stuff her face with fast food, or get dolled up for roll play. She hadn't told Autumn that she actually had fans, nor had she told her about the extra money she was making by exploiting her growing curves.

A part of her was embarrassed, as if she had crossed some imaginary line. That was how she felt when she surpassed the 400 pound threshold, the feeling that she had taken the feeder feedee relationship she had with her fiancé too far. 400 seemed too big, too real, and somehow finite, like there was no going back. The same way there was no going back after creating her Onlyfans account and showing her face on camera.

Autumn was a career woman, and Sydney admired her so much and thought of her as so elegant and classy, she worried she would turn her nose up at such things as silly fat fetish videos.

There was another part of her that feared if Autumn ever did get involved with her newfound online community, her popularity would far exceed her own.

With her face and her body and irresistible disposition, Sydney had no doubt in her mind.

Autumn would make a fucking fortune.

From the bedroom, Autumn entered the master bathroom and Sydney noticed she had to turn sideways to get through the door, while she herself could still enter head on with only a light squeeze of her shoulders against the frame.

Breathing quite heavily, Autumn clumsily pushed her skirt down to her knees after a bouncy tussle with her hips and rump. Wearing no panties, she opened the lid of the toilet and sat down with a gasp. It was a relief in more ways than one.

Sydney took a drink straight from the wine bottle, then set it down. She leaned against the granite countertop next to Autumn's bar stool and despite feeling a little awkward, watched her pee from a few feet away. It was strange to see Autumn, who always seemed so glamorous and stoic, in such a vulnerable state.

From her side profile, her double chin was much more apparent, as a cute little roll slumped from her softening jawline before slopping into an adorably chubby neck. She was resting her arms on waist high aluminum handrails that were on both sides of the toilet, which was something Sydney hadn't seen before.

But god her arms!

Despite her petite and delicate bone structure, and with no muscular strength to speak of, Autumn's arms, upper arms in particular, had become truly enormous. They were now complete blobs of fat and looked to be composed purely of blubber, oozing out at her sides like an extra set of boobs with the thin straps of her bra and camisole cutting into her flabby flesh like dental floss through vanilla pudding.

When she finished peeing she said, "Fuck it (pant) I'll have a cigarette in here real quick before we go outside. Can you (pant) hand me one?"

Sydney glanced down at the open pack of Dunhills between the dual sinks. "Yeah sure, (pant) but don't flush, I need to go too." She turned the fan on, then handed Autumn a cigarette and lit it for her with the zippo that was on the counter next to the bong.

Autumn took a long drag with a look of instant gratification and extreme pleasure across her face. After wiping, and with the cigarette dangling between her lips, she lifted herself up with the assistance of the handrails, then pulled up her skirt with fits of gasps, coughs and vivacious wiggles.

With some squishy bouncing of bellies and tits brushing into one another, the girls struggled to trade places, giggling, gasping and coughing as they moved. When Sydney reached the commode she noticed it was equipped with an oversized seat, in addition to the aluminum side bars. She sat down, gripping the handrail. "So, (pant) is this thing new?"

Autumn turned around and lowered her butt onto her stool. Completely winded, she fanned herself with her left hand and smoked with her right. "Sort (gasp, wheeze) of. It's just (cough, cough) that when we remodeled (huff) Mike got this larger toilet, (gasp, pant) but it's still so low to the ground that you really need something to grab onto just (pant) to get up."

"Wow, (pant) I need to tell Kegan that we're getting one of these."

Autumn puffed on her cigarette and blew smoke towards the softly humming ceiling fan. "They're (pant) only like fifty bucks (cough) and they'll make your life a lot easier."

Sydney gazed at her with drunken eyes. "I've noticed (hiccup) more and more lately (pant) that things are more difficulter…is that a word, difficulter?"

"More difficult."

Sydney finished peeing, then giggled. "Yeah, a lot more difficult than they used to be, (gasp) and I'll probably just keep getting bigger with the way (hiccup) Kegan's been feeding me."

Autumn raised an eyebrow. "Oh really?"

After cleaning herself with a square of bathroom tissue, Sydney flushed and rose to her feet. She gave her belly a slap. "Oooff, (gasp) I think I put on 5 pounds from that cheesecake alone."

Autumn leaned to her left and flicked ash into a bowl that was placed on the fiberglass rim of her jacuzzi style bathtub. She looked at Sydney and her eyes narrowed. "Why (gasp) not find out for sure?"

"Omigod, where's your scale?"

Autumn pointed her smoldering cigarette towards the cabinets beneath the sink. "Under there."

Sydney wobbled into a crouch and after navigating through the numerous bottles of lotions and oils, pulled out the My Weigh XL bathroom scale. "Fewww! (gasp) When's the last time you weighed (pant) yourself?"

"I don't know, (gasp) but it's been a minute."

Sydney placed the scale flat on the tile floor between the toilet and the walk in shower. Through the glass she could see there was a bench-like shower chair, complete with handrails and a small backrest.

She stood up straight and looked at Autumn and the way she teetered atop her stool like an elephant on a tennis ball. Although the seat was wide and had thick sturdy legs, beneath Autumn's hindquarters it was almost invisible and it sounded to be on the brink of shattering into splinters.

Goddamn.

Handrails, shower chairs?

It was easy for Sydney to forget just how fat Autumn had really become. It was almost too hard to wrap her brain around the reality at times because she still had this mental image of her friend as the little 130 something pound hottie she had known in college.

"How (hiccup) much were you? Like the last time." Sydney said.

Autumn placed the cigarette between her lips, sucked in her puffy cheeks and exhaled with a heave of her breasts as the stool creaked loudly beneath her. "I'm usually (huff) in the 440 to 450 range. That seems to be (cough) where my body likes to stay these days, (gasp, pant) although I've gone up a few sizes since the last time I weighed myself so (pant) we'll see." She took another drag. "(gasp)You?"

"405, but that was maybe two months ago." Sydney bit her lip. "Is it just me,(pant) or did it like kinda scare you? Like, passing 400."

Autumn sighed, still audible between slow yet constant wheezing. "It did, (gasp) but when I found out, (wheeze) I hadn't weighed myself in a while and was like way over. (huff) I was like 440ish." She took a puff on her smoke. "I don't know, (cough) it was scary at first, then it just felt(gasp, wheeze) unreal, like I was honestly (hiccup) having trouble believing it."

"I know (pant) exactly what you mean. For me I had to find out at the doctor's office, and I don't (pant) know if it was something about the way the nurse told me or something, (huff) but it like really pissed me off. I felt bad because I ended up taking it out on Kegan."

Autumn fluttered her eyelashes, expressionless. "Oh (pant) god, that's why (cough) doctor's suck. It's 2024 and they're still mostly just fat-phobic mansplainers, they're just all about shaming you for being a woman and having curves."

"Totally. (pant) But Kegan's so sweet, and really good at making me feel beautiful. He gets so turned on by seeing the numbers go up that it makes me really turned on too, (pant) and then I'm just like, you know what? Fuck those stupid doctors, their just doing their stupid job, I'm not going take it personally or let it ruin my week."

After a long drag on her cigarette, Autumn coughed and said, "(cough)I think that's good and (huff) really healthy."

Sydney placed her hands on her hips and smiled. "Ready?"

Autumn looked up at her. "You first,(pant) but make sure to activate the voice thing (pant) so we don't need to bend over and look."

"I love how they (gasp) give you the talking option, like they (hiccup) assume you'll be too fat to read the numbers." Sydney crouched down again and tilted the scale up. "How (pant) high does this thing go up to?"

"700 I think."

Sydney put the scale down and stood up. "Jesus, can you imagine?"

Autumn couldn't help but let out a short giggle.

When the scale was zeroed out and ready, Sydney took her boots off, stepped on and waited with bated breath.

"Four hundred twenty-three point two pounds," the scale said.

Autumn raised her eyebrows. "Wow, (gasp) somebody's been a bad girl."

With slurred speech and a goofy look on her face Sydney said, "Hollllyyyy crap! Omigod! What (pant) the fuck?" She started laughing. "How the fuck did I gain another like, 20 pounds already?"

Autumn smirked. "I think most of it's in your bra."

Sydney cupped her medicine ball breasts and gazed at herself in the mirror. "Mmmm, you think so?" She turned towards Autumn and smiled. "Okay, your turn, I'm just too curious, I can't wait."

Autumn leaned forward and stabbed out her smoke, then looked up at Sydney. "Help (pant) me up."

After rocking her to her feet with a delightful bumping of bellies, Sydney said, "You gonna (pant) take your slippers off?"

"Uhh, (gasp) too much work."

Autumn caught her breath for a moment, then ran a hand through her gorgeous hair, stepped on the scale and rolled her eyes. She put her arms out to her sides to maintain her questionable balance.

The scale sounded like it might crack beneath her weight, and Sydney feared a similar fate for Autumn's knees as well, as she stared at the way her ankles trembled from so much pressure pushing down on them.

"Jesus," Sydney said softly.

"Five hundred and six, point nine pounds," the scale said loudly.

Autumn's face went white and she stood stiff as a board for several seconds, then her breasts heaved as her breathing quickened. Looking like she might hyperventilate, she turned to Sydney. "Umm, (gasp) sooo, wait, what?"

Sydney, who had been leaning against the counter, now stood up straight. She looked at her friend.

Fuck.

What the fuck had they been smoking? Was this real?

When Autumn said she was in the 450's last time, Sydney had guessed she would be in 460's now, maybe 470's, but over 500 pounds?

Not even just 500 pounds, but five hundred and six fucking pounds?

More than a quarter fucking ton?

Was it even possible?

Sydney took a deep breath and stared at her, wide-eyed, bewildered. "Umm, okay (pant) so maybe more than you expected?"

"Shit," Autumn said under her breath as she stepped off the scale. Panting and panicked, sweating and drunk, she looked at Sydney. "Bring (gasp) me that fucking bottle. (pant, huff) I need to sit." She turned towards the toilet, slammed the lid closed, then lowered herself down with a rattling thump. Her voice lowered to a strained, throaty whimper. "I need a (huff, gasp) cigarette. (cough) I want food."

Sydney rushed toward her, handed her the wine bottle, then quickly placed a cigarette between her lips and lit it for her. "Damn (pant)baby girl, are you alright?" She put a hand on the cold, yet sweaty bare skin of her upper arm. "Vibe check on Autumn."

Smoking frantically, yet seemingly regaining some composure, Autumn took a swig of wine. "Uhh, (gasp, wheeze) I give up. I don't (gasp, pant) even care anymore, it just (cough) is what it is."

Sydney peered down at Autumn's body and smiled. "We are so (hiccup) extra it's kind of insane." She gently grabbed a handful of fat from Autumn's waist."Look at this belly, oooh and those hips. You are so goals. If I've been a (gasp) bad girl then I guess you've been a wicked girl."

After a puff on her smoke and in a very breathy voice Autumn said, "Oooh, (gasp, wheeze) I don't know it's not like (huff, pant) I'm even trying, it's just I like gain weight so (pant) fucking easily it's crazy."

"Well, (pant) we did just eat (hiccup) an entire cheesecake." Sydney looked down and bumped her knee in Autumn's hip which was spilling significantly over the sides of the toilet in all directions. "I love the way it all keeps going straight to your ass. You're making me like, horngry. (burp) If Mike was looking at you now I bet his head would explode."

Autumn looked up and cracked a hint of a smile. "His (pant) penis would (gasp) explode first."

Sydney gazed at her blankly for a moment then burst into a frenzy of giggles. "Sorry I'm like seriously still in shock right now. You are over (gasp) 500 pounds! We need to celebrate." She stopped laughing. "Are you gonna tell Mike?"

Autumn took another swig of wine then shook her head. "No, (pant) he'll just get too (hiccup) obsessed." She took a drag on her smoke. "It's (gasp) more fun to keep him…oohhh…(hiccup) guessing anyway, besides a lady (burp) never reveals her weight." She smirked. "But I… oooff…wouldn't (huff) oppose opening a bottle of champagne."

Sydney smiled in a shit-faced kind of way. "Omigod you must drive him nuts."

Autumn looked up at her. "That's (pant) part of a wife's job, that's how you keep them on their (gasp) toes and always wanting more."

"I'll remember that."

Autumn took another drink. "Let's (hiccup) go check on them. (burp) I feel like we've been waiting for our ribs for like (huff) ever already."

"Mmm, ribs sound so good right now."

Autumn placed the wine bottle on the counter to her left, then with her cigarette still wedged between her fingers, clasped the handrails and lifted herself up. "I (huff, wheeze) know and I'm (gasp) getting hungry." She took one more long drag on her cigarette, then dropped it in the toilet.

"I wonder what they've been talking about this whole time," Sydney said, holding onto Autumn's wrist to help her keep her balance.

Autumn stepped around the scale and rolled her eyes "Men (huff) think about sex (gasp) every 8 seconds."

Sydney exited the bathroom and entered the master bedroom. She turned around and watched as Autumn struggled to squeeze past the doorway's white casing. She giggled."I love how you're like wider than the door now."

Autumn let her hips press into the frame, then looked at Sydney with deviously pursed lips. "I know. (pant) Sometimes I like to tease Mike by pretending I'm (huff, gasp) stuck when he's trying to take a shit."

Sydney's eyes widened. "Omigod now that's an image. Pretty (pant) soon you won't have to pretend with the way you've been going."

Autumn smiled seductively, then another intentionally provocative thrust against the casing, managed to squeeze herself through. She fanned herself. "Okay (pant, huff) now you're getting me all hot (gasp) and bothered."

"Um, same."

They started wiggling and bouncing their way towards the double French doors and the living room.

"Omigod," Sydney said. "You should like, (huff) play up getting stuck in the sliding door on our way out."

It took a great deal of concentration for Autumn to put one foot in front of the other, but despite her aching quads, shaky knees and labored breathing, she couldn't help but smirk at the idea. "Yeah, (gasp) I'll be like (wheeze)squishing the door against my (huff) butt and being all like…" She looked at Sydney and gave her an exaggerated pouty face, and then continued in an extremely whiny and sultry voice. "Mike (huff) I'm starving and I (gasp) want my rack of babyback ribs but I'm (pant, gasp) ooohh…I'm stuck!"

Sydney broke into laughter and felt the back of her neck tingle with excitement as they turned toward the kitchen. "Okay now (pant) I'm getting really turned on."

"Ooohh, (gasp, wheeze) me too." Autumn fanned herself as they approached the door to the patio. Through the glass she could see her husband, sitting in a white plastic chair, looking like he was deep in conversation with Kegan. She stopped and placed her hand over the wedding ring on her chest as it sank deeper into her cleavage. Her heart was racing again, this time even faster. "God, (gasp, wheeze) so out of (pant) breath."

531 DUBOIS

"Autumn has always been my favorite, when everything bursts with its last beauty as if nature had been saving up all year the grand finale."

I'M SORRY
I GOT
UPSET.
IT'S
OKAY.

Find Jolene Dubois audiobooks and other Jolene Dubois novels and short stories on Amazon, Audible, Apple Music, Spotify and Patreon.

https://www.amazon.com/stores/author/B0846SNGDD

Visit Jolene Dubois Patreon for lots more stuff,
including the *Plump Fiction Video Series*
https://www.patreon.com/Jolenedubois

JOLENE DUBOIS *is the author of many books, both fiction and nonfiction. She lives on the northern California coast with her cats Bubbles and Badger. She loves to bake, enjoys good food, tending to her garden and watching the sunset over the pacific ocean with a glass of local wine.*

Her other books include:

Plump Fiction
Plumper Fiction
The Girl Next Door
Addicted to Curves
Through Think and Thick
Dangerous Curves
Diary of a Curvy Girl: Eat Drink Smoke
Diary of a Curvy Girl: Tell Me You Like It

Made in the USA
Monee, IL
15 March 2023

0cdfac9a-1cbb-4869-bdf7-895249f006d3R01